WILDFIRE

A Novel

Mary Pauline Lowry

Skyhorse Publishing

Skyhorse Publishing books may be purchased in bulk at special discounts for sales promotion, corporate gifts, fund-raising, or educational purposes. Special editions can also be created to specifications. For details, contact the Special Sales Department, Skyhorse Publishing, 307 West 36th Street, 11th Floor, New York, NY 10018 or info@skyhorsepublishing.com.

Skyhorse® and Skyhorse Publishing® are registered trademarks of Skyhorse Publishing, Inc.®, a Delaware corporation.

Visit our website at www.skyhorsepublishing.com.

Epigraph from Norman Maclean's *A River Runs Through It, and Other Stories* reprinted by permission of the University of Chicago Press, copyright 1976.

10 9 8 7 6 5 4 3 2 1

Library of Congress Cataloging-in-Publication Data is available on file.

Cover design by Kisscut Design
Cover photo credits: girl with braid credit John Markalunas; background photo credit Kari Greer

Print ISBN: 978-1-62914-497-9

Ebook ISBN: 978-1-63220-192-8

Printed in the United States of America

This book is a love song for my boys on the
Pike Interagency Hotshot Crew.
Especially:
Luke Austin
Aaron Bevington
Anthony Loren Deveraux
Josh Edwards
Tim Foley
Shane Greer
Bryan Jack
John Markalunas
Chris Naccarato
Mark O'Shea
Bob Schroeder R.I.P.
Brent Smyth

And for my father and mother

I was young and I thought I was tough and I knew it was beautiful and I was a little bit crazy but hadn't noticed it yet.

—Norman Maclean, "USFS 1919: The Ranger, the Cook, and a Hole in the Sky"

Prologue

After my parents died I started to set things on fire. I was twelve. Old enough to know to be careful about it. When my grandmother headed out for a ladies' luncheon, I'd light votives in my new room in her palatial house, carefully feeding little scraps of paper to the flames. In the bathroom, with the door locked, I would spray hairspray on my hands and wrists and strike a match.

The blue flames would crawl down my forearms and over my fingers. It was just the hairspray burning—it didn't hurt a bit. Those were the moments when the grief burned away—the flames flickering over my skin, edging out the darkness of my fresh hurt. And then just before my skin began to heat up, I'd plunge my arms into a sink full of water.

One afternoon I sprayed my parents' names in hairspray across the tile wall over the bathtub. I touched the wall with a match and there it was, their names in fire. I didn't know I'd forgotten to lock the bathroom door until I heard the knob turning. My grandmother Frosty's exclamation carried all the rage and disappointment pent-up inside her since my parents' accident.

At my parents' memorial service, and every day since, Frosty had maintained a reserved composure. But the sight of the flames dancing across the tile seemed to have scorched away her preternatural calm. She rushed to the tub and wrenched the faucet.

When she turned to me, the sight of her dripping bouffant was more of a reproach than anything she could have said.

"I've taken you in because you are my only daughter's only child. But I will not have you burn down my house."

"But tile doesn't burn." Of this I felt certain.

When she spoke again her words were staccato and angry. "You. Are. Just. Like. Your. Father. He took her. He took her from me." Immobile, terrified, I stared at her as the meaning of what she said hit me, knocking out all my rebelliousness.

My father had been driving the car.

"You have no idea how dangerous—" she gestured to where the flames had burned their names. "I want you to promise me you're done with this. Never again."

I took a deep breath and when I spoke my voice was shaky with the devastation of this new loss. "I promise," I said.

I kept my promise for nine long years.

Part
One

Part One

Chapter One

THE VAST SADNESS OF THE GREAT PLAINS stretched out to the east of the highway, an expanse running all the way to the horizon. To the west, the short-grass flatlands erupted into the beauty of the Front Range, the craggy peaks an oceanic blue against the lighter blue of the early morning sky, their tips snagging little wisps of drifting clouds.

At the Monument exit, I pulled off the highway to fill my tank and ask directions. I eyed a pickup polished to a high shine, the battered deer in the back obviously the victim of a car rather than a hunter's bullet.

Inside the gas station I spotted a muscular man with a compact build wearing blue jeans and a T-shirt spattered with deer blood. He carried himself with the angry confidence of a military man. As I headed to the coolers in the back for a bottle of water, I could overhear his conversation with the cashier.

"Hey Tan, sheriff call you about that deer?" the cashier asked.

"Yup. Someone hit it off County Road 240. This big buck will get us through till we go on the boards."

I walked toward the counter as the cashier set down a tin of Copenhagen. The man called Tan slid money to the cashier and then opened up the tin, putting a pinch of tobacco in his bottom lip.

I set my bottle of water on the counter. "Can you tell me how to get to the Pike Fire Center?"

The cashier's face remained impassive. "Hmm. Tan, can you help this young lady out?"

Tan turned to me. "Pike Fire Center? You got business there?"

"I'm on the hotshot crew," I said. "I mean, I just got hired on."

"Well, then, you'll wanna head west out of here, right at County Road 220, at the tracks head west again. Fifteen miles from the tracks you'll see the signs."

"Thanks." I headed outside, and the door swung shut behind me.

I followed Tan's directions to a T, and after eighteen miles down the county road I still hadn't seen the Fire Center. I kept glancing at the clock on the dashboard. When I spotted an old man pulling a fishing rod from his truck bed, I pulled over.

"Excuse me. Is the Pike Fire Center this way? Or did I miss the turn?"

The old man studied me. "The Fire Center? Go back the way you came, about twenty miles. Take a right when the road hits a fork. Pass the gas station. Go another ten miles. Take a right at Dirty Woman Park. That'll be a dirt road. Keep on that a few miles and you'll see the signs."

My car trailed a plume of dust as I drove past the PIKE INTERAGENCY HOTSHOT CREW sign down the washboard road through the forest. A pond winked in the morning sunlight. Open meadows bursting with lupine and paintbrushes were visible between the stands of ponderosa, which cast long shadows across my path. Up ahead the Fire Center appeared, nothing more than a cluster of old wooden buildings with green roofs tucked up against Mount Herman.

To the right sat what I would soon learn was a big, spacious classroom built into the side of the foothills. Just behind it was the superintendent's office, stone stairs running up the side of the hill to the door. The Piker bunkhouse, to the left of the road, sat low, squat, and plain. Behind it was the little shack of a kitchen. A crew of twenty men, all of them wearing green pants and gray T-shirts, stood gathered outside the kitchen between a stone barbecue pit and three picnic tables.

I sped by, hurriedly parking in the dirt lot. I climbed from my car and jogged toward the group of men, slowing to a walk as I reached them. The man holding a clipboard trailed off and they all turned to stare at me.

"Jesus, the splittail." It was Tan who spoke. He grinned at what must have been my shocked look.

"You're late," the man with the clipboard said. I recognized his voice from my phone interview. This was Douglas, the Pike superintendent.

"I'm sorry, I—"

Douglas held up his hand to silence me.

A tall guy with a shaved head and gap-toothed grin spoke up. "Last time we had a girl on the crew, she gave at least five of us the wild herp."

"Rock Star!" Douglas barked. "Enough."

The crew quieted. Douglas continued as if the interruption of my arrival hadn't occurred. "I was saying— Each of you should know your employment status is conditional. You can't hang with training—you don't pass every PT test—you go home, rookie or vet. Got it?

The Pikers nodded and I nodded with them. "Can we just send the princess home now?" Tan asked.

Douglas ignored Tan. "We'll be doing our yearly classroom training, too."

A red-faced guy with a big belly and a build like a brick shithouse groaned.

"Forest Service regs," Douglas said. "To get your red card, you gotta do your two weeks' training. No matter how many times you've done it before. And we don't need to be in the classroom yet for me to start hammering you about my number one rule of fire. Hawg?"

The big-bellied guy replied, "Keep your backpack on at all times."

Douglas held up a gray backpack with a small rectangular pouch attached to the bottom. "I know some of you've heard it from me before, but I drill it into you for a reason. You keep your backpack on because your backpack holds your fire shelter." Douglas yanked the fire shelter from the pouch on the bottom of the pack. "If the fire ever blows up and we can't get to a safety zone, you climb inside one of these and hope to God it doesn't fail when the fire burns over."

The crew listened to Douglas with a respectful silence.

"I think I'd rather make a run for it than try my luck in that piece of tinfoil." I turned to see who spoke. It was a young guy, who looked a little too soft to be on a hotshot crew. He had on the same green pants as the rest of the crew, but no crew T-shirt, so I guessed he must be the only other rookie on the crew. The Pikers looked at him with disdain.

"Most of the men on Paloma Canyon last year who didn't make it had your same idea," Douglas said. "They were trying to outrun a fire blowing uphill at forty miles an hour. Fourteen firefighters died that day. Ten of them hotshots."

A long silence hung in the air before Douglas clapped his hands. "We're gonna do paperwork and check out gear."

The picnic tables where we stood faced a small dirt parking lot where three Suburbans and a saw truck, all Forest Service green with the Pike logo on the side, sat parked. A stand of trees separated it from another dirt lot for the Pikers' vehicles, where I had parked my car. Alongside the Piker rigs and just across the road from the office stood the two-story Saw Cache. Taller and more imposing than any of the other buildings, the Saw Cache was clearly the heart of the Fire Center. A life-sized cutout of Smokey Bear hung from the side of the building, along with a sign that read, WELCOME TO THE PIKE INTERAGENCY HOTSHOT CREW.

The guy called Rock Star exited the Saw Cache. "Princess, Archie, you're up for checking out gear."

I hurried toward the doorway behind Archie, a tall, lean Piker with auburn hair and a goatee, and stopped just inside, arrested by the space. Work counters had been built out of plywood and unfinished boards. Rows of fire tools hung from one wall, and a grinder for sharpening them hunkered in the corner. Tobacco stains covered the concrete floor. A wooden ladder reached up through a hole in the ceiling. The shiplap walls had long disappeared behind posters—Stihl chainsaw ads and giant black-and-white photographs of men cutting down enormous trees with misery whips hung next to busty blondes drinking Budweiser. The remnants of a small fire had begun to die out in the potbellied stove. Accustomed as I was to the cold majesty of my grandmother's house and the impersonal space of my rented college apartment, the sudden urge to belong in the Saw Cache overcame me.

I stopped in front of a couple of Stihl chainsaws sitting on a work counter. The saw bars glinted in the light. "Don't look too close. Those are for the saw team," Archie said.

Above the chainsaws hung a photo of a younger looking Archie and Rock Star standing with an older man in front of a lake, all three of them holding up fish.

"That's me and Rock Star fishing up at Ice Lakes with my dad a few years ago."

In the photo Rock Star grinned wildly; Archie looked more relaxed. Standing next to him I felt a calm reliability coming off of him.

"Don't even think about getting comfortable in here." I turned to see Tan standing in the doorway. "The Saw Cache is for sawyers and swampers only." He spat on the top of the potbellied stove, and the spit curled into a ball, sizzling and dancing from the heat.

Archie gestured at the ladder, and I climbed it up to

the attic, Archie's reddish brown head popping up through the hole in the floor after me. The attic was bright with sunlight falling through the three skylights above. We walked together toward the giant walk-in storage closet where Douglas stood next to a tall, lanky, weathered man with leathery skin and a smiling face.

"Julie, Sam Magrue. You're gonna be on Sam's squad this season. He's your squad boss."

Sam and I shook hands, and then Sam moved quickly to pile gear up at our feet. Archie and I each received a canvas red bag, a sleeping bag in a stuff sack, a one-man tent, a hard hat, a backpack, a silver fire shelter in a clear plastic box, a head lamp, a space blanket, a red, long-sleeved wool shirt, a knit cap, four quart-sized plastic water bottles, and an MRE.

Archie began to rifle through the big shelves of green Nomex pants and yellow buttoned-down Nomex shirts on the back wall. Many of the shirts, though washed, were still black with ash. I pulled out a bright shirt wrapped in clear plastic. "Look! A new one, a small," I said, excited by my find. Archie glanced over at me and smiled, bemused.

"You sure that's the one you want?"

I tucked the shirt under my arm, a little defensively.

"You let me, I'll keep an eye out for you," he said. "Teach you some things."

"I never fought fire before," I said. "I'm a little nervous."

"Seems to me you should be."

We hiked hard and fast away from the Fire Center toward Mount Herman. Following no trail, we traveled straight through the forest, scrambling over dead and downed trees. Dry needle duff crunched beneath my boots, the air sweet with the resinous scent of ponderosa pine. Meadowy patches between the trees burst with purple alpine fireweed. Blue forget-me-nots pushed up through cracks in gray stones. I wore my new green pants made of fire-resistant Nomex, my backpack full of gear, a blue hard hat listing to one side of my head; I carried a chingadero. The tool looked like a short-handled shovel with the blade bent at a 90 degree angle. All the other Pikers' shirts had been permanently blackened by ash. My bright yellow shirt fresh out of the package was like a neon sign screaming, "Rookie!"

Douglas led the single-file line of twenty, and behind him I could see three sawyers with their chainsaws slung over their shoulders. Behind the sawyers hiked the three swampers and then the rest of us, the diggers, followed suit. I was smack in the middle of the line, behind Hawg. The baggy Nomex felt oddly comfortable, familiar on my frame, but my hard hat kept tilting to one side. On Douglas's recommendation, I had spent $300 a few weeks before on my new White's fire boots. I still wasn't used to their high arch, thick lug soles, and big heel. And the stiff leather uppers rubbed the tops of my ankles raw in no time.

I'd run three marathons in the previous two years, and I'd been hitting the weights hard, so there was no risk I'd fall out, but hiking with a pack was a different enough form of exercise to make me hurt. My legs burned and sweat trickled from my forehead into my eyes. In trying to keep close to Hawg, I accidentally bumped into him. "Watch it, Rookie," he said. After that, he held his Pulaski just below the axhead, swinging it carefully back and forth so that anytime I came too close to him the handle whacked me in the thigh.

The sun had risen higher in the sky, hot and bright at altitude, and I wished myself confident enough to reach back and try to pull a quart of water from a side pouch of my new pack. We'd been climbing straight up the face of Mount Herman for a half hour, my thighs and lungs screaming, when Douglas started yelling.

"Fire in the crowns! We've lost our line."

Sam and the crew's three other squad bosses joined Douglas in hollering at us.

"Grab your shelter, water bottle, gloves," Sam barked. "Drop your packs."

"Shelter, water bottle, gloves. Run for the clearing. Stay together," another squad boss yelled.

I fumbled to undo the plastic clasps at my chest and waist. When my pack hit the ground, I crouched down, trying to unsnap the rectangular canvas holster that held my fire shelter. "Might want to hurry it up, princess," Hawg said. He turned and hauled ass up the mountain. I finally yanked the clear plastic box free, then opened up my pack and pulled out my gloves. I dropped a glove, crouched to pick it up, dropped the other. Most of the crew had already begun sprinting up the mountain ahead of me, so I gave up on my water bottle, and headed after them.

My hard hat wobbled to the side and fell off and I kept running on without it, my lungs burning, sweat blinding me, my boots ripping at the flesh of my feet and ankles. Up ahead I saw the other Pikers pull their shiny silver fire shelters from their boxes and shake them open to complete this shelter training drill. The landscape around me filled with flapping aluminum. I followed suit. "Step on the back with your heels!" Douglas yelled at me. I tried, but my boot heels didn't catch, and the Pikers around me disappeared one by one under their silver tents. Finally, I managed to pin down the back of the shelter with my feet, and I fell forward onto my stomach, pulling the silver shelter over my head as I went. The world disappeared, and I was alone inside the silver pup tent.

I held down the front end with my hands and took shallow breaths in the sudden darkness, the tent tiny and dark and hot. I lay there for what seemed like an hour, the inside of the tent heating up by degrees under the sun, feeling a sudden and overwhelming sense of panic rising inside me. Suddenly I could imagine what it would be like, to be trapped inside such flimsy protection waiting for a forest fire to roll over me. I took shallow breaths as the panic rose and grabbed the edge of the shelter so hard my fingers hurt. My chest tightened and a stabbing pain shot through my sternum. I couldn't breathe at all, and then I was bursting out into the bright air to Douglas yelling, "What are you doing? Julie, you just got burned over. You're dead." The four squad bosses stared at me, smirking and annoyed. Deployed fire shelters littered the meadow around us, every other Piker remaining inside their scant protection, unburned, dignity intact, listening gleefully to my humiliation.

We stopped in a clearing in the foothills bright with wild columbine and white meadow stones baking in the sun. Four Stihl chainsaws that the squad bosses had staged lay there in the grass.

Douglas stopped in front of them. "Gather up!" We gathered in a circle around them. Hawg stood next to me. He sniffed the air. "Princess comes to training wearing her Chanel No. 5." The other Pikers laughed.

"It's called soap," I said. "You should try it sometime."

Douglas quieted us all with a look. "Only three guys on a crew run a saw, but everybody's gonna get their Class A Faller cert. Tan, let's start it out simple for the rookies.

Tan—showing off—picked up the saw, set it on his leg, and gave the cord a yank. The saw roared to life. He let it die.

"I said simple," Douglas said. "Not everyone here was a SEAL."

Tan obliged, demonstrating the much easier move of starting the saw with it lying on the ground. Again, the saw came to life on the first yank. As he let it die, Tan looked up at me. "Princess, why don't you give it a try?" All twenty Pikers turned to stare at me, amused.

I wiped my palms on my pants as I stepped forward, bent down, and grabbed the chainsaw with one hand to stabilize it. I pulled the saw cord hard. A sputter and then nothing. I didn't look up but could feel every set of eyes on me. Another frustrated yank yielded the same lack of results.

"Before you can run a saw, you gotta be able to start one," Tan said, and the Pikers busted up laughing. I gave the saw cord another pull. When it didn't start, the Pikers hooted and laughed harder. I gave two more furious yanks, and the saw came to life with a roar.

That first night I crept down the bunkhouse hallway to the women's bathroom where I stuck my fingers down my throat to bring up my dinner. The roar filled my head, and then the savage, light-headed rush, followed by the holy feeling of being clean, emptied out, and in control.

When I was finished, I brushed my teeth and washed my hands—the meticulous end to my ritual—and then crept back down the bunkhouse hallway and lay on my twin bed, relieved that since I was the only girl on the crew, I wouldn't be sharing the room. I pulled out my phone and finally forced myself to make the call I'd been dreading for weeks.

My grandmother answered on the first ring.

"Hi, Frosty. It's me."

"I was just thinking about calling you. I'm trying to pack, and I can't decide if I need to bring my Burberry coat. How chilly is it there at night?" I heard her take a sip of her drink.

"Frosty—"

"I ran into Louisa today, and she's so excited her granddaughter is graduating from Yale."

"Frosty—"

"But I guess we can't all be Yalies, now can we, dear?"

"Frosty, you shouldn't come."

"Don't be silly."

"I won't be there. I'm not going to graduation." I inhaled deeply.

"Why, of course you're going," Frosty said.

"I already have a job," I said. "It's started."

"We've discussed this. You're going to come home and start your internship. You've been in Colorado long enough."

I thought back to that day when Frosty told me I was just like my father, who took my mother from her by missing that curve in the road. I felt the old resentment rise. She had blamed him.

"I'm not graduating," I blurted. "I flunked out. I've got a job. I'm going to be a forest firefighter."

"My God," Frosty said, and she sounded suddenly defeated, suddenly old. And I didn't feel a hint of triumph at having finally escaped her control and her plans for me, just a great wash of sadness and remorse.

During the two weeks of preseason training at the Pike Fire Center, our days were framed by morning crew runs and afternoon hikes through the mountains loaded down with gear. The rest of the day we spent in the classroom, learning about fire behavior and the effect of relative humidity on fuel. We learned about the holy trinity needed for a forest to burn—oxygen, fuel, and heat. Take away one of those things and the fire dies. As a handcrew, our job would be to take away the fuel. On smaller fires, one or two hotshot crews could encircle a fire with a fire line to contain it. On larger fires, it took many crews to do this work, and the fire line would sometimes be reinforced by fire retardant dropped by slurry bombers, the falling slurry landing along the fire line to help knock out the heat of the fire and prevent it from jumping the line.

We spent long hours learning the dangerous "Watch Out Situations" firefighters might encounter—the list long and daunting. And we learned the theory and history of the burn out or backfire: if a fire burned toward a crew, one strategy was to dig a fire line and then set the forest on fire along the fire line so that when the main fire reached the burn lit by the firefighters, it would be stopped by the lack of fuel created by the burn out.

We also learned that forests need to burn, that fire remains an essential part of a healthy ecosystem. Small fires clear out dead and down trees on a forest floor while leaving the old growth trees still standing and barely touched. Complete suppression of forest fires leads to unhealthy forests. Because of this the Forest Service had begun a program of "prescribed burns"—lighting forests on fire in a careful and controlled way to maintain the forest's health and prevent out-of-control conflagrations later.

The other Pikers looked bored as we sat through long hours of this sort of material, but I remained transfixed by every bit of information about fire and its behavior, by the thought of being paid to dig a fire line along the edge of the flames, and by the idea of setting a whole forest on fire for a good cause.

On our last day of training before we were to be "on the boards" and available to be dispatched to a fire, we drove to the Sante Fe Trail for our timed mile and a half run. Sam, our squad boss, drove the rig. Rock Star rode shotgun. I sat in the backseat between Archie and Hawg.

I felt jittery as hell, nervous about the run. I had wanted to get rid of my lunch after I ate it but knew I'd run much better if I had the fuel.

I looked up at Archie, his eyes greener below his almost red hair, his chin hidden below a full goatee. He told me how he'd grown up in a house two miles from the Fire Center that his dad and uncles had built themselves; his folks and his little sisters lived there still.

When we pulled up at the trailhead, Rock Star turned around in his seat, grinning at me wickedly. "It's the hour of truth, Rookie," he said. I ignored him.

We climbed out of the rigs, the guys wearing cutoff blue jeans or sweat pants. I wore my lightweight running shorts that had helped me through plenty of marathon training runs. I jogged around a little to warm up. The others did some bouncing stretches that any athlete should know would do more harm than good. Douglas called for a group of five of us to line up to run first. "Hawg, Julie, Archie, Lance, and Joe." Hawg and Archie came forward, along with Lance, a fine-boned guy with stainless steel loops in his ears. Unlike the others in their makeshift workout gear, Lance sported shorts made of some fast-dry synthetic material. The one other newbie on the crew, who had already been dubbed Rookie Joe, lined up with us.

I stood with the four of them at the starting line that Douglas had traced in the gravel of the trail with the toe box of his boot. I felt shaky with the feeling of too much adrenaline.

The on-your-mark-get-set part seemed to stretch out forever. And then Douglas said, "Go," and I was running. Lance sprinted far ahead, like a rabbit. Archie loped easily in front of me, too. Only Hawg and Rookie Joe remained behind me; I could hear their footsteps. Lance must've thought a mile and a half short enough to sprint, because he blazed ahead, his baggy blue shorts catching the afternoon light. I knew better than to run full speed. A mile and a half is a tricky distance. The trail was long and flat and treeless and I couldn't help but think it would've been better if it'd been hilly. We could see the end of the run by about a half a mile into it. There was a little box of a structure, a bathroom, way out ahead and next to it a tiny ant, which was my squad boss, Sam, standing with a clipboard and a stopwatch.

I ran hard, but not as hard as I could, and up ahead I could see Lance burn out so that Archie passed him, and then I passed him, too, without either of us having to speed up. Hawg and Rookie Joe's footfalls fell away, and I couldn't hear anything but my own breathing. I looked ahead at Archie's back, and then I forced myself to surge.

I ran harder then and the pain started. At first it was just a burn in my lungs. Then I got that stabbing pain in my side and I could taste copper. The space between Archie and me started shrinking. I tried to pace off him but couldn't, his muscular legs so long he only had to take one step for my every two. I pushed harder, and I could tell he heard footsteps, because he surged, too. The pain dug into me, worse than I'd known I could make myself hurt. All I had to do to make the pain stop was slow down, and I knew it.

I thought, Fuck it if this guy looks like a Greek god and dips tobacco and knows how to fight fire. I surged again and I managed to pull alongside him. I could see him out of the corner of my eye, and he looked surprised to see me catching him. That made me angry enough to run faster, my insides feeling like they were ripping apart. By that time I could see Sam clearly. I gave one final push. I blew by Sam and heard him say, "Way to go, Julie. You smoked them all."

Archie walked right up to me after crossing the finish line and threw his big sweaty arms around me, lifting me up, and spinning me in a big circle. Sweat slick, we clung to each other, and then my feet touched the ground again and Archie let me go.

I wandered away, dazed from Archie's unexpected hug, as Hawg and Lance came across the line, and then finally Rookie Joe.

The sky over Mount Herman turned purple with the magic hour of dusk as we tumbled out of the rigs. The ponderosa swayed in the wind, the air full of the smell of a quick summer rain. "We're on the boards!" Hawg yelled. "Whoo!"

Rock Star dragged a keg from the Saw Cache. "Beer thirty."

"Beer sounds good, but Beam sounds better," Hawg said. He and Tan turned to stare at me.

"What?" I asked.

"Liquor run, Rookie."

I parked in the full dark and began to walk through the stand of ponderosa between the parking lot and the bunkhouse, a plastic bag holding two liquor bottles looped over each arm. I heard a sound like a twig snapping and turned to see the silhouette of a wild animal loping toward me through the trees. It didn't look like a dog, and it was way too big to be a cat. It was coming right at me, and I started running through the trees. Tripping and stumbling over dark, uneven ground, I kept looking over my shoulder at the thing, and it was gaining on me. Up ahead and to my right I saw a path I'd never noticed before. In the darkness I could just make out the stones lining it. I knew if I could step onto that smooth ground I could outrun the animal and make it into the bunkhouse where I'd be safe.

The bags holding the liquor bottles swung wildly, bumping against me. I stepped out onto the path, but instead of hitting flat ground, my foot hit nothing and I fell the three feet to the bottom of the drainage ditch. The plastic bag handles still looped improbably around my arms, I climbed up quickly, dragging myself out of the ditch.

A glance over my shoulder as I ran revealed the glint of bared teeth, the animal at my heels.

Archie stepped from out of the darkness near the bunkhouse.

"Better stop."

Trusting him instinctively, I froze in my tracks; my eyes squeezed shut. Archie let out a shrill whistle. I opened my eyes to see the animal trotting toward him. It jumped up against Archie's leg. In the light from the bunkhouse I could make out that the animal was a fox.

"Thanks."

"Oscar the fox," Archie said. "Damn helitack crew has been feeding him all winter."

"That's nice."

"Not knowing to be scared of people's gonna get him shot." Archie pulled back his boot as if to kick the fox. "Scat! You oughta know you don't belong here." The fox fled into the night.

I broke the seal on a bottle of Jim Beam and took a swig, handed it to Archie. He took a long drink. Mount Herman loomed over us, hulking and enchanted in the silvery moonlight. Archie passed the bottle back to me.

"Way back in high school Rock Star and I used to hang out up there. Skip school for days and sleep in an old abandoned cabin."

Just then Hawg, Tan, and Rock Star came spilling out of the bunkhouse, keg cups of beer in hand.

"Princess brought the Beam!" Hawg said.

Tan leaned back on the picnic table. "Bring it on over to old Dad."

I took another swig as Archie and I turned to join them.

As the party began to rage, I stayed to myself, leaning against the side of the kitchen watching the Pikers drinking beer and singing along to Archie and Rock Star strumming their guitars. I kept a curious eye on Hawg as he carried armloads of firewood to the center of the dirt parking lot between the kitchen and the Saw Cache. No one else seemed to pay him any mind.

Sam came over to stand beside me. He handed me his bottle of cactus juice, and I took a swig. "This time tomorrow we could be headed to a fire."

"I'm scared," I said.

"Nah, you're not. You're excited. I've seen it before."
Sam winked at me and we both grinned.

Hawg had a decent-sized pile of wood. Now he
carried over longer sticks and branches and made them
into a teepee above the firewood. He then ran to the little
shed that held saw gas and oil, and came out carrying a
giant jerry can of gasoline. He stumbled a little, liquor and
wildness clearly running all through him. When he began
to douse the ten-foot teepee of firewood and branches with
gasoline, I stared, rapt.

All the other Pikers turned to watch, too, and even
Rock Star and Archie paused between songs as Hawg lit
a match and tossed it on the wood, which went up with
a whoosh of flame that rose into the dark air, crackling
and throwing up tiny red pinpricks of light. The Pikers
cheered and whooped and pumped the air with their
fists, and then Rock Star and Archie started strumming
their guitars and singing Damon Bramblett's "Nobody
Wants to Go to the Moon Anymore," and the party
resumed.

Sam drank from a bottle of cactus juice, and Tan and
his saw partner, Clark, arm wrestled at the picnic tables.
Hawg did a couple of shots of tequila and then staggered
back to the jerry can. He picked it up and made a run at the
bonfire, stopping just short of the flames to douse them with
gasoline. The bonfire boomed. Pikers laughed and hooted.
Encouraged, Hawg took a few steps back and charged the
flames again. But this time, as the gasoline hit the bonfire and
the flames shot high into the air, they caught the sleeves and

front of Hawg's shirt. Drunk and too discombobulated to think clearly, Hawg dropped the jerry can and started to run.

"Stop, drop, and rooooooollll!" the Pikers screamed in unison, but Hawg was already blazing toward the forest, a luminescent streak lighting up the darkness. Tan was on his feet and chasing after Hawg even as Rock Star sprinted toward the Saw Cache to grab a shovel.

Just before Hawg reached the trees, Tan caught up to him, diving to take him down at the knees. The two hit the ground hard. Tan rolled Hawg to smother the flames. As soon as Rock Star reached them, he shoveled dirt onto Hawg to put out the remaining fire.

Pikers all around me laughed so hard they choked and spit beer. And a strange and new feeling welled up in me, a sense that I had found my people, even if they didn't yet recognize me as one of their own. I felt it clearly now. Before my grandmother walked in on me that afternoon when I was twelve years old, before I gave up fire as a dangerous and childish thing, I had been only a rank amateur, a fledgling pyro. My grandmother snatched the nascent obsession from me by reminding me she'd had no choice but to take me in, by eliciting a promise that I would give up the one thing that assuaged my loneliness and pain. She had taken away my great ameliorator, and now—finally—I had been given it back.

Chapter Two

WE STOOD ON THE MESA, GATHERED around Douglas, the sky a fearless blue above us. The dark, brooding lodgepole pine were interspersed with bright, quaking aspen, their leaves winking in the sun. We'd been dispatched to a fire in Aspen Valley at three the day before, arriving at fire camp after dark. We'd woken at dawn and had been helicoptered in closer to the fire line at first light.

Douglas briefed us calmly, as if giving a presentation in a conference room. "We're digging line from here, need to tie it into a red rock formation to the west." Doug pointed westward. "Sawyers, you guys open up a fifteen-foot saw line. Diggers, the fire line needs to be twenty-four inches. Got that?"

"Got it," the crew said in unison.

Archie and Rock Star stepped forward with the rest of the saw team. All three sawyers set their Stihls on their thighs and yanked the saw cords, and the machines turned into roaring animals, their bars ready to tear through anything they touched.

During those fourteen days of training at the Fire Center, I'd more or less pieced together how a hotshot crew worked. Unlike engine crews, hotshot crews don't use water to quench the flames. Unlike smokejumpers, hotshots don't jump out of airplanes to parachute down to the burning forest below. In the hierarchy of fire, hotshots sit solidly between the two, not quite at the smokejumpers' pinnacle of badassness, but close. The Pikers prided themselves on the fact that during a busy season, the crew was rarely at the Fire Center. Instead they spent days and nights in their crew rigs, burning up the highways, traveling just over the speed limit to reach big, mushrooming smoke columns. They lived to jump out, gear up, and start toward raging wildfires that anyone with good sense would flee. Wherever shit was burning, that's where the Pikers wanted to be.

Hotshots either hike the miles to the fire, carrying everything they need on their backs, or they're flown in by helicopter. Really they're glorified ditchdiggers, using their own brute force to create a firebreak through the forest. The saw team moves out ahead of the diggers, limbing trees to cut a fifteen-foot opening through the canopy above, which prevents the fire from moving from limb to limb. The sawyers also cut any bushes that might be growing near the line and drop any small trees in the way. Each sawyer's swamper grabs what his sawyer cuts and throws it away from the line. Thus, the sawyers create a saw line wide enough that the radiant heat from the fire won't cause it to jump across. The diggers follow behind, working in a line to dig a shallow trench, a fire line down the middle of the saw line. Dug down to mineral soil, this channel prevents the fire from burning across grass or through roots.

When the fire burns up to the line, hopefully it's stopped by the lack of fuel. And if the fire throws sparks from the burning "black" side across the line to ignite spot fires on the unburned "green" side, the hotshots hurry to dig a trench around the spots to keep the green side free of fire. Then the sawyers go through and drop any trees burning near enough to the fire line to throw sparks or fall across. They also cut trees snagged out enough to be in danger of falling suddenly and crushing an unsuspecting hotshot. I had the idea of it down pretty well, but this would be my first time to see it in action—to dig a fire line myself.

I stood beside Sam. "You really ought to keep all that hair up in your hard hat," Sam said.

"I told you I tried. It made it too hard to tighten up the inside band. With my hair inside, the damn hard hat won't stay on my head."

"You're lucky we don't make you cut it," Sam said, winking at me to let me know he didn't mean it. "Seriously though, when the sparks start flying, you got to tuck that braid down the back of your shirt or something."

Nervously, I leaned against my chingadero, watching the saw team as they moved out ahead of the diggers. Rock Star limbed a tree branch, and Archie grabbed it, tossing it out and away from their saw line. The other sawyers and swampers worked behind them, cutting and clearing brush. All six members of the saw team moved ahead and out of sight, disappearing into the timber. I could see the space they'd cut through the forest, an open corridor through the trees. A smoke column in the distance was the only sign there was fire nearby.

"Okay, diggers," Douglas called, "let's move it out." The Piker working lead tool started swinging, opening up a seam in the earth with the blade of his Pulaski, the next digger widened it a little with his combi, both of them bent over, all asses and elbows, their tools rising and falling with an easy, chain-gang rhythm. The rest of us would follow, making the break in the earth into a little trench twenty-four inches wide that would snake through the forest. Sam moved out next, and I fell in right beside him, digging line for the first time. I raised my tool and brought it down as hard as I could, chopping at the soil. On my third swing, my hard hat listed to the side of my head and I had to stop to straighten it. "Hurry it up, Rookie," someone down the line yelled. "Quit messing with your PPE." I rushed to dig again, putting everything I had into each swing.

In front of me, Sam easily skimmed chunks of grass from the top of the earth with the grub end of his Pulaski. The rest of the diggers had spread out in a line behind us, all of them chopping through roots, scraping vegetation, clearing a two-foot swath of ground. Lifting the chingadero, I brought it down hard, aiming to slice through roots that Sam hadn't cut with his Pulaski, but more often than not, I missed them altogether, my chingadero sinking uselessly into the soil. Sweat ran down into my eyes, and I tried not to pant. My arms burned and my throat tasted copper. All up and down the single-file line, the other Pikers worked effortlessly. Even the ones who looked like they hadn't done much all winter but sit next to their kegerator and play video games were digging like pistons.

Sam gestured to a bunch of tiny cabins scattered over the rolling, green foothills in the distance. "Folks who live in cabins like those can't afford to lose 'em. Those ain't vacation homes. We better put in a line that's gonna hold."

Soon the sandy red soil beneath the grass and roots coated my fire boots and the hem of my Nomex pants. Sam stopped over a stubborn root yelling, "Swinging." I stepped back, along with the three Pikers behind me. Sam raised the Pulaski and brought it down on the stubborn root, raised it and brought it down, with terrifying ferocity. He was so tall that the axhead of the Pulaski must've reached ten feet into the air on the upswing and each stroke rang out with a thwack. When the Pulaski severed the root with a pop, Sam moved forward again, turning the Pulaski's handle over in his hands so that he could dig with the grub end, breaking ground with an immutable cadence. "Cut through that root at a second spot," Sam called back to me. I started swinging on the root. By the time I'd halfway severed it, my arms threatened to fly off from the impact. Droplets of sweat rolled into my ears. A digger from down the line yelled, "Bump out of the way."

"Hey feeble one, let me take that root," Hawg hollered. Sam had moved easily out ahead of me, so I hustled to catch up, stepping sideways and swinging my chingadero as I went, looking back to watch Hawg cut through the root in three strong swings. His belly hung over his pants as he bent over, but his barrel chest and his arms were strong and his aim true. I couldn't get over how clearly comfortable he was in his own build. Sturdy and thick with muscle and too much beer, he was a regular fat boy, with bright red cheeks. At the Fire Center he'd worn T-shirts that said *Certified Muff Diver* or *Cure Breast Cancer, Save the Boobs.* We all knew I'd outrun him during the timed mile and a half, but it was already clear he could dig me into the ground.

By the time I drew up alongside Sam I was panting like a rhino.

"You're gonna wear out working like that." Sam skipped a single swing to bend down and scoop up an arrowhead from the ground. He held it up for me to see, dropped it in his pocket, and resumed digging.

"Rock Star soldered two pounds of lead on the top of that ching for a reason. Let the weight do the work for you coming down."

Douglas yelled for us to hustle as the sun rose over the edge of the mesa, the fire rising with it. "We gotta catch this thing before it takes off," he said. "Sam, spin a weather." Sam stepped away from the fire line, pulling a little plastic box from the pocket of his cargo pants. I watched to see what he'd do with it.

"What's the relative humidity, Sam?" Hawg asked.

Sam licked his pointer finger and rubbed it back and forth against his thumb, counting in his head. He stopped when the spit between his fingers went dry. "I'm saying eleven percent." He fiddled with his weather kit. Looking leathery and worn, he wasn't what anyone would call handsome—too thin and too tall. But out there on the fire line, Sam was at home; I could see it. He could tell which way was north by a glance at the vegetation on the mountains or by the moss on the trees. He poured a little water from one of his water bottles over a cotton ball attached to a string, then spun it in a wide circle.

"Doug, Sam," Sam said, holding down the button on his radio. Douglas had wandered ahead of us as we dug, disappearing into the timber.

"Go, Sam," Douglas's voice crackled from the radio.

"Dry ball RH ten percent. Wet ball eleven. Winds coming from the north."

"Sam's the one who tells us when the wind's shifted or the RH has dropped," Hawg said to me, spitting to seal the importance of the fact. The information Sam gathered could easily make the difference between the fire rolling over us or the lot of us hauling ass before a blow up and making it back to our safety zone alive.

Hawg looked at me again, as if noticing me for the first time. "What are you doin' up here anyway? Rookies dig at the end of the line."

I stared at him.

"I'm serious." Hawg looked down the line at Rookie Joe. "You, too, Rookie. Git!"

Rookie Joe and I exchanged a look and headed back to the end of the line.

I dug at the very end of the line of diggers, Rookie Joe in front of me. I could see he struggled worse than me, and he moved so slowly we'd fallen a bit behind the others. Flames shot up from the treetops in the distance. For the first time, I heard the roar of fire picking up speed, a sound like a deafening waterfall.

Rookie Joe swung his tool and struck a rock, which

flew up, nailing him in the forehead. He staggered back, blood pouring down into his eyes. Panicked, I patted down my pockets, trying to find something to staunch the blood. I could see the fire rolling through the tops of the trees toward us.

Another glance up the line showed the Pikers still pounding out fire line, putting in a Piker superhighway as they moved quickly away from Rookie Joe and me, impervious to the danger barreling toward them. I could hear Sam's barely audible voice, yelling, "We're not gonna lose this one. Let's go! Let's go!"

And then I saw Archie running down the line toward us. He yanked a handkerchief from his pocket and quickly wiped away enough blood so Rookie Joe could see.

"You're okay," Archie said. "Just don't fall back."

Rookie Joe nodded, but he looked exhausted.

"Go!" Archie yelled. I turned and sprinted up the fire line, the wall of fire picking up speed as it rolled toward us. I glanced back to see Rookie Joe trip and fall on a severed tree root. Before I could consider the risk of going back to help him, Archie was already dragging him to his feet. I turned and ran at a full sprint, my feet hitting the uneven ground of our fire line, to my left the blinding heat of the flames. Up ahead I could see the rest of the Pikers still digging toward the flat open space of a giant red rock.

Behind me I could hear Rookie Joe's panting and Archie's voice urging him on. Up ahead I could see the Pikers hitting the safety of the rock. They'd tied their line in to the natural fire break of the inflammable red rock and now stood there looking back down the line for us.

I reached the red rock, followed by Rookie Joe and Archie, just as the great wall of fire hit our line. As if by magic, the gap we'd scratched through the forest floor stopped the towering inferno in its tracks. The flames roiled and boiled and exploded into the sky, but stayed on the black side of our fire line. It seemed unbelievable that our work could stop such a force of nature. But there it was before me. The thrill ran up and down my limbs. I had never been so close to such an inferno. I had never helped make anything as powerful as that fire line we'd scratched along the forest floor.

All twenty of us took a few steps back from the scorching heat. We stood together watching as the fire burned hot against our fire line, but didn't cross to the other side. The modest cabins scattered across the hills stood unburned, thanks to the Pikers' hard work and willingness to risk their lives.

I glanced over at Archie standing beside me.

"Thanks," I said.

"I wouldn't leave you to drag that weak link to the safety zone by yourself." He grinned. We turned back to the fire as a giant lodgepole pine along the edge of the red rock exploded, like a rocket trying to launch itself from the earth.

Chapter Three

AS THE FIRE BURNED DOWN, WE COULD SEE the landscape on the black side had transformed into a postapocalyptic wasteland of ash, teetering snags, and demonically glowing stumps, all of it sending up great steaming billows of smoke. But still, on the green side of our fire line, the foothills rolled out untouched, peppered with log cabins and meadows bursting with flowers. The Pikers seemed unaffected by this contrast. They sat scattered over the red rock, swapping entrées from their MREs, and telling fire stories.

The fire management officers met in the early mornings in fire camp to lay the day's plan for exactly where each hotshot crew would dig a line in each division of the fire. We'd completed our designated section of the fire line for the day, tying in to the big natural fire break of the red rock a lot sooner than the fire gods had anticipated, so we were to wait on the red rock until it was time to hike back to the helispot to be picked up and flown to camp.

The late afternoon sun felt good. I drank warm water from my bottle and took in the other Pikers, their Nomex shirts filthy, their faces and hands smudged dark with ash. The saw team sat together, Rock Star and Archie next to each other as always, their blue hard hats almost touching as they leaned back on their packs and had thumb wars. Tan sat next to his saw partner, Clark, a PhD student studying forest resource management.

Hawg lounged on the other side of them, thick from a lifetime of hard work, beer, and red meat. During the six-hour drive from the Pike Fire Center to fire camp the day before, I'd become accustomed to Hawg's penchant for crudeness. It was already clear he was the only digger besides Sam whom the saw team deemed tough enough to bother with.

I relaxed on the red rock as close as I could get to the saw team without exactly being with them. A cluster of diggers sat a little ways away. Most of them could cut it on a shot crew well enough, but they lacked the toughness of the saw team; they didn't have Sam's understanding of fire. I was almost glad none of them made an effort to include me because it meant I could eavesdrop on Sam and Hawg.

Sam opened a paperback dictionary at random and read, "Eponymous."

Hawg pondered the word as he unwrapped a nut roll and took a bite. I could tell this was an old game between the two.

"I can't believe you can still eat those things," Sam said.

"I like 'em," Hawg said. "From the Greek 'eponumus,' given a significant name." He took another bite of the nut roll. "Peanuts tear me up, though."

"So what's it mean?" Sam asked.

"Being the person a literary work is named after. Like

Debbie is the eponymous heroine of *Debbie Does Dallas*."

Sam nodded, then opened the dictionary to another page. "Cotillion."

"It's French. It means 'petticoat.'"

"It means something different in English," Sam said.

Hawg looked uncharacteristically stumped.

"It's a ballroom dance that's sort of like the quadrille," I said.

Hawg turned to look at me. "What are you, a debutante?"

All the Pikers within earshot turned to stare at me.

"That explains it. We got ourselves a high-society rookie. Debbie the Debutante!" Hawg yelped. The Pikers laughed.

I shrugged, my face hot. "My grandma would have killed me if I hadn't been a deb."

"My grandma would have killed me!" Hawg mimicked.

I grabbed my water bottle and threatened to give Hawg a dousing.

"We get in a bar fight, we'll see what debutantes are really made of. Julie, you gonna throw down with the Pike?"

I stared at Hawg, unprepared for this new line of questioning.

"Nah, of course you wouldn't," he said. Something about the unexpected barb stung worse than the debutante teasing.

Nearby, Lance, the crew paramedic, cleaned up the cut on Rookie Joe's forehead and sutured it with butterfly bandages. With his stainless steel loop earrings and fine-boned features of a teen heartthrob, Lance looked like a hipster among rednecks.

Hawg jerked his head toward Rookie Joe. "Bear bait, that one. Major wuss."

Douglas walked across the rock toward Rookie Joe. The group of us sitting just within earshot exchanged a glance as Douglas spoke. "So you barely passed your timed run and your pull-ups. I let that go. Figured I'd see how you'd do on the fire line. But today I got two hotshots risking their lives to get you to the safety zone. I can't have it."

Rookie Joe began to protest, but Douglas cut him off. "Once we get back to fire camp, you can get a ride into Basalt with the catering truck. Bet you can make your own way from there."

A glance toward Rookie Joe showed his eyes shining. Hawg, Archie, Sam, and I were surprised. Hawg looked at me. "How 'bout you? Might as well go out with him." He belched to show what he thought of me.

But I was still feeling a little high from my proximity to those flame lengths rising above the treetops and the way our line had stopped the fire in its tracks.

"I'm in," I said, "whether any of you like it or not."

"Atta girl," Archie said.

We hiked down our fire line toward the helispot. On the west side, unburned forest sloped away from us. Blue spruce and Douglas fir grew around pure stands of aspen quaking in the sunlight. To the east lay the devastated landscape, ash swirling in the afternoon breeze. A giant burned tree groaned and then fell. I could feel the impact come up through my boots as it hit the ground.

Up ahead, the Lolo Hotshots approached, hiking in to work the night shift. We stepped to the side so that they could pass us. The Lolos were a rough bunch from Montana. The shine of piercings glinted from their faces, and I could see tattoos creeping up several of their necks. They were clearly the hardcore opposite of the clean-cut, country music–loving Pikers. As they hiked by us, hackles raised on both sides. When a tall Lolo with a long, blue goatee walked past, Tan said, "Looks like someone's been bobbing for turds in the Port-a-John." We all snickered. The Lolo glared, but was forced to keep hiking with his crew. And then we were back on our fire line and hiking away from them.

A few minutes later, Douglas stopped again as an airplane flew toward us. We gathered in a clump to watch. The plane rumbled low to the ground. Archie turned and glanced down at me, his eyes serious, his goatee glowing reddish in the light. "That slurry bomber's gonna knock some heat out along our line. Make sure the fire won't jump it later."

Sam reached into the front pocket of his Nomex shirt and pulled out a camera as the plane came closer. "Photo op," he yelled. Pikers all down the line lifted cameras as the plane approached. I hurried to pull my shiny new digital camera from my shirt pocket.

"Sam's shot will be the best," Archie said. "He's got the fire mojo, especially when it comes to photo ops."

The plane came barreling along, on track to pass right over us, flying so low to the ground it eclipsed the sun as it approached.

"Motherfucker," Sam yelled.

All around me, Pikers flung themselves down onto the ground without hesitation. Archie dropped gracefully onto his stomach as if he didn't have forty pounds on his back. Disoriented by the gigantic rumble of the plane, I stared up at the plane's belly bearing down on us, so close I could make out the details on the underside of its wings. All around me Pikers lay face down with their hands over the backs of their necks. When the shadow of the plane fell over us, the belly blotting out the whole sky, I was the only Piker still standing, for once looming tall over the others.

I gaped as the bottom of the plane opened up and a vast, bright pink cloud of liquid dropped out even as the plane sped away from it. I took a step to run as the huge fluorescent sheet of slurry slammed into me, knocking me face down onto the ground, the camera falling from my hands.

"Goddamn cocksucking sonofabitch," Rock Star yelled. When I lifted my head, I saw that slippery pink slime covered my shirt. The other Pikers clambered up from the ground, the backs of their pants and their gray backpacks splattered a shocking, synthetic pink.

Tan took a step, jumping back when he heard the crack of my camera below his boot. But when he realized it was mine, he began to laugh. I picked up my ruined camera as I scrambled to my feet.

"Boys, I think our dirty leg might be a natural," Tan said.

"Hotshot?" Hawg asked.

"Photographer." The Pikers loved this. All around me they began to chortle and snort.

I glared at Tan.

"Tan, watch out or she'll hit you with her cotillion!" Hawg said.

"Fucking rednecks," I muttered.

"Oooooohhhh," the Pikers said.

"Debbie the Debutante's mad now!" They laughed harder.

I looked around for someplace to storm off, but there was nowhere for me to go.

As the relative humidity rose and the fire died down, the Pike Hotshots lounged on the ground near the helispot waiting for the choppers. What they called a helispot was really just a big meadow large enough for a helicopter to land in, ringed by a stand of aspen. We leaned back on our packs with our legs stretched in front of us. I plucked a bit of grass to chew on, and it tasted meadow-sweet. There was something magical about the scent of the smoke now that the sun's rays had begun to lengthen and cast dappled shadows through the aspen leaves.

We perked up to listen to the relative anomaly of a female helitacker reading the flight manifest. With her hardhat and sunglasses on, none of us could tell exactly how cute she was, but her pretty white teeth and long blonde ponytail were enough to keep the Pikers interested. Again, I sat close enough to listen to the sawyers and Hawg and Sam snapping and popping and bullshitting.

"Hey, Big Sweet Sam," Hawg said, his eyes lighting

up with a manic excitement. "You ought to go down to Mexico with me at the end of the fire season. You can't even imagine how cheap hookers are in a country with an average income of four dollars a day. They've all got the tortilla gland kickin' in to full effect, too. Latina Rubenesque, I call it. Lard and masa, baby." Hawg puffed out his cheeks and held his hands out in front of his chest. "You've got to come."

"Maybe so," Sam said. Sitting on the ground with his long legs stretched out in front of him, he looked rugged and more than a little worn.

"What do you do all off-season, anyway?" Hawg demanded.

"Collect unemployment," Sam said. "I would work in my yard, but it's buried under all that snow."

"You really ought to get out of your hometown. Renounce your provincialism, see the world," Hawg said.

"If I'm gonna be lost between fire seasons no matter where I am, then I might as well stay in the house where I was born." Out on the fire line Sam had seemed sure of his place, but I began to think his life away from the crew was a different story entirely. "Besides, I see the world plenty with the Pike," Sam said. "How many states did we go to last year?"

"How's about a fresh ground scrod?" Rock Star sang out, pulling a can of tobacco from the front pocket of his shirt. He packed a big dip into his bottom lip and then held the can out toward the others.

"Thanks, Rock Star," Hawg said. "Idaho, Florida, New Mexico," he counted on his fleshy fingers as he spoke.

"Wyoming, California, Arizona, Utah, Colorado, of course. Did we make it to Montana?" Tan shook his head. "So nine, we made it to nine states." But by the time Hawg had finished making his list, Sam had already cracked a well-worn copy of *The Sun Also Rises* he'd pulled from the cargo pocket of his pants.

Out of the corner of my eye I watched Rock Star and Archie clasp their fingers together for a thumb war. Rock Star grimaced wildly as the struggle progressed, but Archie remained calm, watching the two thumbs as if neither was his own.

"A-ha!" Rock Star cried in delight as he pinned his best friend's thumb. "One, two, three, four, five! I won!"

"You got me, buddy, you got me," Archie conceded.

Rock Star looked up and saw me watching them. "How about a thumb war, Julie?" he called out and then started cackling as he held up his open hand. It was twice as big as mine, clearly four times as strong. I stood up and walked toward him.

"I hate flying," Tan said, apropos of nothing. He rubbed his forehead with his hand, leaving a streak of ash, a tangible trace of worry. "One bolt falls off of that goddamn helicopter and it flies as well as a typewriter. The sea's got nothing on me, but the air? Fuck."

The helicopter burst up over the edge of the mesa as if Tan had conjured it. It hovered above us for a moment, the rotor wash kicking up a great cloud of dust, then landed gingerly on the helispot. The blonde helitacker doing the flight manifests had said I was slated to fly with the first load, so I followed Hawg, Tan, and Archie as they walked behind her. Hawg stumbled as he walked, so thick and a little clumsy. Little wiry Tan moved lightly on his feet, and Archie strode along with the ease of a born athlete. As we approached the helicopter, we all hunched over to avoid the rotor blades. The helitacker threw open the chopper door, her ponytail blowing in the rotor wash, and I slipped into an open seat. Hawg sat across from me, his back to the pilot. He suddenly looked young, with his chubby red cheeks and sunglasses that were too big for his face, his bottom lip packed full of tobacco. Archie sat next to me, a Greek god in profile, his face half hidden by a hard hat, sunglasses, and a flipped-up collar. I put a hand to his ear, leaned over, and yelled so that he could hear me. "Where's Hawg going to spit?"

"He'll have to gut his chew," Archie yelled back.

Peering between the two seats facing me, I caught a glimpse of the pilot's face in the side mirror. He grinned, his twisting white teeth like tiny skeletons dancing between cracked lips.

The pilot swooped around over the fire, the decimated landscape glowing red below us, the smoke rising in grayish plumes from between the blackened, brittle stalks of scorched trees. My heart lifted suddenly with the helicopter. I'd done it. Despite my grandmother's disapproval, I'd found a way to escape. I may have left burning buildings behind me, my relationships ruined by my willfulness, and my last year of school a disaster, but instead of ending up back under my grandmother's control, I was being paid to glide in a helicopter above a flaming landscape, the terrain reminiscent of the wreckage of my past. I considered how angry my grandmother must be at me, how disappointed. The thought gave my elation a tinge of self-reproach.

If I could, I would've gone back to Austin, back to the life with my parents that ended when I was twelve. For a moment, I could see it, the funky little house off of South Congress where we'd lived, the three of us. My mom was a potter, her studio in the garage, and my dad a small-time lawyer who helped people write up wills or work through minor litigations. When I came home from school, my mom and I would walk through the twisting streets to the Big Stacy Pool to swim a few laps. In the early fall and late spring when the air was scorching hot, the water was cool, but in the winter the pool was heated so that huge clouds of welcoming steam rose from its surface. When we finished, we'd climb out into the chilly air and run giggling to the heat lamp-warmed changing room, our skin dripping and covered with goose bumps.

When my dad came home from work, we would all walk down the hill together to El Sol y La Luna because my mom only baked, she never cooked. We'd eat bowls of caldo del sol with huge chunks of zucchini and avocado and chicken along with hot corn tortillas and salsa, and then we'd walk across the street to the Continental Club to listen to the happy-hour bands play swing music.

I'd sit on the rickety old bleachers and eat peanuts and watch my parents dance, their feet shuffling in perfect unison, my mother spinning out and back on the end of my father's arm. The song would end, and they'd cling to each other, laughing, before coming back to hug me and tousle my hair.

Every few months the three of us made the obligatory drive to Dallas to visit my grandmother, always laughing on the way back about her proper ways—how she dabbed all the way around her mouth with a linen napkin, how she rang the tiny silver bell at the end of each course, how she would corner my mother and exhort her to give me a chance by raising me right. Back then my grandmother's disapproval was almost sweet because it fell on the three of us together—my mother not the daughter she'd hoped for, my father not the hard-driven trial lawyer she would've wanted as a son-in-law.

During those trips, my grandmother would take me to her ladies' luncheons and ply me with cucumber and mayonnaise sandwiches with the crusts cut off, urging me to sit up straight, use the proper fork, not be such a tomboy. But back then sometimes she would laugh with me, too, and tell me stories about my mother at my age, a delicate girl I wouldn't have recognized who could not be pried from my grandmother's lap. My grandmother missed that daughter, I could see that clearly. She had wanted me to take her place. But even back then I wiggled free of my grandmother's thin hands, reaching out to hold me or work a tangle from my hair.

Glancing across the helicopter to the seats facing me, I saw Hawg's skin had taken on a greenish cast, little rivulets of sweat running down the sides of his face. He gulped, visibly struggling to swallow down a mouthful of tobacco juice. I elbowed Archie and gestured at Hawg. The helicopter had leveled out and was flying so low to the ground I worried the tips of the taller snags might brush the underside of the chopper. We crossed over a fire line, passing out of the burnt forest. On the other side of the line, the landscape changed from swirling ash to dusty orange soil covered with towering timber. Then suddenly the earth dropped away entirely as we flew off the edge of the four-hundred-foot mesa, my pulse racing to see a vast meadow reaching far ahead and then rising abruptly into more mountains, etched against the late afternoon sky. Below, fire camp stretched out, an acre of tents edged with fire engines that looked like toys.

A shimmer of happiness rose up in me as I took in the view of fire camp, which would hopefully be my home for the next three weeks. With no warning the helicopter began a freefall, all of us plummeting toward the hard, dry ground. My stomach flew up into my throat, the helicopter a three-thousand-pound typewriter dropping from the sky. Time slowed down and stretched out as we fell. "Fuuuuck!" Hawg yelled, his mouth wide open, his hands gripping the edge of his seat. Involuntary sobs wrenched out of me and I grabbed onto Archie's arm, my whole body tensed for the helicopter to hit the ground and explode into a fireball. Through the window, the ground hurtled up toward us, and I closed my eyes tight.

The helicopter pulled up with a jerk, sailing forward again as easily as if nothing had happened. My stomach caught up with itself, but for a moment, my eyes stayed squeezed shut, my gloved hands gripped tight around Archie's forearm. When I finally opened them, the pilot's teeth glinted in the side mirror as he cackled at his joke. It took a moment to comprehend that he'd made the helicopter drop just to spook us. "Cocksucker!" Tan yelled.

Hawg grabbed the cotton undershirt he wore below his Nomex, pulled the collar over his mouth and started puking onto his chest and stomach. The smell of vomit filled the closed space. "Oh, God," I heard Tan holler over the sound of the helicopter. Hawg lifted his head up, his chin smeared with regurgitated bits of ham sandwich, then pulled the shirt collar back over his face and started heaving again. My whole upper body shook. Archie gave one of my hands a quick, little pat and then pried it from his arm. When I looked up at him, he shrugged as if to say, "I can't help you keep your shit together."

As we swooped over fire camp, I wiped the tears running down from under my sunglasses with the sleeve of my Nomex. The helicopter lowered down, hovered for a tantalizing moment, and then the rudders touched the ground. The throbbing sound of the rotors slowed, and a helitack crew member ran to open the door of the chopper. My knees wobbled and almost gave out on me as I climbed down, the feeling in my stomach the same shocked, stunned one I'd had when I was fifteen and my grandmother slapped me across the face for calling her a drunk, dried-up old woman.

Hawg followed behind me, a vomit stain seeping through his Nomex shirt. Archie, still somehow radiating a beatific calm, came next. Tan jumped out last, and as we all stumbled away from the helicopter, Archie tapped me on the back and gestured that I should keep my head down to avoid the rotors. The sound of their whirring filled my head and I pushed down another sob, this time of relief. Suddenly I could feel the hot pain of my blisters again, and I wondered how I'd make it through another day of my stiff boots rubbing the raw, ripped open flesh. As soon as we were far enough from the rotor wash to hear, we pulled out our earplugs. For a moment we just stood there looking at each other, and then the anger exploded out of Tan.

"Motherfucking pilot! What kind of a fucked-up fucking joke was that? He ought to have his cocksucking licensed revoked." His face looked colorless, as if all the blood had been leached from his body.

"Seems like he left half a deck back in 'Nam," Archie said. I reached to push my sunglasses farther up my nose, but my hand trembled so badly I missed.

"Never been so sure I was gonna die in my life," Hawg ranted. As we walked away from the helicopters, Hawg stripped off his Nomex and crew T-shirt, exposing his vomit-streaked chest and big belly to the world. "Man, I usually don't have any trouble gutting my chew, but flying backward and gutting my chew and then practically dropping out of the sky? Forget it."

"Way to take one for the team, Hawg," Archie said.

"Thanks."

Archie clapped me on the shoulder. "How'd you like your first day fighting fire, Julie?" He looked down at me with his clear green eyes and smiled.

"I liked it."

"You ready for six months of this?"

"Hell, yeah," I said, hoping to convey a certainty I didn't feel.

"Let's just see if she makes it through her first twenty-one-day tour," Hawg said.

"You're a long way from Dallas, aren't you now?" Archie asked.

The sun shone brightly enough to make me squint. Shielding my eyes with my hand, fire camp appeared before me. Since we'd arrived in darkness the night before and had hiked to the rows of helicopters just after dawn, the sight was still new to me. A sea of tents stretched out ahead, reaching almost all the way to the mesa. Hundreds and hundreds of flimsy dwellings shimmied in the breeze. Along the dirt road, a row of fire engines sat parked with their crews lounging on top drinking Gatorade. More men walked along the side of the road, all wearing Nomex pants. Some of the guys still wore their long-sleeved, yellow shirts and hard hats, but most had shed their safety gear as soon as they arrived back in fire camp and just had on their crew T-shirts.

Out ahead of us, a group of vendors' stalls sold toiletries and T-shirts with "Shutts Fire" emblazoned across the front. A long line of firefighters stood waiting for a few phones set up on a table, and I saw others with towels and Dopp kits headed toward the portable showers. Rows of Port-a-Johns stretched out behind them, and I could see the catering truck in the distance, where a long line of hotshots and engine guys stood waiting for their dinners. Before arriving the night before, I had never imagined such bustling, makeshift cities existed. I'd been expecting a few guys moving quietly in the eerie stillness of a meadow, nothing more. I tried to take it in again, the tents pulsing in the breeze, the hotshots joking and shoving each other good-naturedly or sitting on the ground tinkering with chainsaws or sharpening tools, an instant city inhabited exclusively by burly men in green pants.

Chapter Four

DOUGLAS CALLED FOR US TO GATHER UP. As we stood around him, our hands gray with ash, our faces streaked, his cleanliness was conspicuous—his Nomex spotless, his hair parted and combed to one side, his teeth so white they must've been bleached. "Good day today, Pike."

"Eventful day," Sam said, and the Pikers laughed. By that time Hawg had given himself a whore's bath with water from his bottle and all of us had changed into clean Piker T-shirts and Nomex pants that weren't covered in slurry.

"Everybody fill your water bottles, sharpen your tools, get lined out for tomorrow before we eat dinner," Douglas said. My mouth watered at the smell of dinner cooking in the catering tent.

Sam picked up a five-gallon box of water called a cubitaineer and began filling Tan's water bottle from the spigot sticking out of the side. I grabbed a second cubie and poured for Archie and Rock Star and the Pikers who reached out their empty bottles. Nearby, Douglas told an uninterested Clark about some Broadway play he'd been to during the off-season with his oncologist girlfriend. When all the Pikers had watered up, I sat on the ground with my legs splayed and my chingadero between them, struggling to sharpen the tool's edge with my file. "Rookie, put on your PPE if you're going to sharpen your tool," Hawg yelled. I grabbed my gloves from the carabiner on my belt loop and pulled them on.

"How's your day coming along?" I looked up to see Lance standing above me. Expensive sunglasses covered his blue eyes and the stainless steel loops glinted in his ears. I'd felt a little embarrassed for Lance after Archie and I had so easily flown by him during the timed mile and a half, but even then he hadn't seemed embarrassed. And today he'd patched up Rookie Joe with a competent calm I hadn't expected.

"Pretty well," I said. "Nice sunglasses."

"Thanks. The snowboard company I ride for gave them to me." He crouched down on his heels. "They ran two full-page ads of me last winter in *Snowboarder Magazine*. And they might be coming out with a whole 'Lance' line of clothing. Lance pants, Lance jackets, everything. I just have to win a couple more contests."

"If you're about to be the Tony Hawk of snowboarding, what are you doing out here?" I asked.

"Fighting fire's what pays for my winters. This last year I went up to the northwest to ride Mount Hood for a few months."

My sharpener slipped from the blade of my ching, catching one of my gloved fingers. I shook out my hand and carefully aligned the sharpener's flat edge against the ching's diagonal blade.

"You look like you could use a foot rub," he said, arching an eyebrow.

"You wouldn't want to come near these stinky feet right now," I said, and we both laughed. I didn't mention that they were too covered in blisters to tolerate a rub. Lance stood up to walk away just as Archie approached. I pushed the file along the edge of the bent-over shovel blade, the motion still foreign and uncomfortable.

"You're not making much progress sharpening that thing, are you?" Archie asked. His long frame folded easily as he settled on his heels. He watched as I pushed the rough file along.

"I'm trying."

"No offense," Archie said, his tone kind enough. "But you must've fallen into this work ass backward."

"Growing up in Texas, I'd never even heard of forest firefighting," I admitted.

"So how'd you get into it?"

"I went to Colorado College. My best friend there, Della, last summer she worked on a timber thinning project up on Mesa Verde. She got to fight some fires there on the mesa. When we met up back at school last fall, she told me all about it. Said she wanted to try to hotshot this summer."

Archie didn't say anything. But I could see he was listening.

"I didn't have a clue what I was going to do after I finished school, just knew I didn't want to go back to Dallas. Figured I'd pretty much burn up on reentry." Archie laughed and I went on, encouraged. "So last winter Della helped me fill out apps for hotshot crews. Her mom has been working for the Forest Service fifteen years, so Della knows just how they rate the apps. We trained hard all winter. Then Douglas offered me a job." What I didn't tell Archie was how inevitable it had seemed. When Della told me about hotshotting, about crews that traveled all over the West chasing down towering infernos, I had felt that solid thunk inside me. Everything in my whole life clicking into place. It felt as if I had always been moving toward this thing, ever since the day my parents died. Without my knowing it, the universe had been pushing me toward it.

"So you had a soft place to land after you finished school." Archie laughed. "Not that anyone except Tan could call a spot on a shot crew 'soft.'"

When I met Archie's eye I was surprised to hear the truth coming out of my own mouth. "I didn't finish." Because I had barely spoken of it, it had never crystallized, had never become real. I'd been lying to myself even, almost convincing myself that I'd refused to attend my graduation ceremony, not fully admitting that after the phenomenal sum my grandmother had spent on four years of tuition and bills, I'd flunked out of school in the home stretch. Now that I said the words, a hot flush of shame filled me. But there was another feeling, too—a sort of exultant triumph. My grandmother had thought that because my parents had died, she could force me to be a certain kind of woman, that she could mold me into the person she had wanted me to become, and here I had somehow bested her.

Archie gave me a questioning look but didn't pry any further. "I remember how that phone call from Douglas felt," he said. "Like I was falling and the Pike was the net that would catch me."

The smell of smoke and sweet grass filled the air. The sky behind Archie had turned purple. The magic hour of dusk had arrived, and the edges of the silhouetted mountains and the mesa rising above glowed beautifully.

"Line it out for dinner, Pike," Douglas called. I tossed my chingadero in the rig and fell in behind the other Pikers winding out from the catering truck. At the nearby folding tables, firefighters from other crews scarfed down fruit cocktail, mashed potatoes and gravy, chicken-fried steak, and white rolls. The sight of the food made me feel almost faint with hunger.

A tray of fire food in my hands, I walked along scouting for a table. Scanning the faces of the crews I passed, I didn't see any other women. Something about the intense, low-lidded collective gaze from one crew in orange Nomex jumpsuits made me shudder. Rock Star, Archie, and Sam sat together at a small table.

"Mind if I join y'all?"

"Y'all?" Rock Star turned to Archie and Sam. "Did she just say y'all? Are you for real?"

I slid into the chair, ignoring him.

"Look what I found today," Sam set his arrowhead on the table.

"Man, Big Sweet Sam, you've got the fire mojo," Archie sighed. "Always the first to spot an arrowhead."

"It's beautiful," I said, examining it.

"Sam's fire mojo gets us called out to half the fires we make it to," Rock Star said, running a hand over his shaved head.

"I didn't realize y'all are so superstitious," I said.

"Fire mojo isn't superstition. Out here, it's the law of the land."

"Hey, Julie," Sam said, "how do you like being one of the only gals in fire camp?"

"There aren't any women here, but there are plenty of bitches," Rock Star said.

"What do you mean?" I asked.

Rock Star jerked his head toward the crew who'd been scoping me out. "You know why those guys are wearing orange jumpsuits, right?"

I shook my head.

"That's a prison crew."

"A what? Prisoners?" I asked, alarmed.

"Yeah, so you know plenty of them have been somebody's bitch. You better be careful not to go wandering around fire camp after dark."

After dinner I went behind a stand of bushes a ways from the edge of fire camp. I glanced around quickly to make sure there was no one close enough to see me, and then I shoved my fingers down my throat. It was something that started just after Frosty made me promise to give up playing with fire. The flames I'd lit in those early days after my parents' death had given me momentary respites from grief. But somehow I couldn't break my promise to Frosty. Her horror and rage that I'd risked burning down her house after she had taken me in had filled me with such compunction that I knew I had to keep my word. But still my pain was too powerful, and if I couldn't burn away my grief, I still needed a way to assuage it. I still needed some escape, some quiet rebellion. And so I began to stuff my pain way down with food that I then brought back up with a violent ritual that purged my grief and left me hollowed out, feeling empty, holy and pure, without needs and momentarily without pain.

The subject of my parents wasn't one I could broach with my grandmother, she made that clear enough. But still in her own way she tried. She'd take me to the Kimbell Museum with watercolors and drawing pencils and thick white sheets of paper and we'd sit in front of the Rothkos, the Motherwells, the Gottliebs, trying to recreate them with our boxes of color. Only I was twelve and too disinterested and too much of a tomboy for the ballet classes she insisted on. Not that I ever would've enjoyed such a girly activity, but at five perhaps it would've been more palatable. And as I stood at the ballet barre I could hear her words ringing through my head. "You. Are. Just. Like. Your. Father. He took her. He took her from me—" I knew exactly what Frosty had meant by those withering words. My birth had severed my mother's close ties to Frosty. And my father had ended my mother's life.

After suffering through an hour and a half at the ballet barre in a pink leotard, I'd go back to my grandmother's house and then ride my BMX bike to the grocery store and stand in the ten items or less line to buy junk food I would binge on and then purge. The ten items numbed out the reality of my new life in her immaculate mansion, and the toilet held all of my secrets.

The chicken-fried steak came up quickly, efficiently, and then I was headed back to the Pike with the old sense that I'd gotten away with something. I pulled my red bag from the back of my squad's Suburban. None of the other Pikers had pitched tents, so I didn't bother grabbing mine, either. The ground looked suddenly hard and rough and real. Archie, Rock Star, and Sam stood clustered together, and I headed their way, hoping not to be rebuffed. "Can I come sleep by y'all so I don't have to worry about being assaulted by a stray prisoner?"

"Yeah, sure, if you'll go grab your ching," Archie said.

I threw my red bag on the ground and headed back to the rig, walking under the twilight sky, the mountains to the south etched black against it, the moon rising up above giving a silvery wash to the world around me. When I handed Archie my chingadero, he used it to carve a little hollow in the earth.

"Hey, let me use that," Rock Star said. He scraped the ground clear of sticks and dug a little groove in the earth a respectful distance from Archie.

I carved my own hip hollow between the two. After pulling off my fire boots, I examined the savage, ripped open blisters pulsing on the top of my ankles and along my heels. "Oh yeah," Sam said. "You're going to keep getting it from those new boots for awhile. Last time I broke in a pair of White's I had White bite the size of quarters."

"At the end of last season I sawed the calluses off the tops of my ankles with my Leatherman," Rock Star bragged.

"That same Leatherman you used today to cut up your apple?" I asked.

"Of course."

"Yuck."

"Don't be prissy," Rock Star said.

Archie stood up and walked over to the rigs. When he came back, he tossed a couple of little paper packages at me, each about half as big as an envelope.

"What's this?"

"It's called Second Skin. Cover your blisters with it in the morning. Otherwise you'll be in for it."

"Thanks."

It took a moment of rummaging through my tightly packed red bag to find my boxer shorts. Slurry still coated the long rope of my braid; I unbraided it and tried to brush it out, but was so tired I didn't even have the energy to untangle my hair.

"You're skipping your shower tonight, right?" Rock Star asked. "When there are showers at fire camp, only shrimpers use them the first couple days." Rock Star gestured at Lance, who walked toward the showers with a towel tucked under his arm, a peach loofah in the other hand. "Look at super snowboarder Lance's pansy ass shower jobby."

"Back at the Fire Center I piss on that thing every time I shower," Archie said.

"Me, too," Rock Star cackled. "Julie, don't let Lance scrub you down with that thing." I made a face.

In college, before bed I'd take a long hot shower, shave my legs, scrub myself down with a loofah. Then I'd comb out my hair, floss and brush my teeth, wash my face, pluck a few stray eyebrow hairs. At least my toothbrush and toothpaste felt familiar in my hands. The mesa loomed above me, raven black against the deep purple sky, and the air had turned cold with a bite never felt in Dallas, except in the middle of winter. Summer Dallas air was like hot, evaporated lake water. Here the air was light and clear, more absence than substance. Much as I hated home, a sudden longing filled me, perhaps for the way my childhood would've been if loss had not blotted everything else.

Lying on my back in my sleeping bag, I looked up at the vast smear of the Milky Way shining so brightly above me. I'd never been camping before.

"Your pants are gonna be mighty cold in the morning if you leave them outside your bag," Archie said.

I reached my arm out of my bag and grabbed my Nomex pants, pulling them in with me.

We all stared at the night sky. "Ah, now that's what I love about fighting fire," Archie sighed.

"Can you make out Scorpio, Rock Star?" Sam asked. There were Pikers lying on the ground all around me now, which felt odd since I had always been an only child.

"Oh, tell me again where's its tail?"

"See up over there?"

"I see it, I see it!"

I strained my eyes to the sky, but couldn't discern any patterns in the countless stars. The cool air chilled me, and I wiggled down into the bottom of my bag. My hip fit into the groove Archie had showed me how to carve in the earth. I was a joint that had finally and for once found its socket.

"And there's the Big Dipper," Sam said, "looking like

it could hold a million gallons of water."

"Hey Sam?" Rock Star asked.

"Yeah?"

"How're things going with that Bitterroot dispatcher you been seeing?

"Remember that engagement ring I bought for Nellie, the Western Slope gal? Well, I traded it in and got an upgrade. A pear-shaped diamond this time. You get more bang for your buck with a pear-shaped."

"So you're gonna propose?" Archie's voice sounded steady and calm.

"Sure am. Fighting fire's what I love," Sam said. "But it'd be nice to have a woman to come home to."

Quiet settled over us, and soon I could hear my new friends' breathing and farther away a snoring loud enough to keep the entire fire camp awake. "Shut the fuck up, Hawg," Tan barked. In the moonlight, I could see a fire boot sailing through the air before hitting Hawg with a soft whump.

Hawg snorted awake, "Sorry, sorry." Everything stayed quiet for a moment and then Hawg's ripping snores commenced again.

Chapter Five

I WOKE TO THE UNZIPPING OF SLEEPING BAGS. Rock Star and Archie clambered to their feet on either side of me as I picked crusted bits of slurry from my braid.

"Hey there, big buddy," Archie said. "Can I get a morning hug?"

"Surely," Rock Star said, throwing his arms around Archie.

"You two act like littermates."

"Archie and I haven't always been like this," Rock Star said. "We used to hate each other."

"And then one night in high school we got into it at a party at Rock Star's dad's house," Archie added, slinging his arm over Rock Star's shoulder.

"I broke one of Archie's ribs."

"And I fucked up Rock Star's shoulder."

"And we've been best friends ever since."

I fumbled to open a package of Second Skin, my hands stiff with cold. Inside was a three-by-three square of a clear gelatinous substance about the thickness of a bandage. Archie knelt beside me, pulling out his Leatherman to cut pieces of the Second Skin to fit on top of my blisters. He was so close to me I could almost feel his breath. "This is gonna fix you right up."

When I pulled on my boots and stood up to walk around, I felt like I had new feet.

The only open chair I spotted was at a table occupied by Hawg, Tan, and Clark. Where Tan was loud, gruff, and dark-haired, Clark was reserved, studious, and blond, but the two were almost as inseparable as Rock Star and Archie.

"Nice hair, Rookie," Hawg said, as I slid into the open seat. He reached out and rumpled the top of my head.

"I didn't think this was a beauty pageant," I said.

Tan glowered at me, but Clark said, "That's right. You don't have to take Hawg's shit." Clark's boyish face belied his age, and he didn't seem nearly so set on disliking me. He and Tan always looked a little strange together, Tan so small, his wiriness perfectly proportional, and Clark top heavy from wrestling for so many years, his arms and massive shoulders and chest set atop legs so skinny he looked like he was riding a chicken. It was Clark who had a certain stillness about him that came from long hours reading books.

"So how's your dissertation coming along, Clarkie?" Hawg asked.

Clark shrugged. "In a way, studying fire ecology makes it harder to fight fire. I can't swallow the bullshit the way I used to."

I shoveled in bacon, sausage, and eggs.

"Jesus, girl," Hawg said. "You're stomach sure is capacious. Maybe you oughta be the one people call Hawg." For a moment I felt a quick flash of shame, but reminded myself that none of them knew.

"Anybody want my eggs?" Clark asked.

"I'll take them," I said, before I could stop myself. Clark spooned them onto my plate. "You don't like them?"

"I'm allergic as hell."

"What happens if you eat them?"

"My eyes swell shut."

"Yikes," I said.

"No shit. It's fucking terrifying."

Hawg farted audibly. "Shaggy." He pulled a postcard out of his pocket and slapped it down on the table. "I'm sending a postcard to my buddy on Los Padres Hotshots, so I need everybody's best fire booger." Hawg reached into his nose and yanked out an inch and a half long black slug of a booger and smeared it onto the postcard, covering it with a piece of scotch tape he pulled from his pocket.

"Gross," I said.

"Jesus," Hawg said. "Don't be a fucking priss. You've heard about the LP shots, right Julie?"

I shook my head.

"They're one of the toughest crews in SoCal. Finally got a gal on the crew last year after lots of pressure from the district sup. She used to be a Division 1 soccer player, a real badass. Only the LPs wouldn't let her even dig line. She had to trail along behind the last digger with a rake."

Tan, Hawg, and Clark all looked at me expectantly. I reached into my nose and pulled out a big, black booger, wiping it on the postcard as the others cheered.

"So you're not hopeless, Rookie," Hawg said as he

covered it with scotch tape. "Okay, everybody give up your best boog." Tan and Clark just looked at him.

"You're not going to do it?" I asked, strangely disappointed.

"Go hit up Rock Star and Archie," Clark said. "Tan and I aren't about to give you our boogers. We're grown men."

As soon as we stood up from the table, the old panic at how much I'd eaten hit me. There wasn't much time before we'd gear up and head over to the helipad, so I hurried toward a stand of mountain sage on the eastern edge of fire camp. Hidden in the sagebrush, I crouched down and, for a moment, hesitated as I stared at the dry red ground. In my sleeping bag, between Archie and Rock Star, my hip had fit so well into that groove I'd dug in the earth. And the mountain sage smelled so fresh and so good. I almost returned to the camp, but the urge remained too strong. My finger disappeared down my throat to quick, controlled heaves. Worried that not every bit of my breakfast had come back up, my finger went back down my throat.

"Julie! What are you doing?"

I wiped my mouth on my sleeve as I stood and spun around, and my eyes met Hawg's. We stood for a moment, speechless. Horror at being busted overcame me, and my face flamed red. It wasn't the first time someone had discovered my secret, but it was the first time I'd ever been caught in the act.

The plumber had been the one to tell my

grandmother what I'd been doing. A year before, when I was home for summer break, I'd managed to stop up the toilet, shower, and sink in my plush bathroom at my grandmother's house. She'd pieced it together then, why I'd been on the verge of flunking out of school for two semesters in a row. Despite all my begging and pleading that she let me finish school instead of sending me straight to treatment, Frosty had patted her bouffant with her French manicured nails, tossed back a martini, and dryly insisted I needed help.

But after thinking about it all afternoon, my grandmother reconsidered. She came to my room where I sat huddled on my bed. She seemed at first as composed as ever, only her eyes were red-rimmed. "Perhaps I could've done better," she began, haltingly, "after—" She stopped, abruptly. "I thought time with me, plenty of exercise, ballet . . . would be . . . curative." I wanted to scream, throw something, anything to split open the shell of her reserve, which seemed, for the first time since she walked in on me in the bathroom that long ago day, dangerously close to cracking. But I did nothing. Perhaps, as much as I hated her composure, I myself had come to depend on it.

"I'll send you back to school," she continued, "if you promise to get help. I've called around, found a very good counselor in Colorado Springs. Specializes in this sort of thing." I could imagine how humiliated she must have felt seeking such information. "You'll get what you need, straighten up, do better in school, *feel better*." Her stress on the last two words sounded more aristocratic than reassuring. But *she* was reassured. She patted my leg and nodded at me as if we'd had a good talk. I spotted a slight wobble as she left, her ankles balanced as they were above her three-inch espadrilles. And I wanted to yell out after her, "It wasn't his fault!" My father had loved my mother with all his heart. He never meant to miss that curve in the road. He had never meant for Frosty to have to take me in.

What would her friends think of her having a granddaughter in rehab? It would be a reflection on how she'd raised me. I was glad to have dodged that bullet. I went back to school, and there Della told me all about her summer thinning timber and fighting wildfires. She and I were running and lifting weights every day that fall and talking about our dream of a summer on a hotshot crew. Nights we spent working hard on our applications. I was going to class even, and keeping up with my studies, more or less. But I was still purging. That I had been powerless to stop.

And now here in the mountain sage on the edge of fire camp, Hawg gave me a look reserved for people thought to have been mentally sound, now understood to be totally insane. Revulsion twisted his face, but below it I thought I could see puzzlement and perhaps even concern.

"What are you doing out here?" I stammered.

"I didn't want to have to grump in the Port-a-John. I don't have to ask what you're doing, apparently."

"No kidding," I said. "I'm puking like a monkey. I think those eggs I ate were bad."

"Oh," Hawg said, obviously relieved the explanation was plausible. "I thought you were . . . you know . . ."

I laughed. "Me? Oh, god, I'd never. I may be fucked up enough to be out here with you guys, but I'm not that fucked up."

Hawg fixed me with a quizzical stare and then he shrugged, and I knew he would let my lie stand.

We dug a fire line right along the edge of the fire, working so close to the flames I could feel the skin on my face burning pink from the heat. With the sawyers out ahead opening up a corridor for us, there was no one to drop the inevitable, dangerous, catfaced trees right alongside us, so that Sam was constantly yelling, "Watch the snag!" as we pounded line past tottering trees half-burned through their trunks.

Sam worked in front of me breaking ground and Hawg dug line just behind me. My arms shook with exhaustion, and I regretted having puked up my breakfast.

"Hey debutante," Hawg asked as we worked, "why don't you show us your bow?"

"Ugh," I groaned. "Never."

Looking up now and again at the forest burning hot alongside me, I realized the enormity of my coup. I was not supposed to be here, certainly. According to my grandmother, I was supposed to be home in Dallas, being courted by some pompous med student, or perhaps studying for the LSAT. And since I seemed too stubborn to look for a husband and had ruined my chances for anything my grandmother would consider a real career, I should be locked down at some eating disorder treatment center, sitting on a veranda with a bunch of emaciated, upper-class girls in wheelchairs, their hearts too taxed by starving and purging to risk ambulation, all of us staying still through the horror of digesting a meal.

"Watch the snag!" Sam yelled again. Hawg repeated Sam's cry, and it echoed down the line of diggers. We hustled to scratch line under the tree. Flames had eaten away at its roots and then skittered up the trunk, so that the high limbs still burned. Not a pecker pole, but a sizable tree, it stood at least twenty-five feet tall and a foot in diameter. Relief washed through me as I passed from under it, moving out of its falling range. Sam stepped back and radioed Douglas, telling him to send a saw team down to drop the burning tree. "This thing falls in the green, it's gonna be a mess," Sam said.

I swung at a clump of grass and somehow missed it entirely. "What ineptitude," Hawg said. "Somebody call the incompetence police."

"Shut up, Mr. Dictionary," I replied, but Hawg had stopped listening. He dropped his combi and ran back down our fire line, which looked like a raw wound gouged into the forest floor. He passed several other diggers as he yelled, "Falling!" The flaming snag was pulling up at the roots, beginning to fall over our line into the green. Hawg ran right up under it, braced his shoulder against it, and with a cry of "Huhhh!" pushed with all his might. The tree groaned with him, and for a long moment, Hawg and the tree were stalemated, like two arm wrestlers whose arms remain tilted a bit to one side, yet perfectly still, each immobilized by the other's counterstrength. The tree had an advantage, it had already begun to fall, and its weight bore down on Hawg's shoulder, as if to crush him.

Every muscle in his thick body strained, and his face turned a deep purple, veins popping out in his neck. Then with one more great cry from his gut, the tree creaked and moaned and began to move against gravity, to rise up and then tip the other way, crashing down into the black, sending up a puff of flame and a swirl of ash. Diggers all up and down the line stared drop-jawed at Hawg, who looked suddenly self-conscious, momentarily lost without the tree to struggle against. Someone down the line put his hands together, releasing one or two solitary claps and then a great cheer went up from all of us, a gleeful cry of wild, animal victory, of pride in a Piker capable of such stupid and profound strength, such dedication to keeping fire from crossing our line.

Douglas's call for a lunch break came as an echoed answer to the cries of pain coming from my cramping hands, my strained lower back, my eyes stinging with ash-streaked sweat. I was so tired from digging I stumbled as I walked. The saw team sat together, except for Rock Star, who announced he had to go take a grumpy and then clumped off into the bushes. I sat down next to the others. "Rookie, who fucking asked you to come sit by us?" Tan clenched his hard, SEAL jaw with displeasure.

"What's up with the hot and cold?" I asked. After all, Tan hadn't given me such a hard time at breakfast.

"Oh, there's no hot with regards to you." The others

laughed. "And you don't know shit about cold. In the first hour of the first phase of Hack It School, they take us down to the surf in fatigues and boots. The water's sixty degrees and we get wet, take a roll in the sand. Do a couple hundred push-ups and ten sets of ten pull-ups. You don't know shit."

My face flushed red. "Last I heard this wasn't Navy SEAL training, Mr. Glory Days." I stood up and walked over to the diggers.

"That's right," Tan called after me. "Stay in your place."

The diggers, who'd heard everything, snickered at my approach. Only Lance patted the ground beside him. "Come on and sit by me." I gratefully lowered myself to the ground next to him, a little ways away from all the other Pikers. "Don't worry about anything those guys say. They're obsessed with their own machismo."

"I just don't understand," I said, low so that even the Pikers sitting closest to us wouldn't hear. I pulled my sandwich out of my lunch bag. "Half the time they're nice enough to me."

"Don't worry about what they think of you," Lance said. "I don't." I thought of Lance heading off to the showers the night before carrying a peach loofah in full view of everyone in fire camp. "I had to get over the fact that those guys don't like me." He smiled at me, his straight white teeth flashing in the sun. "Did I tell you I was superintendent on an engine out of Boise last year?"

"No," I said, inspecting my sandwich before taking a bite. "You were too busy talking about your snowboarding triumphs to mention it."

Lance just laughed as if I'd said something charming.

Chapter Six

DUSK LOWERED ITS CLOAK DOWN AROUND fire camp as I threw my sleeping bag on the ground again between Archie and Rock Star. "How was dinner with super snowboarder Lance?" Rock Star asked pointedly.

"Don't be stupid," I said. "At least he wasn't picking on me this afternoon."

"Julie, you're going to have to have a thicker skin to make it as a hotshot," Rock Star said. "A little good-natured hazing is part of the beast."

I lay in my sleeping bag between them for a long time, looking up at the stars, my spine pressed against the earth. Sleep evened out Rock Star and Archie's breathing. Snores that could've only been Hawg's ripped out thirty feet away.

Every sinew and muscle ached from my long day of digging, and I hoped I'd fall asleep before I had to climb out and go pee. Finally I gave up, creeping from my sleeping bag and shoving my feet into my White's. When I was a good ways from the others, I squatted behind a bush. Walking back toward my sleeping bag, I saw a silhouette moving toward me, and I thought of the leering prisoners in their orange jumpsuits. "Who is it?" I whispered. "Who is it?" I hissed again, and then I could see Lance's delicate features illuminated by the moonlight.

"It's me," Lance said, almost inaudibly, and when we met in the darkness, he put an arm around my waist and pulled me to him. Before I could stop him, he leaned in to kiss me, but I stepped back quickly, pushing him away.

The sound of Pikers stirring all around woke me, and I peeked out of the top of my sleeping bag. "Morning Sweet Lips," I heard Rock Star sing. "Oh, Lance," he said. He grabbed Archie around the waist and pressed his mouth to Archie's, only his hand in between. "Mmmmm, oh, oh, Lance." Rock Star let go of Archie. "I'm surprised Lance didn't start licking at the old salt block."

"Shut up," I said. "That's so gross!"

"You can't hide from the Pike, Julie," Rock Star said. "We know what you've been up to."

By the time we geared up to hike to the fire, the gossip about my nocturnal encounter with Lance had spread through the crew like wildfire. My chest burned from the stage whispers spoken more than loud enough for me to hear as I pulled my ching from the back of our rig.

"Hundreds of guys here at fire camp and one woman, and Lance is the one with the stink finger," Hawg mused. "But how could Julie help herself? He's so debonair."

"I couldn't sleep last night for all the slishing and slurping," Rock Star muttered loudly. "It about made me sick."

My face flushed hot. "That is the biggest bunch of bullshit."

"The rookie girl was off to a decent start this season," Clark said, wandering over from his squad to join in, "but looks like she crashed and burned early."

"Disgusting!" Tan barked, like an angry drill sergeant. "That's why women shouldn't fight fire."

I rolled my eyes.

Nearby, Lance chatted away with the other diggers as he pulled on his hard hat and pack. He certainly wasn't getting slapped with the kind of shit I was taking. He looked up. Our eyes met and he gave me an appalling, slow-motion, conspiratorial wink.

As terrible as the morning had been, I figured the Pikers were over their glee at my imagined tryst. During an afternoon break, Hawg, Tan, and Clark leaned back on their packs, talking and laughing and eating trail mix. As I approached, their conversation ceased and I sat down on the ground amid an awkward silence. After a minute Tan started throwing trail mix in my lap saying, "Here birdie, here birdie, birdie."

"What are you doing?" I demanded, brushing the trail mix off like it was hot ash.

"It's lovebird seed," Tan said, straight-faced, and every Piker within earshot howled with laughter.

Back on the fire line, a burned-out tree teetered and fell over our fire line into the green. Tan hustled toward it, started his saw, and began to cut up the tree trunk.

Archie picked up a section to carry it over to the burning side. Hawg picked up another. Sam dug a line around the fallen tree to keep the fire from spreading. I squatted down and took hold of a section of the bucked-up tree trunk. I strained with all my might, but couldn't get it to budge. Hawg returned just as Tan turned off his saw.

"Bump," Hawg barked. I stepped back, frustrated, as Hawg picked it up and carried it across the line.

As soon as I was in my hotel room, I shucked my filthy Nomex, took a long hot shower, and put on jeans for the first time since leaving the Pike Fire Center. I blew my hair dry and found a lip gloss and mascara deep in the side pocket of my red bag, stashed in anticipation of just such an occasion. Downstairs I found at least half the crew drinking in the otherwise deserted hotel bar, decorated to look like an old-time Western saloon. As I sat perched alone on a barstool, the pretty bartender's smiling face came as a relief. She slid me a strongly poured gin and tonic. The first sip came with the bite of quinine, the fresh zing of lime, and the luxury of crushed ice unimaginable on the fire line. Two seats over, Tan and Clark sat drinking Coors, but they didn't acknowledge me. Though I knew by then they were both thirty, baby-faced Clark didn't look old enough to be in graduate school and Tan's face could've been fresh off of a Navy recruitment billboard. Archie and Hawg came in and headed over to Clark and Tan.

Hawg called out to me. "What's up, oh effete and dainty one?"

I gave him a look and took a long sip of my drink. When I spoke, it was to Tan. "You'd bucked up that tree trunk into smaller pieces, I could've carried them just fine."

"And if I get splanged by some big rock right as the fire blows up, you gonna be able to carry me out just fine?" Hawg asked.

"I'm not even sure I could carry you out, buddy," Archie said. And we all laughed.

Hawg walked up to the baby grand piano and sat down, oddly comfortable there in his unbuttoned flannel shirt and stained T-shirt, his hair wild. "Play us a tune, fat body," Tan joked. We all looked at each other, wide-eyed with surprise, as Hawg began to pound out "Great Balls of Fire." Hotel guests wandering back from dinner trickled in, and people walking down the street pressed their noses against the window. And then the Lolo Hotshots started coming in, just a few at a time, until it seemed their whole crew was there. With their arms covered in sleeve tattoos, they looked more like an overgrown death metal band than a hotshot crew. The Pikers and Lolos eyed each other like warring clans.

But before long dancing couples and laughter packed the lounge. On the other side of the room I could make out Lance and his weaselly roommate Gary talking and laughing with a cluster of diggers. Lance met my eye and raised a slender black brow. I shook my head and looked away.

Across the way Sam dropped down in the middle of the dance floor to do a set of one-armed push-ups, and Rock Star and Archie two-stepped with a couple of pretty young girls. Couples who'd wandered in off Main Street to investigate the music swung their hips, Pikers and Lolos tossed back shots of whiskey, and I sat on my barstool alone, watching it all, an old familiar loneliness rising up in me. My grandmother had dragged me to a hundred and one coming-out parties and as many fund-raiser and debutante balls, and I'd learned well how to assume this very pose and watch the tigerish women swish by in bright gowns, the men all portly, identical penguins. Only here in this hotel bar in the mountains, I didn't want to be apart.

Hawg finished a passable cover of "Tiny Dancer" and then headed over to talk to Sam. Archie and Rock Star tuned up a couple of old acoustic guitars the bartender had brought out for them.

The Lolo with the blue goatee and one of his buddies pressed in beside me at the bar. Blue Goatee pulled out a wad of bills and threw down a twenty. "What'll that buy me?" he asked the bartender suggestively.

"Vulgarian?" Sam asked Hawg. It was the dictionary game with no dictionary.

"Nouveau riche, churlish, ignorant, turd-bobbing Lolo lout."

Archie and Rock Star began strumming the guitars hard, the sound filling up the room. They looked confident and too handsome for their own good. Everyone turned to watch them as Archie began to sing the Marshall Tucker band's "Fire on the Mountain," Rock Star joining him on the chorus. "And there's fire on the mountain/lightning in the air."

Even the Lolos watched without speaking. Archie took a few steps forward as he strummed, until he stood almost directly in front of me. We looked right at each other as he sang the last refrain. Everyone joined in on the final chorus. As the song ended, the bar exploded into applause. I took a step toward Archie, but he was already turning away, clapping Rock Star on the back.

Just under the noise of the crowd I heard Sam say to Hawg, "Puppy love?"

"Smitten. Twitterpated. Eat up with it," Hawg replied.

Flustered, I turned back to the bar, accidentally knocking over Blue Goatee's beer in the process. "I'm sorry," I said, mopping up the beer as best I could with a napkin.

"You missed some," Blue Goatee said, pointing to his crotch.

Hawg stepped up beside me. "You say something, turdbobber?"

"You deaf, fat boy?" Blue Goatee asked.

Hawg hauled back and punched Blue Goatee in the face. The impact of his fist against Blue Goatee's cheek released all the pent-up tension between the Pikers and Lolos. The bar erupted into a giant brawl. I pressed my back against the bar to stay out of the way of the sudden violence.

I saw a Lolo grab Archie in a headlock. Archie elbowed him to escape. Another Lolo prepared to jump Rock Star, but Archie smashed the Lolo with a chair, and the Lolo dropped to the ground.

In front of me, Blue Goatee took a flying leap at Hawg,

knocking him down. Before I could think, I rushed toward Blue Goatee, grabbed a handful of his hair and pulled him off Hawg. Blue Goatee turned around and gave me a shove that sent me stumbling backward. I knocked over a couple of chairs as I went down. As I scrambled to my feet, I saw a flash of Hawg's outraged face, and then I was charging Blue Goatee. I rammed him in the gut with my shoulder and he fell back, landing on a table and then rolling off onto the floor.

"Out!" a voice yelled, and we all turned to see the bartender standing on top of the bar, holding a baseball bat.

The Pikers congregated in a dive bar across from the hotel. They sported bleeding cuts and buzzed with the energy of the fight. I sat on a barstool with Hawg, Tan, and Clark standing all around me. I was giddy with the thrill of the fight, light-headed with the fresh memory of my own bravery.

"Who's got a fresh ground scrod?" Hawg asked. "I'm jonesing."

"You're always bumming scrod off of me," Tan complained. His dimples popped out as he made a sour face.

"It's true," Clark added.

"Seriously, Tan, I'm gonna stock up on about fifteen cans of scrod for our next tour, and then when you run out, I'll be the one hooking you up," Hawg said.

Tan rolled his eyes. "When whores work for free, I'll believe that one." But he pulled a can of tobacco out of his back pocket. Tan put a pinch in his bottom lip and held the can out to Clark and then Hawg. All three of them sighed with communal satisfaction.

"It sucks we didn't make our full twenty-one," Hawg lamented. "I hate to go home tomorrow."

"Eleven days of overtime and hazard pay. It's a start," Clark said. "It's not a twenty-one, but it's not bad."

The eleven days I'd just spent on the fire line being ostracized by the crew had seemed like a full year. This feeling of sudden belonging and confidence that had come with the bar fight was something I wanted to keep going.

"I'll take a fresh ground," I said. Tan raised an eyebrow, but wordlessly stretched out his hand. I grabbed a pinch of tobacco and put it in my bottom lip. The tobacco tasted pungent, dark, and good, and I felt a brutal, punch-drunk rush. The edge of the bar against my back steadied me; my feet remained hooked inside the bottom rung of the barstool. Hawg leaned forward to talk to me over Clark. "Man, Julie, the first time I put in a scrod I was eight years old, and my cousin and I were hiding out on the roof of the barn. I puked over the side just as my dad came out. He beat my ass with the business end of his belt for that one." Hawg's tone was surprisingly friendly.

"You're probably going to yeep," Clark agreed.

I shook my head, flagging down the bartender for a paper cup to spit in. "I'm not much of a puker." The lie rolled out easily.

"Except when you eat bad eggs," Hawg said.

"Every egg's a bad egg as far as I'm concerned," Clark said.

"How does all this seem to you after grad school?"
I asked him, gesturing at the Pikers around us eagerly
recounting their part in the bar fight.

"This sure ain't academia, but I'm used to it. I'm
the only grad student I know who's written most of a
dissertation on the fire line."

"I'd love to read it," I said. "I don't know a thing about
forest ecology, but I'd like to."

"You're the only Piker besides Tan and Hawg who's
shown any interest in the damn thing." For a moment,
neither of us spoke.

"You love it, huh?" I asked.

"Fighting fire?"

"Yeah."

"Well, let me put it this way," Clark said. "You wake
up at dawn, dig line for fifteen hours, then at night you
lie on the ground under the stars and fall asleep. Life gets
real simple." I spit tentatively into the paper cup, wiping
a dribble of tobacco juice from my chin. I felt buoyed
up by nicotine and hope. "And the land's more beautiful
somehow after you spend fifteen-hour days working on it."

The walls of the bar pulsed and whirled around me. The
edge of the barstool bit into my fingers and I swallowed hard.

"That's the thing about the Pike," Clark continued.
I'd never heard him string so many words together. "It
takes us out to country so remote, places almost no one
who's alive today has ever seen before. I love the forests
and good God but this is a prettier country than people
ever have a chance to realize. Being on the Pike, it makes
me feel like I'm really living, that's all. Living in a way so

many folks never do."

The nausea overwhelmed me, and I bolted from my barstool and out the door of the bar. I puked in the street and then again in my hotel room. Throwing up from the scrod brought the old familiar rush. Once the nausea lifted, I lay on the soft bed for awhile, feeling my breath going in and out of me.

When I heard a light knock on the door of my hotel room, I staggered to my feet. A peek through the peephole revealed Lance standing in the hallway holding a flower he must've plucked from the table of the hotel restaurant. I opened the door a crack. "What are you doing? Are you crazy?" I hissed.

"Can I come in? I brought you a flower."

"No, you can't come in," I said. "Come on, Lance, I'm trying to be a hotshot here."

"Quit worrying so much what everyone else thinks of you," Lance said, "and we could really have something."

I shoved the door shut, double locking it for good measure, hoping furiously that none of the Pikers would come down the hall and see Lance in front of my door clutching the stolen flower.

Out on my hotel room balcony, I sat in the chill night with a blanket wrapped around me, looking up to the sky where the city lights washed out most of the celestial lights above. I wished I had someone to call to tell about the glory of the bar fight. I would've called Della, but she was probably on a fire herself. I would have called her except for the fact that after she helped me apply for hotshot crews, after we'd spent the fall months training together, somehow she'd figured out about my bulimia. She confronted me, told me she didn't think I had any business on a hotshot crew. "You're gonna be the representative female," she said. "You can't do that if you're sick with this thing." I'd stopped talking to her then, so angry at her, so righteously indignant. Just because I couldn't stop myself from puking, it didn't mean I shouldn't have a chance at fire.

After Della and I fell out, the binging and purging got worse, much worse, because I no longer had anyone to pretend for. I stopped going to class, stopped studying for exams, gave up on my thesis entirely. I saved all my energy for eating and throwing up, and for working out to prepare myself in case a job offer came from a hotshot crew. And then Douglas called me for an interview.

As I sat there on the balcony, for one unlikely moment I considered calling my grandmother. To tell her this was the hardest thing I'd ever done and that I wanted her to be proud of me. But I knew I never would.

The sound of a glass door sliding open two balconies down startled me from my thoughts. Two tall figures appeared, one carrying a big bundle in his arms. Quietly I slid my chair over into a dark corner of the balcony.

"Would you watch out?" Archie demanded.

"I got it, buddy. I got it," Rock Star said. Their drunken whispers carried easily on the thin summer air.

Both figures knelt down before the balcony rail with the bundle in front of them, and for a moment it looked as if they were joining together in some strange ritual of prayer to the gods of fire. But then Rock Star let out a little whoop of triumph, and Archie shushed him. They stood up, and one silhouette tossed the bulky bundle over the rail and the knotted-together sheets cascaded to the ground. Rock Star swung his leg over the balcony and shimmied down. As soon as his feet hit the grass below, Archie followed suit, and then the two ran across the green hotel lawn in their boxer shorts, wailing like banshees, all efforts to be quiet forgotten in the sheer easy joy of flying on fleet feet toward the glowing blue of the hotel swimming pool.

Lights popped on all along the side of the hotel. Pikers and groggy, irritated hotel guests stepped out onto their balconies just as Rock Star and Archie dive-bombed the swimming pool, its flat surface erupting as the compact cannonballs of their bodies cracked the water. Douglas stepped out onto the balcony next to mine, anger radiating from him into the darkness. When the two delinquents surfaced, Douglas's low tone carried like a dog's warning growl. "Archie. Rock Star."

"D-oh! Sorry, Douglas," Rock Star said. Archie stayed characteristically silent.

"Oh, you'll be sorry," Douglas said and disappeared back into his hotel room, sliding the glass door behind him.

Chapter Seven

AN EERIE QUIET HUNG OVER MY SQUAD AS we hit the road, the sun beginning its bright white rise from behind the mountains, all of us groggy from the night before. Sam looked red-eyed and grim as he drove the winding road through the looming mountains; his usual levity had disappeared, and he didn't glance up once to wink at me in the rearview. Rock Star and Archie actually acted a little cowed. The only one behaving normally was Hawg. "It's like a cat shat in my mouth while I was sleeping," he said, smacking his lips. "I need to remember not to mix my libations." He leaned his head against the window and conked out minutes out of town, and no one even commented when the snores started ripping out of him.

"How many hours to Monument?" I asked, ready to be back at the Fire Center.

"Six," Sam said, "but we're not headed straight home."

"We're not?"

"No, we're gonna stop on the way. Hike Paloma Canyon."

"Paloma Canyon where all the firefighters died last year?" I asked.

Rock Star jabbed me in the ribs with his elbow and made a face.

"That's the only Paloma Canyon I know," Sam mumbled.

As I opened my mouth again, Rock Star shook his head and gave me a look.

"Everyone's in such a mood," I complained, but I kept quiet after that, feeling uneasy.

We'd driven so high up into the mountains that even with sunglasses on we shielded our eyes as we stood at the trailhead. The mountain sloping up above us had been burned hot. All the snagged out trees had been clear cut, and so the landscape rose above us ashy and desolate. "We'll be hiking in our Piker T-shirts, no need for Nomex shirts, no need to carry our packs," Douglas said, all of us erupting in celebratory hoots and hollers. "But our friends Rock Star and Archie will be carrying their chainsaws up the mountain as a reminder that the guests of the Basalt Hotel didn't appreciate their antics last night."

"Yeah, you woke me from a dream where I was banging a delectable little fat chick," Hawg said.

"Jesus Christ, Hawg," Tan barked. "We don't want to hear it."

"Enough of that Pike, let's line it out," Douglas said. I would've gladly taken the punishment of hiking with a saw over the scorn I'd received since arriving on the Pike. Piker sentiment toward me seemed to have warmed a bit since the bar fight, but I was obviously still on probation. The thought of it had made me want to get rid of my breakfast in the bathroom of JB's where we'd stopped for the breakfast buffet. With a long drive ahead, I told myself I wouldn't need the food for fuel to hike and dig. But for some reason I stayed at the table, Archie across from me, both of us drinking our coffee and the rest of the Pikers all around. It was a quiet morning, no one talking much, let alone to me.

"Enjoy those saws, men, enjoy them," Tan called. He'd spent his early twenties on the sea for Special Forces operations he would never discuss, perhaps scared shitless and too proud to show it. It was clear how it must've changed him. He never talked about why he'd left the service. He welded now in the off-season up in Casper, soldered iron, bent rebar to his will—a fitting profession for an intractable, severe nature.

Sam stood a little ways off from the rest of us. He suddenly bent down to the ground and then straightened back up to his full height, holding a perfectly carved arrowhead aloft.

"Shit, man," Hawg said. "You're like half Indian." Sam held the arrowhead out for the rest of us to inspect. There was an aching, haunted look in his eyes I'd never seen before.

I slipped in behind Hawg as the crew began moving up the trail. Archie and Rock Star hiked up front just behind Douglas, each of them with a chainsaw balanced on his shoulder. "Did you puke last night, Julie?" Hawg asked.

"What are you talking about?" I asked, ready with a defense.

"From the scrod?"

"Oh," I said, relieved. He didn't know. "Yeah, sure did."

He laughed. "The first dip of scrod'll get you."

My breath had started coming faster, and when I glanced to my right I could see the highway down below us, cars crawling like insects along the black ribbon of road. We were definitely climbing. Across the valley I could see the unburned mountains, lush and green in the sunlight. As we zigzagged up the steep dirt trail through leftover ash and new growth oak brush, I could hardly imagine Dallas, the skyscrapers and spaghetti freeways packed bumper to bumper with cars, all of it wavering in the heat. Out there on the path up Paloma Mountain, Dallas seemed to me like a figment of an unhealthy imagination.

Somewhere up the line of Pikers, Tan's voice rose up loud and clear, singing cadence. "Oh I used to be a liar."

The rest of the Pikers responded, echoing Tan's song, "Oh I used to be a liar."

"Now I'm fighting forest fires."

"Now I'm fighting forest fires," the Pikers sang back to him, and I joined in, a chill traveling down my spine to be part of the sound.

"Hawg's always looking for fat chicks," Tan sang.

"Hawg's always looking for fat chicks," we echoed.

"Who like to suck on big old sticks."

"Who like to suck on big old sticks."

Grass came up thick and green from the ash. Marmots galloped along over rocks and clumps of oak brush just barely starting to come up again. Blue sky arched over us, and the sun rose up, warm, but not too hot. The terrain stretching out below us would've been gorgeous if it wasn't for the highway cutting through. Halfway up the mountain and already I was tiring, but singing along with the cadence lifted my thoughts from the effort of hiking the steep slope and reminded me that I was part of the line of Pikers moving up the switchbacks in the trail ahead.

"There they are!" someone called, and looking up, I could see the fourteen white crosses scattered across the mountain. As the crew approached them, our line broke up, and Pikers wandered toward the crosses. Little offerings lay cluttered around their bases: laminated poems, bottles of beer, shirts and stickers from other fire crews, arrowheads, and silver dollars. Engraved on each cross was a name, birth date, and whether the person had been a hotshot, a smokejumper, or an engine crewmember.

Just ahead of me Sam stepped off the trail, almost stumbling. He looked suddenly slump-shouldered and too thin. Clark stepped up to him and took his elbow. "You okay?" Sweat had popped out on Sam's forehead and he looked woozy. Either he'd drunk way more the night before than I'd realized, or he was coming down with something.

"I'm alright," Sam said, his voice like a heartache.

"When a mountain's been burned this hot, it takes a good while for the new growth to come in. But it'll come," Clark said, patting Sam on the back.

Sam made a weird little sound, shrugging off Clark's hand and trundling away toward the two crosses that were highest up the mountain. Clark took a step to follow, but then stopped himself and merely watched as Sam hiked away from him. When Sam reached the crosses, one ten feet or so above the other, both so close to the top of the ridge it made my chest hurt to think how those two had almost made it over to safety, he bent down and touched the first cross. Then he walked up to the highest one and lowered himself down to the ground next to it, slowly, as if the effort of hiking up the mountainside had aged him considerably.

I sat down by myself next to a cross that had been decorated with seashells, a beer bottle, and a rotting crew T-shirt. A shadow fell over me. Archie loomed above, the saw still over his shoulder. He set it down and collapsed next to me on the ground. Sweat ran down his temples and his breath came hard. "I'm whupped from carrying that saw, and I haven't even been digging line all day. Makes me realize how beat they must've been when the fire started barreling up the mountain. Fire rips uphill, you know. Radiant heat dries out the fuel above and—" He made a gesture to signify fire blazing uphill.

"It could happen to us," I said.

"Any day it could. It reminds me it's only by grace that we've still got the breath God blew into us." I didn't believe in God, not the way Archie did, but it meant something to me, the way he said it. Longing for the belief Archie clearly felt stirred like a broken sparrow behind my breastbone. "You know," Archie continued, "I looked up 'grace' in the dictionary one time, and it said, 'A gift freely given and undeserved.' Fight fire long enough and you mess with some serious odds, and being alive becomes a sort of grace."

Grace had only ever come to me in tattered scraps. Archie who had always had his solid family, his best friend Rock Star, and memories of a happy childhood in the woods could believe.

"Can I ask you a question?"

"Fire away," Archie said.

"What's up with Sam?"

"He's like a vet at the Vietnam Memorial," Archie said.

"He was here?" A shudder rippled through me.

"Sure was. He was working a three-week detail last season with an engine out of Green Lake so he could get his Strike Team Engine Leader checked off in his Task Book. He also wanted to hang out with a couple of his buddies, Mike Letz and Dan Mosano. They'd been on that engine for years. When the wind shifted and that fireball ripped uphill, Sam and his buddies tried to hike up and over the ridge. They knew they'd be safe if they could just get over the top—fire burns so slowly downhill. Sam just barely made it. Mike and Dan were right on his heels, but they weren't so lucky. Sam said he hunkered at a rockslide over the ridge until the fire passed. He was the first to hike back over and find them." Archie gestured to the crosses around us.

"Oh my God," I said, "I had no idea."

"Nobody around here is exactly confiding in you," Archie said, not unkindly. A quiet settled between us. "Looking at these crosses makes me think. You can't tell by looking which of these guys were strong on their crews and which were weak. You can't tell which of them couldn't stand each other and which were best buddies from way back. The crosses, they remind me of how, from a distance, no one could've told Jesus from the two thieves."

We were quiet again, and I felt jealous of Archie. Perhaps he could be so certain in who he was because he believed all the things that had always seemed like bullshit to me. It came radiating off him, the certainty that he existed in the center of an ineffable grace, while I myself had always lived on its terrifying fringes.

"Hiking up here with your saw must've been brutal."

"Nah, Rock Star and I like sweating out our badness. The saws are our own tiny crosses to bear, right? And they aren't so rough. I mean, Jesus didn't get to hike the thirteen stations with his best buddy, that's for sure. It would've been a whole other story if he had."

"Oh, so now you and Rock Star are Christ figures." I gave Archie's shoulder a hard push. Our laughter came as a wash of relief, and I had the sudden irrational feeling that if Archie would just throw a big arm around me and pull me to him, everything in my life would be set right. We quieted again, something humming between us. I moved my hand a tiny bit so that the edge of my fingers touched his.

"The girl who was on the crew last season?" Archie said. "Everyone liked her just fine until she started hooking up with Hawg. From then on her nickname was Wild Herp. And she got nothing but disrespected."

"I kind of figured," I said.

"I don't want that for you." Archie looked at me, a great longing between us. "Pals?" he said.

"Pals," I agreed.

He stood up and slung his saw over his shoulder, then started up the hill toward the crosses higher up the mountain.

With my eyes closed, I put my head down on my knees, trying to focus on breathing, but it was almost as if

I could see them, the burned bodies, hot still, glowing and smoking, all of them letting off a terrible stench.

Walking back down the mountain was easier. We wove our way along the trail between the shoots of new oak brush, the Pikers ahead of me looking vulnerable without their long-sleeved Nomex and hard hats, without heavy gray packs on their backs. Chipmunks and marmots zigzagged in front of us. Tan sang cadence again, and the rest of us responded with one voice that drifted through the thin summer air of the canyon. To me the song said that we would always be young, that we'd always be part of a group soldered together by the risks we faced and survived together.

Right before the crew dropped down below a ridge I turned around to look at the crosses, small and far away, the fire scar already disappearing beneath the green of new growth.

As soon as we hit the road and Archie, Rock Star, and Hawg fell asleep again, I asked Sam how he was holding up. He shrugged, and for a long moment it didn't seem he'd speak. "It's burned into my nostrils, that terrible smell. My friends. And I keep thinking what I could've done different. Like if I'd spun a weather just before and had known the relative humidity had dropped, if I'd said we should deploy instead of trying to make it over the ridge. I tell you what, though, Julie, it may sound strange, but that's the day I realized it: I'm gonna be fighting fire for life. Being a hotshot, it means everything to me." Sam cleared his throat.

"Everything?"

"I never had a real family of my own. My ex and I are still friends, sure, but our marriage couldn't hold up to hotshotting. I never seen one that could."

"And your folks?" It was a question I almost never asked because I dreaded it myself.

"Living in their old place, the house I grew up in, makes me feel sometimes like they're still with me."

"You mean—"

"Both of 'em. Of cancer within two years of each other, back when I was in high school."

"I was twelve," I said. Our eyes caught in the rearview mirror.

"Your mom and dad?" he asked, his voice low.

"Together," I said. "They were on vacation in Mexico, driving from Cuernavaca to Taxco. Their car went over a cliff." Suddenly I couldn't stop myself. "The car, it exploded, or caught fire, whatever. Burned right up. They had to be identified by their dental records." As soon as the words were out, a profound exhaustion coursed through me, the fatigue laced with relief that I had finally spoken them aloud.

Sam nodded slowly. There was no need to comment further, but in the silence the understanding of orphans drifted down between us and held us fast together.

"So you made it through your first tour with the Pike," Sam finally said.

"It wasn't a full twenty-one."

"Still, it counts. You fought some fire, you dug some line." He paused. "You gonna make me proud?"

Suddenly, unexpectedly, my eyes filled with tears. I nodded.

Sam reached over his shoulder and dropped the arrowhead he'd found into my hand. "An arrowhead from Paloma Canyon. You keep it." It gleamed in my cupped palm, and I realized I'd never belonged anywhere before in my whole life.

Our four crew rigs pulled into a gas station, and all of us hiked into the store to buy snacks. With twenty Pikers crammed into the aisles there was barely enough room to pick out something to eat or drink, but I liked it, having them jostling around me and how the other customers turned to look at us in our matching Nomex pants and crew T-shirts, how they saw us as one entity. "Look at this," Hawg said, shoving a box of individually wrapped wedges of cheese toward Archie and me. "In French these are called 'petite fromage.' Little cheese. Listen to the sound of those words, so beautiful, so lilting. Petite fromage," Hawg exclaimed, delighted with the sound rolling from his lips. "In English, you know what they're called?" He pointed at the box. "Pasteurized cheese snacks," he read in disgust. "The butchery of a gorgeous phrase. Travesty."

"You are such a paradox," I said.

"Shut up, Rookie," Hawg said. "Don't you have a former engine slug to smooch?" But I could tell he was only joking. Hawg opened up his round box of pasteurized cheese snacks and held up one V-shaped wedge still wrapped in tinfoil. "Petite fromage," he said. "Petite fromage. I can't wait to knock the bottom out of some fat chick's petite fromage."

"Yuck," I said, turning away just as Lance brushed by me to reach the rack of candy bars. I jerked back as if I'd been singed. He looked at me with plaintive eyes, and I spun around, heading to the cash register.

We drove south from Denver along I-25, the jagged mountains of the Front Range running alongside us to the west. The afternoon light played over them, revealing deep blue creases, the stodgy, dark fir brooding together, the bright aspen flirting lighthearted with the breeze. A few thunderclouds rolled up from behind the mountains. To the east, the flat plains stretched away endlessly, a vast expanse of loneliness hiding nothing. Douglas drove ahead of us in the saw truck, the other two Suburbans rolled along behind us, all four vehicles pulling off at the Monument exit. Rock Star and Archie had grown up there in that town of two thousand, knowing everyone, running wild in the mountains. Sam had done the same before them.

Their childhood and adolescence must've been wholesome and good, time spent outdoors in the forest, cold lakes and sunshine in the summers and, in the winters, snow. Even Sam had his parents nearly through high school. I felt suddenly faint with jealousy. From twelve on I had suffered through endless rounds of tea parties and dinners with my grandmother and her friends, held in country clubs and ostentatious houses icy with air-conditioning. And always there were my grandmother's exhortations to me to act like a lady. I had not had a chance at fishing barehanded in a mountain lake or learning that moss grows on the north-facing side of trees.

We passed the fast-food restaurants and gas stations that lined the strip along the highway, but as we drove west from the highway into town, we wound our way by little mom-and-pop shops, the Coffee Cup Café, the post office. We rolled over the railroad tracks and out of town on the black asphalt ribbon, the land opening up and turning beautiful, the road winding right alongside the mountains. We passed occasional houses with wide stretches of open space and trees between them. In fifteen minutes we'd be back at the Pike Fire Center, tucked against the mountains of the National Forest. Once out there, it was hard to imagine that we weren't in the far reaches of wilderness, hard to believe that the little town of Monument was so close by and Denver just forty miles to the north. The CB crackled and Douglas's voice came over the radio, crisp as an ironed shirt. "Sam, Doug."

"You know, Douglas was a Class C faller," Rock Star said. "But he hasn't touched a chainsaw since he made superintendent. He wants to be all white-collar, he's trying to keep up with his girlfriend, the oncologist. But really he's just turning his back on what he's really good at."

Sam frowned and gestured for Rock Star to hush before pushing down the CB button. "Go Doug."

"There's a single tree lightning strike up on Mount Herman. I want your squad to peel off and take care of it."

"That's what I love about being on Sam's squad," Archie said. "We always get the sweet ops."

Sam followed the saw truck as it took a right onto

a dirt road, but then as Douglas turned left at the stone Forest Service sign for the Pike Fire Center, Sam kept straight, taking the road that twisted and turned for miles up Mount Herman, through the dense ponderosa pines. When he pulled over on the shoulder, the five of us climbed out, putting on our hard hats and packs, then lining it out. Sam led the way, hiking quickly up the mountain, through the forest. Rock Star followed him, carrying the saw, then Archie and Hawg. I brought up the rear. The crunch of our footsteps on the duff was the only sound, and the thin air smelled of summer and pine needles. I could hear the babble of a creek somewhere nearby. There was no trail, and Sam didn't carry a compass or a map, but he hiked without hesitation, somehow knowing how to find the tree. He seemed guided by an instinct I doubted I'd ever have, no matter how long I fought fire. I smelled smoke and saw that we were standing at the base of the tree, looking up at the smoldering split in its branches. "This probably wouldn't have gone anywhere," Sam said.

"But it sure gets us hazard pay for the day," Hawg said.

"What do you say we have a scrod before we drop it?" Sam suggested, and the others nodded. We sat on the ground, leaning back against our packs, and for a moment I envied them the ritual of their shared addiction. Suddenly Rock Star said, "How would you like to drop that tree, Julie?"

My mouth went dry and my insides fluttered at the thought of wielding a chainsaw. "Fuck yeah."

"Sam?" Rock Star asked.

"Go for it, Julie," Sam said.

I climbed to my feet, wiping my palms on my Nomex.

I hadn't touched a saw since the Class A Faller training my first week at the Fire Center. "Nah," Rock Star said. "I want to drop it after all."

Disappointment coursed through me. "Come on!" I said.

"Nope. But you can swamp for me, if it's okay with Archie."

"If Julie thinks she's up for swamping, it's fine by me." There had never been a woman on the saw team, not a woman sawyer, not a woman swamper. It was something I'd known before anyone had ever told me. I wiped my palms again, and tightened my hard hat. Rock Star yanked his saw cord, and the chainsaw came to life in his hands.

He stepped up to the tree and I stood behind him, looking up at the top branches as he put in his pie cut. I didn't glance at him as he pulled out the wedge and flung it away. I wanted to see if the treetop started to tremble. I wanted to be ready. Rock Star stepped back around to my side of the tree to put in his back cut. Archie, Sam, and Hawg's eyes burned into me from where they stood fifteen feet or so behind us. When the tree started to wobble I yelled, "Falling!" Rock Star and I both stepped back and the tree crashed to the ground.

"Help me stump it," Rock Star yelled over the idle of the chainsaw, and I rushed to him. He crouched down and put the saw up against the very bottom of the tree, as close as possible to the ground. The chain spun on the bar and the teeth dug into the stump. Rock Star looked up at me, and though I couldn't see his eyes behind his sunglasses he lifted his chin at me to signal that, as he cut, I should lean my weight against the stump to push it over. It wasn't yet ready to budge, and I leaned a little harder, wanting them all to see my strength.

The saw bar was three-quarters of the way through the stump when it started to move. I pushed harder still, and suddenly it gave, the stump completely freed from its base in that fraction of an instant and me still shoving on it with all my might.

I lost my balance, pitching forward with the stump. It began to fly over, and I could feel myself going with it. The realization of what was happening hit me, and the moment hung suspended. An overturned gray stone caught my eye, a batch of ragged blades of grass crowding together, the saw bar slick and hungry below me. I willed myself to somehow undo forces of gravity and physics, but my equilibrium was already lost, the weight of my backpack working against me. I hurtled forward, my arms outstretched, falling toward the roaring bar of the chainsaw. Each second stretched out to a long lifetime as I plummeted toward the ground, my hands extended in front of me, on a perfect trajectory to be cut off by the ravenous, growling saw bar.

On instinct, Rock Star straightened his arms, his shoulder muscles straining below his Nomex. With all his might he threw the running saw away from us and for a moment the saw, the stump, and I were all hurtling through the air. The stump crashed to the ground and I hit the earth, and the saw bounced and moaned and idled just in front of me. I rolled over onto my back and held my hands in front of my face, wiggling my fingers, twirling my hands on my wrists, too overcome by the miracle that they were still attached to my body to be mortified by my clumsiness.

"Thank God we didn't let you run the saw," Rock Star said. "Jesus, I think you should stick to digging." Sam made a sound halfway between a laugh and an agonized, choking cough, and then Archie was there above me, his grip solid and true as he grabbed my hands and pulled me to my feet.

Chapter Eight

THE SHOCKED FEELING HADN'T QUITE WORN off by the time Sam took a right at the dirt road to the Pike Fire Center. We drove down past the pond, the stands of ponderosa, the wide open PT fields, and at the end of the road I could see the dark green roofs of the Fire Center nestled in the pines. Mount Herman rose up behind them, as if sheltering the buildings from the worst of the elements.

The other two Suburbans and the saw truck were parked in the dirt lot between the Saw Cache and the kitchen. The Pikers bustled around the Saw Cache, sharpening tools, cleaning out the trucks. My squad spilled out of our rig as the Lama helicopter came circling around overhead, disappearing out of sight as it lowered down to land on the helipad on the hill up above us. "Slappy ass helitack crew is gonna come strutting in thinking they're hot shit 'cause they've been to some dinky little fire," Clark said.

"Those guys are such sorry fat asses."

"Jimmy finally filled that open spot on the helitack crew," Douglas said, his eyes dancing. "Some of you guys might be interested to meet the new helitacker."

"I've never met a helitacker I liked," Rock Star said. "None of those slappies could hack it on a hotshot crew for five fucking minutes."

When all of our tools had been sharpened and our water bottles filled, Douglas called for us to gather up. "We're gonna work a little later than usual this afternoon. Get our shit wired tight so we're ready to go and be gone again for twenty-one days. Idaho's burning and we're still on the boards."

"Idaho, we're going to Idaho," Rock Star cried as he danced in a circle, his muscular arms shaking in the air around his shaved head.

"What are you doing?" Tan asked. Though he pretended to be annoyed, his eyes showed amusement.

"It's a fire dance to get our fire mojo going," Rock Star said. "I want to see Idaho."

"You can dance all you want," Hawg said, "but Big Sweet Sam's the one with the fire mojo."

"Whatever it takes," Tan muttered. Even he wasn't immune to the odd superstitions and rituals hotshots sometimes engaged in to conjure burning forests.

Suddenly the Pikers' bullshitting dropped away and a hush blanketed them, all nineteen of them holding a collective breath. I followed their gaze to the unlikely sight of a woman walking toward us on the trail snaking down through the woods from the helipad. The sun glinted off of her blonde ponytail. With her gray Monument Helitack T-shirt tucked into her Nomex pants, she managed to look both voluptuous and muscular. She sensed us watching her and the attention made her radiate, her lashes sooty and her eyes blue and bright. Though when I'd seen her before she'd been wearing a hard hat and sunglasses, I recognized her immediately as the helitacker who'd read our flight manifest before we flew down off the mesa my first day fighting fire. My stomach gave a sick shift. It had meant something to me, to be the only woman living at the Fire Center.

"Hey there, big guys," she said, somehow managing to flirt with all twenty of us at once.

Rock Star stepped forward, already reaching for her hand. I saw him as if for the first time, his six feet four inches and lean physique, the way even his big ears and the wildness in his eyes added to his charm. Their eyes met as they shook hands. Though I could've bet her grip was firm, for a moment her fingers lingered in his and something torched out between them. Disappointment shot through the rest of the Pikers. I felt only relief.

"I'm Bliss," she said.

"I'm Rock Star and this is the Pike," he gestured at the rest of us. "When did you get here?"

"About three days ago." Though she spoke only to Rock Star, she seemed well aware the rest of us listened to every word.

"I remember you from the Shutts fire—you shuttled us down off the mesa."

"Yeah, the pilot on my crew was a certifiable maniac."

"No kidding! That bastard almost killed our first load," Rock Star said.

"Oh, we had complaints about him every day. Nothing about fighting fire usually scares me, but flying with him—forget it. So when the Monument Helitack crew called and offered me a GS-5, I couldn't turn it down." She turned to me. "You must be Julie. Looks like we'll be rooming together. I hated to move in on your turf when you were gone."

"Don't worry about it," I said.

Bliss and Rock Star fell back into conversation, and the rest of us milled around, fiddling with our red bag buckles, shuffling and reshuffling tools, eavesdropping unabashedly. "Alaska? You're really from Alaska?" Rock Star asked. "One of my dreams is to fight fire up there. The Pike went to Canada last year, but we didn't make it up to see the midnight sun."

"That's one thing I'll miss being down here this summer," Bliss said. "Summer solstice is the biggest party of the year. Last year I woke up the morning after, had no idea where I was. Turned out I'd pitched my tent in front of the bar where I'd been partying the night before."

"Party at my house tonight," Sam called, and all the Pikers cheered. "Bliss, you'll have to come. I'm Sam, by the way." Even with a steady girlfriend, Sam couldn't resist a wink.

"You don't live here?" Bliss asked.

"Nah." Rock Star jumped in, not giving Sam a chance to answer. "Sam lives down the road in Palmer Lake."

"Okay, Pike, let's get back to work," Douglas called, but even he left Rock Star to stand there yapping with Bliss as the rest of us went back to oiling saws and sharpening our tools.

Sam came up beside me and spoke so quietly no one else could hear, "Meet me behind the classroom as soon as we're off the clock."

My boot heels dislodged gravel as I walked up the hill

and around the back of the classroom. I came around the corner to see Sam standing there with a chainsaw over one shoulder.

"What?" Sam asked. "I see you staring at these Stihls like a fat kid looks at a cupcake." He turned, and I followed him into the woods. We hiked until we hit a patch of dead trees. Sam stopped. "Now if you're up for it, I'll teach you everything you need to know about how to run a saw. So first you're gonna put in your pie cut."

I started the chainsaw and then lifted it up, my arms trembling with the weight. I thrilled at the sound the saw bar made as it bit into the bark of the tree trunk.

Darkness fell as Sam and I hiked back toward the Fire Center. I felt myself glowing with it, the great joy of having finally found my true calling. "Same time same place tomorrow?" he said.

"Shit yeah," I said. "And thank you."

"De nada," Sam said. "See you over at my place in a bit."

I dropped the six-pack of Tecate as I tried to pull it out of the fridge, picked it up, and headed outside. Rock Star and Bliss sat on the picnic tables that fit between the kitchen and the stone barbecue pits, the two of them so close their knees almost touched. They talked with a tall figure almost lost in the darkness. As I approached I saw it was Archie, one foot up on the picnic table bench, his White's emerging from the hem of his jeans. When he turned to me, his eyes glinted green in the light seeping from the kitchen windows. Something about the way

Archie looked at me made me stand up a little taller. Rock Star spoke low to Bliss and she giggled, and again I felt relief to see them so close to each other. A big half moon hung over us, the forest quiet. Perhaps Oscar the fox looked on from the shadows, momentarily timid. There was a sudden stillness to things, a waiting for life to rush in and sweep us inexorably along together, and I somehow sensed that Archie could feel it, too.

"Give me one of those beers," Rock Star demanded. Without thinking, I handed him one, and when he popped the top, it sprayed all over him. Bliss held up her hands to shield herself. Archie and I collided as we stepped away from the Tecate fountain, laughing and grabbing onto each other for a moment to keep from stumbling.

Bliss and I both rifled through our dresser drawers, looking for something to wear to the party at Sam's. She hadn't brought much with her when she moved in. Except for the map of Alaska she'd tacked up over her bed, my room didn't look any different than before her arrival. "So how many years you been fighting fire?" she asked, holding up a neon blouse. I shook my head at the blouse, making a face. "What?"

"Too bright?"

"I tone it down during fire season, but when winter comes, I rat my hair, wear tons of makeup. Julie, I'm the girl in neon."

I laughed.

"So how many years?"

"Never set foot on a fire line before eleven days ago."

Her mouth fell open. "And you got hired onto a shot

crew? My God. How'd you manage that?"

I shrugged.

"You know, I'd about kill to be a hotshot."

I held up a calf-length skirt.

"That's gonna do nothing for you."

I held up a shorter skirt.

"Better. But shit, I guess I'm doing all right. My folks think I should've settled down by now and started popping out kids. I could be sitting around the house changing diapers, folding some man's laundry, but instead I'm down here in the lower forty-eight fighting fire."

I smiled. I liked her in spite of myself.

In the end I chose a little blue sleeveless dress and Bliss borrowed a red sundress with big white flowers. As soon as she put it on, I wished I'd picked it for myself.

Later we stood next to each other at the bathroom sinks, blow-drying our hair, turning ourselves back into women. With the full force of Bliss's magnetism turned toward me, my resentment cracked open and fell away like a dried-out husk. By the time we were halfway through putting on our makeup, I'd told her the story of my disastrous near-encounter with Lance. "I'm never messing with hotshot love, that's for damn sure," I said. "I've got to spend the next five months with these guys." For a brief moment I considered confessing the sharp longing I had for Archie, but decided I'd better keep it to myself until I could discern if Bliss was to be trusted. "And the crazy thing is how much I like being on the Pike, really. It wouldn't be right to say they're like a family, more like a—"

"A tribe, a clan."

"Exactly, something a little more savage than family. I want to be a part of it and I'm not gonna blow it. 'Cause if I wasn't here I'd be home in Dallas, waiting for my manicure appointment. Not even because I wanted it, mind you, but because it'd be easier to get one than to listen to my grandma bitch about how bad my nails look."

"Get the fuck out. Really?"

"Oh yeah."

"You're a long way from a nail shop, girl," Bliss said, a note of admiration in her voice.

"Exactly. What about you? You and Rock Star sure seemed to hit it off."

"Did you notice?"

"We all noticed."

"The boy's got it goin' on." She shrugged. "We'll have to see, won't we?"

I parked along the dirt road in front of Sam's. Bliss walked ahead of me down the long drive running alongside his vast yard, which was hemmed in by a fence made of irregular, weathered cedar four-by-four fence posts connected by two longer four-by-fours. Bliss's strong thighs emerged from the bottom of the dress and her blonde hair hung in a thick sheet midway down her back. In the light of the moon I could look across Sam's yard and see erupting lilac bushes, dense shrubs, long rows of flowerbeds bursting into summer bloom, and a ghostly white hammock suspended between two trees that melted into the night. Archie's truck, Brown Betsy, sat parked in the driveway with Rock Star's Gypsy Mama just behind.

I opened Sam's front door and Bliss followed me into the kitchen and dining alcove, which was packed full of Pikers. Rock Star and Archie sat on the kitchen table, like handsome giants, strumming their guitars.

Sam staggered up to Bliss and me waving a bottle of cactus juice.

"Sam, what happened to your teeth?" I said. "They're as pink as your gums."

"Just finished off a bottle of Hot Damn," he said. He poured a shot of cactus juice into a tomahawk-shaped shot glass and handed it to me.

"I'll do one if you do one," I said to Bliss, surprised to hear the edge of competition in my voice.

Bliss and I took turns tossing back the cactus juice and laughing.

"Your garden is amazing, Sam," I said. "Who takes care of it when you're out on fires?"

"My ex-wife. She cleans my house, too."

"Your ex-wife cleans your house? My God," Bliss said.

A slender woman wearing Wranglers and round-toed cowboy boots appeared at Sam's side. "Julie, Bliss, I want you both to meet someone very special to me," Sam said. "This is Cheryl."

"You're the Bitterroot dispatcher," I cried. "It's nice to finally meet you. Sam talks about you all the time."

Cheryl blushed. "I just drove down from Idaho for a quick visit."

"That's where we're hoping to go," I said. "I hear it's burning."

Rock Star and Archie finished their song, and Rock

Star wandered over to the liquor cabinet for a drink. The front door banged open, and a woman came in with a baby on her hip. "It's Sam's baby," the Pikers cried.

"I didn't even know you had a kid," I said, but Sam was already on his way over to give the baby and the baby's mother a kiss. Bliss chatted away with Cheryl, who didn't seem at all ruffled by the arrival.

"Is that Sam's ex-wife?" I whispered to Rock Star.

"Nah, that's Cookie. She'd never marry Sam."

"What's her deal?"

"She's sitting on a heap of money so she can do whatever she damn well pleases. She raises horses and has about five kids, all with different daddies, and she has a pet monkey that'll try to screw your ear if you're not careful."

"A monkey?"

Rock Star nodded gleefully. "What'll we play next?" he asked Archie.

"'Cocaine Blues,'" Archie said.

"Genius," Rock Star said, and they sat back down on the kitchen table and started strumming.

Sam's girlfriend, Cheryl, held Sam's baby while Cookie talked to Hawg. Bliss seemed dangerously close to flirting with a cute engine slug from a crew out of Palmer Lake. I wandered to the refrigerator, plastered with Sam's fire photos. In one, a slurry bomber passed low behind Sam's head, dropping a pink cloud. In another, Pikers blurred by fire and smoke dropped coughing to their knees. Framed photos from fire seasons past lined the shelves behind the kitchen table, too. There were no images of friends or family, no pictures of Sam's baby either, just Pikers and flames.

I made my way through the kitchen to the living room. The stereo blared Robert Earl Keen's *Picnic* album, and the TV played an alien invasion movie on full blast. Clark and Tan wrestled on the living room floor, bumping into the furniture. A freestanding lamp came crashing down, but no one seemed to notice. A cow skull with an arrowhead piercing it sat on a side table, and dream catchers hung from the ceiling. Glass cases full of arrowheads lined one whole wall, and Pikers kicked back on the big, comfy L-shaped couch and the two recliners. A shelf lined with old bottles ringed the room all the way up to the ceiling. The bottles were different shapes and made of various colors of glass— green and blue and ones that had once been clear but now were so opaque with age they almost looked white. "They're prettier than you'd think old junk could be, aren't they?" I turned to see Lance standing beside me. "You know, most guys couldn't pull off all this Indian crap."

"Yeah, it's a cool place," I managed, wanting to flee.

"Look, Julie, I've really been wanting to talk to you . . . about us."

Just then Hawg emerged from the bathroom, and I mouthed the word, "Help."

"I feel like giving someone a wedgie," Hawg roared, lifting his arms out and puffing up his brick shithouse chest. He reached down the back of Lance's designer jeans, grabbed Lance's underwear, and lifted him up so that his feet dangled a few inches off the ground. Clark had just pinned Tan, but he looked over his shoulder and rolled off his saw partner, laughing hysterically, while I bolted back to the kitchen.

Rock Star and Archie had disappeared from the kitchen, and even with Pikers drinking, Sam kissing the Bitterroot dispatcher in the corner, and Cookie chasing after the crawling baby, the room seemed quiet without them.

Sam tapped a fork on his cactus juice bottle. "Hey, hey," he yelled. "I need everyone's attention. I've got something I want you all to hear." The room quieted down. Sam pulled a little ring box from his pocket, dropped down on one knee in front of Cheryl, opened up the box, and said, "Baby, will you marry me?"

"Oh, Sam, of course I will," she said. Sam put the tacky pear-shaped diamond on her finger, then picked her up and kissed her as she wrapped her legs around his waist, hooking her cowboy boots behind his back. Pikers stomped their feet and beat on the kitchen table. Hawg scooped up the baby and covered her eyes. Cookie stood in the corner smiling the genuine smile of a woman who doesn't need men for anything more than sexual pleasure and sperm donation. Tan, Clark, and the other Pikers wandered in from the living room to see what all the fuss was about. Even Lance came in, and I was careful to avoid his eye. I looked around for Bliss, but she was nowhere to be found. Not seeing Rock Star either, I smiled to myself, realizing they were off together somewhere.

Archie had missed Sam's proposal as well, and I couldn't stop myself from looking for him to tell him the news. The living room was empty, and I opened the sliding glass door and stepped out onto the deck. A chill had arrived in the summer night air, and I shivered in my sleeveless dress as I moved across the yard, passing the lilac bushes, their bud-filled limbs reaching in lovely arches to the ground. Up ahead the white hammock appeared ghost-like from the darkness. A solitary figure was sitting cross-legged in its center emanating a distinct crunching noise. "Who's that?" a panicked voice called.

"It's Julie." Peering ahead, I made out Rock Star, shivering and clutching a box of honey mustard pretzels to his chest. The moonlight illuminated his face. He had what looked like a half a can of scrod stuck between his teeth and a mouth full of honey mustard pretzels. "What's going on?" I asked.

"I found a bag of dope in Sam's yard and I smoked it, and now I'm freaking out and the spit's dried up in my mouth and I can't swallow these pretzels and I'm never smoking anything I find in Sam's yard again," he said in a rush.

"Oh is that all?" I laughed and stretched out in the hammock, made languid and happy by cactus juice and the easy joy of partying with the Pike. For a moment I floated in the night, the breeze running over me, causing us to sway. At that instant I wasn't the girl who spent those long orphaned years in Dallas, my grandmother driving me to fancy dress shops in her Lincoln Town Car, AC revved, windows rolled up tight, *Madame Butterfly* pouring from the stereo, to buy me clothes I didn't want in the hopes of transforming me into the granddaughter she would have me be. "Where's Bliss?"

"How should I know? I figured she was with you. She sure as shit doesn't want anything to do with me."

"What do you mean?" I asked.

"We were talking and she was asking me about my ex, Lysle, and I told her Lysle's a dumb hooker. She got all prissy and said I shouldn't talk about women that way and then she stalked off."

"So she didn't realize 'dumb hooker' is your favorite epithet and that you mean nothing by it."

"Exactly. You can't swamp for shit, but every once in awhile, Julie, you get things right. Maybe you can explain it to her."

"I'll see what I can do."

I left Rock Star alone in the hammock and instead of going back inside the way I'd come, I headed across the yard toward Sam's front door. Out of the corner of my eye, I saw movement in the shadows. Slipping behind a lilac, I peered back around the bush. I could make out my new roommate sitting balanced on a four-by-four connecting two fence posts, Archie between her legs. They were kissing and then his hand slipped up her dress—the dress Bliss had borrowed from me.

I turned and moved silently back the way I'd come. Sitting out on Sam's back deck alone, I forced myself to start breathing again, a dull, numb shock setting in. When I finally collected myself, I slipped back through the sliding glass door, sitting down next to Clark on the couch. "How's it going?"

"It's going alright, except that I'd rather be out on a fire, dropping snags." Clark scratched Sam's dog's ears as he spoke. He looked so boyish and sweet that, for a moment it was hard to believe he was a sawyer on a hotshot crew. Unlike Sam or Rock Star, he certainly wouldn't be spending the rest of his life in Monument. In a couple of years, he'd probably be a college professor somewhere, or so far up the Forest Service food chain that he'd be writing policy himself.

"I'd love to be on the saw team someday," I blurted, "even if I was just a swamper."

"Whoa there, I heard you couldn't even pull off helping Rock Star stump a tree."

Rock Star came barreling in from the kitchen, looking revived. "Julie, you want to wrestle?" he asked and I felt glad that I'd worn little biker-type shorts under my dress.

"I'm going to kick your ass," I said, menacingly, a real rage welling up in me. The anger came from what I'd seen in Sam's yard, came too from Clark's not-so-subtle warning about me trying for the saw team someday. Rock Star stepped toward me, wrapped a leg around mine and pulled it toward him, so that my knee buckled and we crashed to the ground. Pikers came flocking in from the kitchen to see what was going on. "He's going to pin her in thirty seconds," I heard someone say. But no one had counted on my sudden fury, which gave me enough strength to rival Rock Star. We rolled over and over each other, banging into the coffee table, my long, curly hair catching and pulling. Pikers gathered all around, hollering encouragement and placing bets. "Look at the girl go," Clark said.

"Pin her, Rock Star," someone else cried.

"Pin the rookie!"

Rock Star tried to hold my arms down to the floor. I drove a knee into his nuts and the others groaned. I scissored my legs around Rock Star's and tried to grasp hold of his arms, but he twisted free and then he had me down, both arms pinned firm against Sam's carpet, and the Pikers screamed, "One, two, three, four, five!" They cheered Rock Star's victory, and as I stood on my feet again, straightening my dress, Sam handed me a shot of cactus juice.

"You held your own there pretty good," he said.

"Thanks. And hey, Sam, congratulations on your engagement to Cheryl. She's lovely."

Sam lowered his voice. "True love's amazing, Julie, but there's nothing on this earth like fire and friendship. Nothing. Remember that."

My eyes stung. I tossed back the shot, and the sweet burn felt good going down my throat. "I will, Sam," I said. "I promise I will."

Chapter Nine

I STARED AT THE STARLESS CEILING ABOVE MY bed, waiting to see if Bliss would make it back to our room, wondering what I would say to her when she did. Bliss could mess around all she wanted. She wasn't on the Pike Hotshot Crew, so she wasn't subject to the unspoken rule that female shots shouldn't hook up with their crewmates. Besides, the fire season promised to be a busy one. Her helitack crew and the Pike Hotshot Crew would be out on different fires, so she wouldn't have to put up with the Pikers much, not like I would.

A little after five, I finally dropped off to sleep, but was awakened by a loud pounding on my door. My clock read 6:30 a.m. "You hoot with the owls, you got to get up and soar with the eagles," Tan's stern voice said. Bliss's rumpled blonde hair emerged from twisting sheets for a moment before she pulled a pillow over her head.

"What in the hell?" I mumbled, my mouth dry, my head pounding from the beer and cactus juice I'd guzzled the night before.

"Get up, Julie, we're going to lift weights," Tan declared. The crew wouldn't gather for our morning run for another hour and a half, but I decided that if Tan was going to be up in the classroom lifting weights, then I was going to be there with him. I exited from my bedroom two minutes later to find Rock Star, Archie, Clark, and Hawg standing there glumly and Tan looking like a perky Chief Petty Officer pleased to have fresh recruits to torture.

Outside the classroom, the pull-up bar shone silver in the morning light, and Tan climbed up on a post to wipe the dew from it with a spare towel. His compact figure rippled with muscle, and even though there was a chill to the air, he wore tiny blue shorts that fit perfectly over his taut bottom half.

"What's up with your shorts?" I asked.

"They're from boot camp," he said.

"So you've had those little shorts for ten years?"

Tan grabbed the pull-up bar and began cranking them out. When he hit fifteen, he was obviously tiring; after eighteen, I was sure he was done. "One for the Chief," he yelled, hauling his chin up to the bar again. We laughed.

"One for the SEALs!" Clark yelled, and Tan obliged him by squeezing out one more pull-up. I went next, managing seven before Archie stepped up and put his hands under my ankles, helping me to crank out five more. I dropped to the ground, forcing myself to meet his eye. "Thanks."

Archie jumped up and grabbed the pull-up bar. Because he had seven inches and sixty-five pounds on Tan, pull-ups were more of a struggle for him. "Look at the boy, go," Clark said.

"Oh, he's been going alright," Rock Star spoke with real anger. "Going all night long."

"That's my boy," Clark said, puckering and unpuckering his lips in little twitches.

Archie pulled hard to finish his ninth pull-up. His face turned red but didn't quite reach the bar, so he let himself drop to the ground. "Going all night long with Rock Star's girl," he said. He smiled, and Rock Star, who had seemed almost raring for a fight the moment before, laughed.

"She's not my girl," Rock Star said. "Yucky. I wouldn't have her."

Archie shrugged beatifically, as if to say, "To each his own."

The thin cool air smelled of ponderosa pine trees and dew. The sun rose into the blue sky above Mount Herman, its warming rays striking my face. In the distance, I could see the sandstone slab of Monument Rock jutting up above the pines. Clark's arms looked like pistons pulling him up to the bar over and over with the relentless rhythm of a machine. The weaker Pikers, the ones deemed unworthy of Tan's early morning wake-up knock, had been left in their beds to get another hour of uninterrupted sleep. The helitack crew was still in bed, too. Bliss included. But I was up and standing in the fresh air among the Pikers I'd want by my side if the shit really hit the fan on a fire.

Oscar the fox came flitting out from between the trees and trotted up to us. Seeing him made me blush—in the morning light he looked cute, nothing dangerous or threatening about him. He certainly wasn't the terrifying wild animal I'd imagined coming after me in the dark. Clark dropped to the ground, picked up a rock, and threw it low so that it hit Oscar in the side. Oscar looked at him for a long, unnatural moment before darting back into the woods. "Damn fox doesn't know he's supposed to be scared of us. Come hunting season he's gonna trot up to some redneck and get blasted."

"That motherfucking aberrant little fox creeps me out," Hawg said.

The air had lost its chill by the time we finished our workout, so I peeled off my long-sleeve shirt and went to the bunkhouse to toss it in my room. The door opened to Bliss sitting on her bed wearing her running clothes, brushing out her tangled blonde hair. "Morning," I said, taking care to keep my voice even.

"Hey, Julie."

"Late night for you, huh?"

Bliss smiled. "Girl, was it ever."

"Sam sure knows how to throw a party," I said, forcing friendliness into my voice. "Did you and Archie—?"

"You know it, sister."

I tried to smile. "Look, I gotta go so I'm not late for PT."

"Yeah, me too."

"What does helitack do for PT anyway?"

"The other guys are too old and fat to run very fast or far, so I've just been going on my own. They say they run, but I honestly think they hide out and drink coffee. Makes me wish I was a hotshot."

Perhaps she was a little jealous of me, too. After all, I was the Piker. "It has its advantages," I said, closing the door gently behind me.

All of the Pikers sat on the picnic tables in our PT gear as Douglas came down from the office, his hair neatly combed, his Piker shirt looking like it'd been starched. "I've got a special treat for you today. I know you might be feeling a little rough around the edges." He held up an orange rubber ball. "Indian run." We all groaned, then headed down the road, all twenty of us single file. I ran at the very end of the line. Tall, handsome Archie was at the front, the orange rubber ball tucked under one arm. He reached around and handed the ball off to Rock Star, who passed it back. The ball continued down the line until it reached me. "Go, go, go," the Pikers yelled and I sprinted up the line of twenty, cutting in front of Archie. The pain felt good, something to take my mind off what I'd seen the night before. I handed the ball back to Archie, and it moved down the line again, but as Lance reached back to hand the ball off, Hawg bobbled it and it fell to the ground. "Drop and give me twenty," Douglas yelled and we obeyed, my arms quivering from the pull-ups and weight lifting I'd already done that morning.

"One, two, three, four, five . . ." Douglas counted as we did our push-ups in unison, all of us straining and sweating together without complaint. We were up and running again, the orange ball continuing down the line with the last Piker sprinting to the front each time to begin the cycle over again.

The ball dropped a second time as Lance tried to pass it back to Hawg. "I don't want to run behind Lance anymore," Hawg protested. "He's screwing me up."

And so it went, with us running hard and stopping to do push-ups whenever anyone dropped the ball. We ran down the dirt road, taking a right when it hit asphalt, then looping around to a trail that cut through pine trees and then stands of oak brush and wildflowers. The physical agony numbed the aching feeling of loss I felt now that Bliss and Archie were an item. As we finally crested the last hill of the four-mile loop, I could make out the roof of the Saw Cache through the trees. I started praying no one would drop the ball again. My arms were so exhausted I could barely manage the twenty push-ups. "Sprint it out, Pike," someone yelled and we all surged together toward the Fire Center, slowing down as we hit the area between the Saw Cache and the bunkhouse, gasping and raising our hands to the back of our heads to walk it out. I felt worked, punchy, and euphoric, but tired, too, from the night before, ready to climb back in bed for a nap. Archie walked by me. "How you doing?" I asked, as casually as I could.

"Pretty good," he said, but he didn't look me in the eye.

"Nice PT, Pike," Douglas called. "Now go get showered up. We just got a dispatch. Headed out in thirty!" We all cheered. Another day on the Pike had just begun.

Part Two

Part
Two

Chapter Ten

EMPTY PINT GLASSES LITTERED OUR TABLE AT O'Shea's Pub by the time Rock Star started bitching to Clark, Tan, Hawg, and Sam about how he never saw Archie anymore when we were at the Fire Center, not since Archie and Bliss had started sleeping in a tent hidden away in the woods. "I'm the one who's going to get old with Archie. We'll sit out on the front porch together and play guitar, at least that's what I thought. But who knows now. I mean, I've been riding shotgun in Brown Betsy since Archie bought her, but now it's Bliss sitting in my seat." All of our phones went off at once, interrupting Rock Star's rant, and we pulled them out to read the text message from Douglas.

"Drop your cocks and grab your socks, Pikers," Tan yelled in his best military voice. "We're going to Idaho!"

"Whoo-wee!" Sam yelled. "Maybe I'll get to see Cheryl."

"You'd really have the fire mojo going if we got dispatched close enough for you to manage a visit with your lady."

An hour later all the Pikers were back at the bunkhouse, just like we were supposed to be, making sure our tools were sharp, our shit wired tight, our red bags loaded and ready to go and be gone for twenty-one days. All of us except for Archie, usually punctual and reliable as granite, but now nowhere to be found.

"He's off with that goddamn splittail of his. Somebody needs to go get him. Where's that hazmat tent, anyway?" Tan asked me, as if it was my fault Archie hadn't turned up. I could hear Tan's brain clicking away, thinking about how women have no place in fire.

"Shit," I said. "I don't know where that tent is. It *is* hazmat."

At twenty-two hundred we all started combing the dark woods, calling Archie's name. Oscar the fox wove his way between our flashlight beams. Archie finally stepped out from between the trees, hair licking out in all directions like little flames. He stood tall and kept quiet—bull elk don't apologize for rutting—and it must've been the right tack to take because nobody gave Archie the shit he deserved.

We drove along through the black, western night toward Idaho, Sam behind the wheel, Archie riding copilot. I sat in the back between Rock Star and Hawg, my feet stretched out to the front seat. Archie rested his arm on the top of my boots, his forearm on my shin. My head dropped back onto the seat behind me and I conked out.

When I woke up, it was dawn. Looking out the window I saw slick, jagged gray mountains rising up, less like land than like ice. "What the fuck is that?" I asked.

"God, Rookie," Hawg said. "Where the hell have you been?"

"I'm from Texas," I said.

"Those are the Grand Tetons," Sam said, and then we were all quiet looking at them. I reached around behind the seat to find the atlas.

"I'm just glad we're not going back to the desert. That was brutal."

"I know, the whole time we were in Arizona and New Mexico, I was hoping for a fire in the mountains," I said. "We're headed to the River of No Return Wilderness Area, right?" I put my finger on the map.

"That's it. Let me see," Hawg said, yanking the atlas from my hands. "They usually let wilderness areas burn. Probably decided to put us in there because of the salmon in the Salmon River. Been classified as an endangered species for twenty years. If the fire burns right up to the river, the runoff will fuck up their habitat."

The idea of fighting fire *for* the salmon appealed to me. Usually we didn't fight fire for anything but adventure and a fat fire check. We knew well enough by then that the forests themselves needed to burn in order to stay healthy—Clark had taught us that.

Archie turned around in his seat to listen to Hawg, and I could tell he liked the idea of fighting fire for the salmon, too. Watching him made me wonder what I would've been like if I'd grown up like he did, tramping through the woods carrying a fishing pole with a backdrop of mountains and streams instead of skyscrapers, overpriced boutiques, perpetually humming air-conditioners, who I could've been without the constant pressure from my grandmother—if I'd had a chance at quiet afternoons by a burbling river.

We parked our rigs and then climbed out to hike to the fire. The black mass of the Salmon River Mountains towered above us, the dark stands of Douglas fir and lodgepole pine interspersed with sun-washed, treeless slopes—the beauty of the landscape austere and a little foreboding. During the long, steep hike we passed in and out of stands of lodgepole protecting sloping meadows bright with purple aster and white stones lying hot in the sun. I walked behind Tan because he was one of the only Pikers short enough to have a stride about the same length as mine.

Hiking through that gorgeous country all I saw were Tan's boot heels. I glanced up every once in awhile to take in the tall lodgepole, their branches whispering to each other, the forest floor thick with bushes, squirrel caches of needle duff and downed trees needing to burn. About an hour into the hike, a stunned whisper, "Sam fell out," and "The Bear got Sam," went up and down our line. I looked back over my shoulder, and there was Sam, a long way back behind us, unable to keep up or even, for the moment, to go on. Sure Sam was getting old for hotshotting, and creaky, but he never, ever fell out. Only shrimpers fell out.

The whole crew had to stop and wait for Sam to catch up, and my face burned with embarrassment for him. It didn't help that we were coming up on a huge smoke column—the fire ripped through the trees up ahead, moving toward us, but downhill. My Nomex caught on some bitterbrush and a big hole tore open just below my knee. Douglas told us to hold, and we sat on the ground and watched the fire coming.

"Who's got a needle and thread?" I yelled.

"I do," Lance said.

"Why is that not a surprise?" Tan muttered, and the others laughed.

Lance reached into his pack, and when he walked over and handed me his little sewing kit, our eyes met. "Thanks," I said, looking away.

He shrugged. "No worries." I hurriedly stitched the ripped part of my pants as we waited to see if the fire was going to make a big run or lay down enough so that we could dig line. We all heard it first, then we saw the flames blowing up from the top of the trees. They must've been a couple hundred feet up in the air. Douglas yelled, "RTO," and we turned around and scrambled back down the mountain.

The whole landscape behind me blazed orange, and my face heated up when I turned to look at it. I tripped over my own boots, but it was worth it for a glimpse. When we arrived back down in the open flat space where the rigs were parked, we watched the fire make its run, like watching an orange band pushing forward across a green mountain, only after the band passed the forest was black. The smoke column mushroomed up like a big fluffy cloud, the fire burning hot enough to make its own weather. As the sun lowered itself down through the haze, the sky lit up a brilliant, unnatural pink. I sat on the grass to lean back and watch Archie, Rock Star, and Clark play hacky sack.

The next day, digging line next to Sam, I looked down and saw that he'd written "I FELL OUT" across the knuckles of his gloves with a ballpoint pen. "Sam," I said. "I'm going to the supply tent tonight to get you another pair of gloves. That's ridiculous, you're just being mean to yourself."

"I'll wear these the rest of the season," Sam said, his hazel eyes full of the haunted look I'd seen on Paloma Canyon. His voice dropped down to a whisper. "I've got to remind myself, because if I can't keep up with the Pike, what am I gonna do with myself?"

As we sharpened tools and lined things out for the next day, a pickup came bouncing down the dirt road toward fire camp. "Sam, your lady friend is here," Archie called. The truck pulled up alongside the Piker rigs, and Cheryl leapt out wearing tight, dark blue jeans, a pearl-snapped shirt, and ropers. Her long chestnut hair curled at the ends, her lashes were thick with mascara, and her lips tinted pink with gloss. I noticed myself then, covered in soot and ash, my clothes and hands grimy, my tangled hair wrestled into a long braid, and I knew with a sudden helplessness that, even though I had the old urge less and less often and could sometimes talk myself out of it, I'd sneak away from the crew after we ate to puke up my dinner. Cheryl and Sam threw their arms around each other and kissed a long deep kiss that elicited catcalls from several Pikers.

They stood in line for dinner together holding hands, looking so thrilled to be in each other's company that I felt a pang of regret at what I gave up to be a Piker. "Way to take your girl to a classy place for dinner," Hawg called, and we all laughed.

"It's plenty good enough for me," Cheryl said. "I've got the world's best date."

After dinner Sam threw his tent into the back of Cheryl's truck and climbed into the passenger seat. "I'll be back before y'all wake up at oh five hundred," he called, waving to us as they drove away.

I set my sleeping bag down between Rock Star and Archie. "Sam sure looks happy," Rock Star said, with uncharacteristic earnestness.

Clark stood close enough to overhear. "Sam's engaged to a different woman every year."

"Hopefully this one's different," Rock Star said.

"Yeah, he's getting older," Archie said quietly. "He needs something besides the Pike to keep him going. After that hike in this morning, even he's got to see that."

"You're right," Clark concurred. "The writing's on the fucking wall. He won't be able to do this work forever. But Sam, he doesn't think past life on the fire line. Cheryl's a smart enough woman, so she's thinking about it."

"Who's up for a game of spades?" Archie asked. Because he'd spoken, I didn't have to feel self-conscious looking over at him.

"I am, buddy," Rock Star said.

"I'm in. I'll go grab my spades partner." Clark returned a moment later with Tan in tow. I lay in my sleeping bag listening to the soothing sounds of their game, my stomach hollow, holy-feeling in its emptiness.

"Hey, buddy," Archie said. "Whatcha got on my mo?"

"Oh, I got a little something something all right," Rock Star said.

I heard the sound of tobacco slapping inside its tin as I drifted off to sleep.

Chapter Eleven

THE NEXT WEEK OR SO WAS FULL OF RUNNING and gunning with the Pike, digging line for twelve or fifteen hours a day, trying to do what we could to put a line all the way around the fire and have it contained. I pounded line between Sam and Hawg, the other diggers trailing out behind, the sawyers up ahead, so that during the day I only saw Archie, Rock Star, Clark, and Tan when we tied our line in and hunkered down for a well-earned break. During those days, all of us, diggers and sawyers alike, just tried to stay two steps ahead of the flames and one step ahead of our own exhaustion. Except for the evening that Cheryl had come to see Sam, I was too tired to even think about making myself throw up. I needed the food to get me through the long hikes and longer hours digging line. And with no mirrors and only baggy Nomex to wear, it became harder to think of myself as not-thin-enough, easier to wish I could pick up logs as heavy as those Hawg could lift from the ground with a grunt and a heave.

Finally the fire was contained, and the morning we were to start mopping up, we lined out and stumbled through the darkness at 5:00 to eat breakfast, the ground all around us shimmering with frost, the sky and the mountains eerily drained of color in the predawn light.

When I sat down next to Archie with a bowl of oatmeal, I looked over to see his eyes drift shut and his red goateed chin dropped down to his chest. I elbowed him hard. "Archie, wake up." He opened his eyes and turned to me with a look that said that for me, his big buddy, he had endless patience.

"I was blessing my food," he said.

After breakfast we made the long hike to the fire that had been completely encircled with fire line. Trapped by the fire line, with nowhere to go, the fire had burned down and gone out, leaving only drifts of ash, steaming tree stumps, and giant torched-out trees. The fire was dead, and now the boring work of mopping it began.

We all loved the exciting work of digging fire line, especially hot line right along the fire's edge. I would fall into the rhythm of swinging my tool, so that I felt I could do it for days. In contrast, mopping was mind-numbingly tedious. Usually when we mopped up a dead fire, we had no water except for what we carried on our backs in "bladder bags." Bladder bags were a misery we all hated, the extra thirty pounds of weight on top of our packs always lopsided and heavy and usually leaking down our legs. One Piker would hand pump a blast of water from his bladder bag onto steaming hot spots while other Pikers would stir the hot ash with their tools.

But for this fire we were lucky. Instead of bladder bags, a helicopter had sling loaded in a couple of pumps and a bunch of fire hose for us to use. So we set up the pumps on the edge of the River of No Return, hooked the fire hoses to them, and ran hose lays all over the mountain. Then it

was time to begin spraying down hot spots with the water
pumped up from the river.

Archie and I paired off together without discussion.
Only Rock Star protested, "I see how it is. My saw partner's
ditching me."

Archie slung an arm over Rock Star's shoulder. "You
know I love you, big buddy. I just need a break from you
every once in a while."

On a normal fire, the sawyers would go through the
area we were going to mop and drop all the snagged out,
teetering trees to make the work safer for the rest of us,
but because we were in an officially designated Wilderness
Area, we had to leave the snags standing. "Light on the
land," Douglas told us, and we resented it. Despite what
we felt for the land's rugged beauty, we didn't want to risk
our own lives to protect a small margin of its torched-out
purity.

Archie and I spent that first day spraying down tree
stumps and hot pockets of ash, one of us holding the nozzle
of the hose, the other dragging it, unhooking it from stobs,
and watching for snags. The ground was a foot deep in ash,
and I was so filthy my Nomex had turned black and my
pores were full of soot. None of us had showered for days,
but I started feeling clean in that way only being dirty in
the woods can make you feel.

The mountains were steep, and the ash swirled up
around the bottoms of the snags. Most of the trees had
torched out, big trees, Idaho old-growth trees, some of them
eighty, a hundred, a hundred and twenty feet tall. They
loomed above us, charred black spikes stabbing at the sky

ominously. The jagged stumps of branches like amputations, the bases burnt and catfaced, all ready to fall at any second. I could look down the sooty gray mountain at the River of No Return running there, a flat glassy green below the clear blue of the sky. The only sound was the water coming out of the nozzle of the hose and the hiss when the water found a hot spot and turned to steam. On the other side of the river, a mountain rose up pristine and untouched by fire. Lodgepole covered most of the mountain a dark green, but in the center of the mountain, a large, bright stand of aspen shimmied in the breeze.

"Aspen connect at the root system," Archie said. "So the whole stand of trees is all one organism."

By early afternoon Archie and I were going long periods of time without saying anything, and I settled into the silence, the two of us somehow closer as we walked through the ash, ten feet apart, than I'd ever been with any of the number of boys I'd wrapped myself around for nights in college.

Most of the time, he sprayed and I followed behind dragging hose. This suited us both—Archie because spraying hot spots was more fun than dragging hose and me because it gave me a chance to stand behind Archie and study him unobserved. He was six foot six with his fire boots on, his broad shoulders tapering down to a trim waist, his legs long and strong in his loose Nomex pants. When he took off his sunglasses, his green eyes squinted against the sun, and even covered in ash, with his hard hat hiding his thick auburn hair, it was easy to see he had angular, even-featured good looks. Every so often he glanced over his shoulder and threw me a smile, that quick flash of white in a soot-streaked face for me, his big buddy, his friend.

Days went by like that with just the two of us together, out of shouting distance from the rest of the crew. Rock Star had mostly given up complaining that Archie and I had paired up to mop. I started to feel so calm and quiet that I didn't need to talk all the time. When we spoke it was because Archie wanted to tell me about fishing. It was hard on him, I think, to look down at that river full of salmon and not be able to fish it, to not be able to be down there, where the land was still green. After all, he'd grown up in the unburned woods, kneeling by streams full of fish, and I knew he was comfortable there in a way I hadn't been since my parents died.

"If I was down there fishing that river," Archie said, one bright afternoon when we were both wishing for a cold soda, "I'd turn over rocks to find insects. That way I could see what's hatching and what the salmon are eating." I didn't ask the questions about the point of fly fishing that flooded my head, didn't want Archie to think I didn't get it. I could see it then, how he loved the unburned forests and the rivers and the fish, more than he loved fire, even. It was just that fire was what brought us to places with names like the River of No Return Wilderness. It was just that Archie understood the beauty of the flames as well, understood that eventually healthier forests would rise again from the desolation and the ash.

I didn't just want to understand fly fishing, I wanted Archie to love me like he loved Rock Star or Bliss. I wanted to be that essential to him. I told myself that it was only because of the ash, and the looming black snags of trees. Because while we were hosing down hot spots, alone together, talking or not talking, there were snags coming down in the forest all around us. We would hear them crack and then crash, and if the tree was big and the branches all burnt off, I could feel the impact coming up from the ground through my fire boots. There in that burned forest, there in the black, I started wanting to be more important to people than I was. I started to think about my grandma Frosty and how she was the only blood relation I had and how I knew I needed more than that if I was ever going to feel really okay.

Archie spoke as if he'd been reading my mind. "Have you talked to your grandma lately?"

"It's been a few weeks," I said. "She's still furious. I'm not sure if she's madder that I flunked out of school or that I'm doing a blue-collar man job." I was starting to take it in, to really process the fact that I'd truly made a mess of things, and that the Pike had somehow transported me out of all the wreckage of my school career and my relationship with Frosty. The job offer from the Pike had come like a deus ex machina that airlifted me out of my life and into a whole new set of problems.

"You really ought to call her," he said.

"You really ought to not lecture me."

He blasted a hot spot with the hose, the steam rising up with a hiss, then turned to give me a look. "She raised you, right?"

"You could call it that."

"It wouldn't hurt you to call her is all. I call my folks."

"If I had your parents I'd call them, too," I said.

"You don't give your grandma an inch, do you?"

I shrugged. "You think Rock Star's still mad at you for mopping up with me instead of with him?"

"If anything, he's still mad 'cause I'm with Bliss. Girls weren't ever something that came between us before. There have always been girls around, sure. But we never had a problem about any of them."

"Rock Star liked Bliss first," I said, trying to keep the hint of accusation out of my voice.

"Rock Star laid claim to her the second he laid eyes on her, but she's a grown woman with the free will to choose."

When it was time for a break I walked down the length of the hose to turn off the water. I sat at the hose to be by myself for a minute and to look down at the river. The forest along the opposite bank was still lush and green, and I imagined Archie as a little kid out in a boat with his dad. It was fucked up, to imagine other people's childhood memories, but all my memories after twelve were of my grandma, and if I thought back before that, it was just memories of my parents, times so vanished they hurt to consider.

So I daydreamed about Archie at nine and his dad, a young dad then with a big beard. His dad opened up his fly case, and inside was a bunch of flies, all different sizes and colors, that he'd tied himself. They looked to Archie more amazing even than real insects. His dad said, "Son, if you're going to make something you might as well make it beautiful." He didn't say, "Make it beautiful for Jesus," but that's what he meant. That's how I imagined it must've been for Archie as a kid.

And his dad taught him how to cast that day, and Archie caught his first fish on a fly. He held that fish in his hands and looked down at its gills working to suck in water that wasn't there. He probably thought then about loaves and fishes and the disciples who laid down their nets. I'm sure he'd learned it all at Sunday school by then. He looked down at just how beautiful God had made the fish. Then he dropped the fish into the water and watched it swim away.

While I sat there at the hose, I felt like I suddenly understood fly fishing and Archie and why Archie could just be exactly who he was, so sure in it and why no one ever slapped him much shit. He about missed a dispatch because he was out in the woods scrogging Bliss, and no one said a word. Sitting there I figured Archie probably caught that fish on a day my parents were driving me to Dallas to see my grandma. Then I knew I was letting the whole daydream get out of hand, and I walked the hose back to Archie and sat with him while he had a scrod.

Afterward, he ran the nozzle again and I dragged the hose. We worked along slowly, my eyes trained on Archie. He stood below a monster Douglas fir the fire hadn't even touched. It was nice to see a tree like that after a fire, a tree hundreds of years old that had made it. It grew straight up from the slope of the mountain, its branches reaching out in an enormous circle. Archie stood under its huge umbrella, spraying a hot spot. I held the hose up in the crook of my elbow, and I gazed at the back of his neck, grimy with ash. I wasn't thinking about anything. I was just there, glad for the chance to be watching him. Then I saw Archie turn and drop his head back so he could see the top of the Douglas fir. He looked like he was listening to it. I tried to listen, too, but I didn't hear it at first. But then I did.

A deep wrenching sound came from the tree.

By the time I heard it Archie was jogging toward me, still looking up, still holding the hose in his hand. I could see the very top branches of the tree moving then. Archie threw down the hose just as I was screaming, "Run, Archie! Run!" I watched him take a step and the tree falling. It was pulling up from its roots, slowly for a moment and then as soon as it began to lean, gravity had its way, and it toppled with sudden speed. Archie was running to make it out from under it, and for a long, frozen moment I didn't know if he'd be fast enough. He cleared the tree just before it hit the ground, the trunk scraping against his pack as it fell. I'd expected a great crash, but the tree still had all its branches and needles, so it just made a soft sort of *wump*.

Archie didn't stop to turn around until he was beside me. For a minute we looked at the tree lying there and didn't say anything. His breath came in strange, ragged little gasps, and he reached out and put a hand on my shoulder to steady himself, his big fingers gripping me tight. I grabbed onto his arm, my hand wrapped around his bicep, and I could feel him shaking. We stood there like that for a while, as close as two Pikers could come on the fire line to clinging to each other. Then Archie said, "Way to look out for Archie. Good thing old Archie looks out for himself." He was teasing, perhaps to cover up the fear that had jolted through him, perhaps to make me feel better about my failure as his lookout. I felt sick, as if I'd lost my big chance. I hadn't known before the tree fell that I would've liked to have saved Archie's life.

We walked over to check out the tree, my hand still somehow gripping his elbow. The uphill side of the trunk, that we hadn't been able to see, had been totally burned out, the catface four feet tall and big enough for a grown man to crouch in. The fire had crept through enough of the root system that the weight of the tree just pulled it over. Archie and I toured that tree like it was a museum. We touched the clots of dirt in the roots, rubbed the shiny charcoal of the catface, walked all the way down its length, and crushed handfuls of needles in our fists.

"How long do you think it would've taken the rest of the saw team to cut you out from under it?" I asked.

"There probably wouldn't have been much of me left to get to. I would've been crushed like a bug."

There didn't seem to be anything to say after that, so I asked Archie if he wanted to break for lunch, because it was either that or keep dragging hose. We sat on the blackened ground, a big flat rock the table between us. I thought about how my afternoon would've gone if the tree had fallen faster or if Archie wasn't so quick. I passed him the bloody roast beef from my sandwich, and he took it without comment.

Then he looked up at me and smiled like I think he would've if I'd heard the tree falling first. If I *had* saved him, like I wished I had. Right then it was like the space between us dissolved just because I'd seen the tree falling and him almost being crushed. Just my witnessing it was something. It wasn't being a girlfriend or a best buddy from way back, but it was as important, maybe. I'd seen something about Archie that no one else had—I'd seen him almost killed and how it had rattled him—and I'd never tell anyone, and we'd always have that between us.

Chapter Twelve

DOUGLAS CAME BACK TO THE CREW AFTER his morning briefing with Command. We all knew that any time we were away from a shower for more than a few days, his neck became a torment of red, viciously itching ingrown hairs that he battled meticulously. So before he called for us to gather up, he hung a little shaving mirror from a tree and stood in front of it for twenty minutes, prying them free with the sharpened tip of his knife. When he finally yelled for us to gather, I stared with fascination at the little wounds he'd dug into his neck, the only chink in his armor of fastidiousness. He reported that we were being dispatched to another, smaller fire about a hundred miles away.

"Whoo-wee!" Rock Star yelled. "Get us off of this dead ass fire. I'm ready to dig me some hot line!"

"We'll be spiking out," Douglas said, and we all cheered. Spiking out meant we'd be alone with just a couple of other crews, our only connections to the wider world the radio and the helicopters that sling-loaded in food each evening. Spiking out seemed so clean to us, without all the slamming shitter doors and little tent cities of fire camp.

Helicopters flew us in before dusk. As we rose I could look out the window and see the Salmon River Mountains, their craggy slopes running down to disappear in the flowing waters of the river. Squat hackberry trees and mountain mahogany clung to the riverbanks. The chopper lowered us into a little basin, covered in lush grass and encircled by lodgepole and Douglas fir, set like a bowl in the middle of a ring of small mountains.

There were already two crews spiked out there, the Logan Hotshots and a prison crew called the Flame 'n Gos. That night our three crews stayed separate, each sleeping in a scattered group of sleeping bags. Crews didn't mix on the fire line, that's just how it went. We woke in the early morning dark, packed up our red bags, and ate breakfast as the first light of dawn brought an empty gray color to the sky. As the sun began to appear, so did the beautiful green hues of the mountains and the blue of the sky. We hiked out, each crew going to its own section of the fire.

Our hike in was long and the landscape dense with towering ponderosa and singing streams, which we crossed on the slick backs of fallen logs.

At the fire line we broke into squads. "Huddle up," Sam said, and Rock Star, Archie, Hawg, and I gathered around him. "Okay, squad, who needs to take a grumpy?" I waved my hand above my head with the rest of my squad.

Before I started work on the Pike, it would've been a chance to sneak away into the woods and throw up my breakfast, but now the thought barely crossed my mind. It was truly all about the privacy of the grump.

By then we all knew Rock Star carried a tiny little reporter's notebook with him, and if he took a particularly strange-looking grumpy, he'd draw a picture of it and bring it back to show us. "Taking a big shit out in the woods is my favorite part of the job, I swear," he said as we waited for Archie and Sam to come back from grumpying.

"I don't love it," I admitted.

"Well, how do you do it?" Rock Star asked.

"What do you mean, how? I just squat," I said, trying to hide my embarrassment.

"Squat?" Hawg roared as if he was a gourmet chef and I'd just admitted to microwaving my pork chops. "Good God, woman."

"No wonder you're not enjoying your morning grump," Rock Star said. "You've got to have a shitter. You can make one out of rocks."

"Or," Hawg continued, "you can find a natural shitter like a nice, big downed tree with a forked branch to sit on."

Archie and Sam headed toward us. "Go on," Rock Star said. "And when you come back we want you to rate your grumpy. View, comfort, location, and then give your grumpy an overall score. I've got to go next, though. Hey, Hawg, do you want to come with me? We can build shitters and eat snacks."

"Holy shit," Hawg said. "You are such a freak show. And you complain about my snoring!"

When we were all done, Sam said, "Okay, guys, enough for the squad meeting, let's go tie back in with the rest of the crew."

"What does Douglas think we talk about at our squad

meetings?" I asked.

Sam winked at me, his eyes twinkling. "We're taking care of squad business, Julie."

Once we met up with the rest of the crew, we spent the entire day digging line. That night we hiked back up to our basin, and the walk seemed longer and my pack heavier in the twilight. When we got back to spike camp we sharpened our tools as the purple sky turned dark. We filled our water bottles and watched the moon rise up over the edge of the mountains until it hung just above us in the middle of the Idaho sky.

After we went through the chow line we sat down on the ground to eat our chicken-fried steak and talk. The other Pikers eyed the convicts, but I tried to not even look over at them. The Flame 'n Gos looked at the ground when I walked by, not wanting to risk getting in trouble for leering at me, but I sensed they all knew where I was in fire camp at any given time.

The fact that the cons scared me so badly reminded me that I wasn't like the other Pikers. None of my buddies feared being grabbed, having a dirty sock stuffed in their mouths, and pulled away into the bushes in the darkness. I tried to tell myself it was silly to be afraid of the prisoners. Convicts who went out on fire crews were short-timers who had a day commuted from their sentence for every day that they were on the fire line. On fires, prison crews always kept to themselves, not mingling with the hotshots. I guess it seemed safer to them that way. Then there was less chance that someone would start a fight or say something offensive and get them all sent straight back to the clink. I told myself none of them would mess with me, but I didn't really believe it.

"I've said it before and I'll say it again," Sam insisted as we started eating. "I don't look at the prisoners the way you all do."

We sat cross-legged on the ground, our paper plates in front of us. "What do you mean?" Rock Star spoke with his mouth full.

"You guys eye them like they're animals, a zoo exhibit. But I see it differently. I've done just about everything those short-timers are in for. I've sold a few bags of dope in my day. I've driven home drunk more than a time or two. The only difference is that I've never been caught. Those guys are just like me with bad luck."

After dinner I dug a dip in the ground for my hip. As I set my chingadero down, I saw Sam out in the middle of the basin talking to a Flame 'n Go, the tallest, skinniest, blackest dude I'd ever seen. Sam must've been inspired by our dinner conversation to make friends. I'd never seen a black firefighter except on the prison crews. The implications made me sick, but I figured that's just the sort of world we live in. If Sam had been black, he would've been imprisoned, sure enough. That's how justice works in America.

The prisoner started telling a story. I could tell by the way he waved his arms as he spoke and by how Sam nodded and laughed. Hawg headed that way to see what was going on, and then Rock Star followed after him. A couple of Logan Hotshots stopped to listen to the prisoner's story, and then three convicts wandered up as well. I'd never seen crews mix like that on the fire line.

I sat down on my sleeping bag, leaning back on my elbows. I wanted to go join in, but with all of the prisoners clustered around, it just didn't feel like a good idea. My headlamp illuminated the pages of my novel. What I really needed, I told myself, was some quiet time to read, but I hadn't finished a page before I put *Jane Eyre* down and trotted over to the cluster of hotshots eagerly conversing in the middle of the basin.

The moon hung almost full above us, and the dark mountains encircling our little basin threw down long shadows. A chill cut through the night air. The tall black prisoner stood up straight, talking in a booming voice and waving his arms for emphasis. "That was the damndest afternoon I ever spent in my life, sure as I'm Slim Jimmy."

I nudged Hawg and whispered, "What's he going on about?"

"He said one time he saw another prison crew put on a nut roll eating contest at fire camp."

"I say let's do it," Slim Jimmy said. "Let's spice things up around here. Let's go on and have our own nut roll contest. Long as we out here, we might as well have us some enter-tain-ment!" A ripple went through the growing circle of firefighters. Voices came out of the light and the shadow, and it was hard to tell who was speaking, since we were all black with ash and still wearing our crew shirts. In the moonlit darkness I couldn't tell the convicts from the other hotshots, and suddenly, being able to distinguish the prisoners seemed a little less crucial than it had before.

"We'll all put money in and then see who can eat fifteen nut rolls first. And whoever wins gets the pot," Slim Jimmy said, waving his arms above his head.

"I'll put in five bucks," Rock Star called out, and the betting went from there. From all around people were saying:

"I'll put in ten."

"I'll put in five more and that's twenty."

When the voices fell silent, the grand total stood at $160.

A Logan shot shouted, "Who's gonna be in the contest?"

"For a hundred and sixty bucks, I'm in," a blond prisoner yelled.

"But think how tore up your stomach will be," Rock Star said. "It's not worth it."

"After working in the prison laundry for three bucks an hour, the money sure sounds worth it to me," the blond prisoner said, which shut Rock Star right up.

A nerdy looking prisoner with dark hair and glasses said, "I'll do it, too," in a voice almost too quiet to be heard. A couple of prisoners murmured in surprise and one gave him an admiring slap on the back.

"So, we've got two Flame 'n Gos in," Slim Jimmy said. "I hear some say in fire camp that prison crews ain't real hotshots. So who outta you *hotshots* is in?" A long silence ensued.

"Hawg, what about you?" Rock Star said.

"Full clout and I'm out," Hawg said. "I ate that big

grub worm on the Saltillo fire last season for sixty bucks and no one ever paid up."

"Rock Star, you up for it?" Archie asked. No one would ever suggest Archie for the contest. He was the serious of the pair—the grounded, dignified one. Archie always encouraged Rock Star's antics, but in the end it was Archie who tethered him, too.

There was a long pause as Rock Star considered, the rest of us waiting in silence. Out of that pause, I saw a chance for myself and I seized it.

"I'm in," I yelled, jumping up and down. They all turned to me, a surprised look on every face. Even the prisoners had forgotten I was there.

The Logan Hotshots and the Flame 'n Gos and even the Pikers looked me up and down, thinking I didn't look much like a hotshot, I'm sure. There was no getting around the petite factor, and my Nomex pants hung baggy from my hips. I'd unbraided my hair and pulled it back in a thick ponytail. A guy in a Logan shirt standing next to Rock Star leaned over and stage-whispered, "Can this pretty lil' gal eat?"

"Makes me sick to watch her," Rock Star said, looking a little relieved, and a little jealous that I'd yanked his spotlight so quickly.

"But where does it go?" the Logan shot asked. Rock Star shrugged.

The circle held together until late that night, everybody talking and excited. I abandoned it early on to try to get some good rest. As I lay in my sleeping bag, surprised at myself for volunteering, but not sorry, I thought about how strange it'd been to see three crews all hanging out together. And I'd certainly never seen prison crews talking like that with regular crews before.

The next morning I was elected to tell Douglas about the contest. I trotted up to him as he stood before a little pecker pole, his shaving mirror dangling from one of its branches. He studied his neck in the reflection as he dug into his soft skin with the knife from his Leatherman, trying to free one of the multitude of ingrown hairs that plagued him. "What is it, Julie?" he asked, obviously annoyed to be disturbed. But when I explained to him about the contest he struggled to keep from smiling and said he'd radio fire camp and request that a couple cases of nut rolls be brought in with the next sling load. I turned to go.

"Hey, Julie," Douglas said.

"Yeah?"

"Sam tells me you've really been getting the hang of the chainsaw."

I smiled, pleased and a little surprised Sam had told Douglas about the chainsaw lessons he'd been giving me every day we were at the Fire Center.

At breakfast we all went back to sitting with our own buddies—I guess it was old habit coming back with the sun—but all three crews waved good-bye to each other as we hiked off toward different sections of the fire line.

That evening as we returned to camp we followed a stream, weaving our way between the huckleberries before finally jumping across at a narrowed bend in the creek. When we arrived at our basin, we set up for the contest, making a start line and a finish line with three rows of nut rolls lying end to end between the two. There were also three white buckets, emptied of their chicken-fried steak, vegetable medley, and mashed potatoes, and on the outside of each Slim Jimmy wrote, "1st Place, 2nd Place, 3rd Place," with a permanent marker someone had stashed in his pack. Sitting on the ground, the Pikers ate their dinners off paper plates, watching the sky darken and then light up again as the sun set and the moon rose over the edge of the mountains that looked like black silhouettes against the great purple of the night sky. A dull hunger gnawed at me, but I wanted to save every bit of room in my stomach for nut rolls.

When dinner was over, all three crews gathered around the nut roll course. The superintendents set up electric lanterns, and the circle of men stood still, but I could feel how amped they all were. The palpable energy zinging through them was the energy of savage sport, of bullrings and boxing and cockfights.

Slim Jimmy stood in the center of the nut roll course. "Contestants, take your marks!" he cried. I stepped out of the group and into the lantern light, which played over the sixty sooty faces encircling me, all smiling like goblins. The towheaded prisoner stepped out into the circle and stood beside me. His arms and chest bulged under his T-shirt, and it was easy to imagine him locked in his cell, doing endless push-ups and sit-ups to make the hours pass.

"How's it goin'?" I asked him, quietly, so the others couldn't hear.

"I'm not sure what I've got myself into," he said.

"Me, either." The third prisoner stepped out into the

middle of the circle to stand on the other side of me. With his dark hair and Coke-bottle glasses, he looked a bit addled, as if worried that the ring of men might close in and start pummeling him.

"You okay?" I asked, under my breath.

"Maybe not," he said, and I had the sudden urge to comfort him.

"We'll be all right," I said. The three of us sat on the ground at the end of the three lines of nut rolls.

"Contestants, are you ready?" Slim Jimmy cried, enthusiastic as a game show host.

"We're ready," I yelled, and the hotshots and cons all laughed at the high pitch of my voice. From where I sat on the ground looking up at them, the men appeared freakishly tall, like giants, and I suddenly felt very small. But then the thought of how beyond horrified my grandma Frosty would be to see me sitting on the ground between two convicts cheered me a little.

"On your mark," Slim Jimmy yelled. "Get set," all the other hotshots joined in. "Go!" they all cried.

I picked up a nut roll, the first of fifteen, and tore off the wrapper. The blond prisoner dunked his nut roll into his water bottle to soften it up, and the one with glasses crammed a whole nut roll into his mouth at once. I began eating, chewing quickly. The nut roll was salty, and the nougat made for hard chewing. When I finished the first nut roll, I quickly unwrapped a second.

As scared as I'd been of the Flame 'n Gos, I sat easily between those two convicts on the green Idaho grass. All three of us were going for the same thing, but it was funny, because even though we were competing for the money, it felt more like we were on the same team. And whatever it was between me and those two prisoners kind of spilled out to fill up the basin. I'd swear that's what made the grass look such a dark green, that's what turned the shadows purple, and that's why the sky took on that navy color.

I realized then that I had more in common with those convicts than I did with my own grandmother, or with any of the girls I'd debbed with. The convicts were all out there under the clear night sky to escape something, just like I was. They were there to elude the confines of prison walls and bars, while I was fleeing my grandmother's expectations. But suddenly those differences between myself and the cons didn't seem to matter at all. The Flame 'n Gos all loved the dirt and the thin air and the unburned forests and sleeping under the stars, just like I did. They all loved fire, the way it burned hot and high and made afternoon runs that had us scrambling for our safety zones, reminding us how precious life is. They were on a crew together, and they had each other's backs when the shit went down on the fire line, and I understood all of that.

I smiled the whole time I was eating nut rolls, a little embarrassed to be there, the center of so much attention. But it felt so right, too. It was an eating contest, after all, and eating was always what I'd done best. It had always been my escape hatch, my secret glory, my greatest shame. After six nut rolls or so, my jaw was getting tired from chewing through nougat, and the peanuts started scratching my throat as they went down, but I kept at it. The muscled blond prisoner sat to my left. He had the kind of white hair that you usually only see on old people and little kids. Laughter ripped out of him as he ate, and he really tore into his nut rolls, seeming pleased to be in the contest. He looked happy like maybe he hadn't been for years. Nut Roll Champ may not sound like much in the regular world, but if you are spiking out on a fire in Idaho and you are the Nut Roll Champ, then it means something.

The prisoner with dark hair and glasses still looked a little scared and surprised at what he'd gotten himself into. Maybe that's how he felt about being in prison; maybe he'd woken up every day behind those walls and tried to connect the dots between what he'd done and where he'd ended up. I'm sure it hadn't made much sense to him. He probably sold a few quarter bags, or knocked back a few drinks at a party, and then drove himself home, and next thing he knew he was living in a seven-by-ten cell with some guy named Yack.

The electric lanterns gave off a strange sort of light, so that the faces of the hotshots gathered all around looked hollow and hungry. I didn't want to let the Pikers down. I wanted to make them proud of me, so even though my stomach was stretched taut and my jaw ached, I kept forcing myself to eat nut roll after nut roll. Rock Star danced around while he sang, "The nougat is gonna get you" to the tune of some old pop song. Someone from Logan said, "Man, that fucker is funny." Glancing around in the lantern light it was hard to tell the prisoners from the hotshots.

Eight nut rolls into the contest the prisoner with the

glasses walked to the edge of the basin and crept over the lip, dropping into the bushes below to puke his guts out. The spectators all groaned because the guy hadn't thrown up in his 3rd Place bucket out in front of everybody. I could tell the audience all felt the way they would've if the theater shut off some action movie right at the very end, at the most exciting part. They grumbled and complained and then they watched me and the blond prisoner even more carefully than before.

The blond convict's laughter had stopped bubbling up from inside of him. His bites looked forced, and the lantern light showed the muscles of his neck working hard. Even so, I stayed calm, eating my nut rolls. I was the underdog up against two cons, and the hotshots liked watching me. Everyone likes an underdog. But I realized suddenly that what they really wanted was to see me puke. For all forty hotshots and twenty cons gathered around, the excitement was in waiting to see the pretty young girl with the audacity to try to be a hotshot force-feed herself until she barfed in front of them all. That was what drew them in. It would be my punishment, in a way, for daring to try to be a hotshot at all. That's what they were thinking. It made me mad, and then it seemed inevitable, really. Sixty rough-ass men out in the woods—it wasn't like I belonged among them; it wasn't like there wouldn't be a price to pay. My heart sank. If I'd realized the true purpose of the contest, I never would've volunteered for it in the first place. My stomach roiled in protest, and with each swallow the nut rolls scratched the inside of my throat, but I kept eating.

At nut roll number eleven the blond prisoner started

gagging. His mouth filled up with puke. I was right there next to him and saw it, but he clenched his lips shut. He swallowed his own mouthful of barf and then kept eating, but he was about to burst. I could see that just by looking at his face. The crowd roared, and it echoed off the mountains. I felt a little queasy, too.

I looked away so I wouldn't lose it myself. Rock Star stepped up and set the 2nd Place bucket in front of the prisoner, but he pushed it away and took another bite. The crowd went crazy, proud of him for sticking it out, but knowing that he was done for. He made it through one more roll, then grabbed for the 2nd Place bucket and puked into it with big heaves, and the hotshots all cheered. I made the mistake of looking, and I saw the wet nut rolls jump up and out of his belly, shining in the moonlight.

By that time the prisoner with the glasses had come back out of the bushes, his skin pale and sweaty, to take his place in the ring of spectators. When the pale convict was done throwing up, he went to stand next to the contestant with the glasses. He held his stomach with one hand and they both watched me. I took a deep breath and kept eating. Whether I belonged out in spike camp with them or not, I was going to eat all fifteen nut rolls. I was going to win. That sort of determination was something I'd learned on the Pike.

As I unwrapped nut roll number twelve, I looked up and saw all my friends looking down at me: Archie, so handsome and stoic, his reddish hair almost brown in the moonlight; Rock Star, silly and playful; Hawg, red-faced and ridiculous; Big Sweet Sam, so lanky and worn. I could see it in their faces, they felt sorry for me. They saw that my fate had been sealed, and they wondered if I wanted to back out. But they knew as well as I did that there was no way that I could, not at that point with all three crews up an hour past their bedtime, dying to see the one sweet-looking little woman among them vomit into a white bucket that'd been a container for their chicken-fried steaks the night before. Determined as I was, I'm sure I looked a bit grim. The crowd all wanted to cheer me up, I think, so when Rock Star started his song and dance again they all joined in. All sixty of them shook their asses and sang, "The nougat is gonna get you. The nougat is gonna get you. The nougat is gonna get you. The nougat is gonna get you. . . . Tonight!"

It must've taken me a full fifteen minutes to eat that last roll, but I got it down. As I swallowed the final bite the crowd around me went crazy, cheering and jumping around and hugging each other.

Then the cheering stopped as suddenly as it had begun. All sixty of them turned together to look at me as I reached for the white 1st Place bucket. I could've finished my last nut roll and then rushed off to the privacy of the bushes, like the prisoner with glasses, like I'd always done in secret before, but I realized my obligation. I knew what the heart of the contest was, and I carried it out. I giggled in between heaves. Sick as I was, I still felt high on winning the contest. The nut rolls tore my throat as they came back up, but it was worth it to feel like a hotshot through and through, tough as nails.

As soon as I was done puking, Rock Star and Archie came toward me. They picked me up, lifting me onto their shoulders. All three crews swarmed us as Rock Star and Archie marched me around the basin, with everyone chanting, "Nut Roll Queen! Nut Roll Queen! Nut Roll Queen!" Only Tan stood back from the crowd, arms crossed over his chest, scowling at me. I knew he'd never change, and in that moment I didn't care.

"I'm glad Julie's on the Pike," Hawg yelled. "Even though without her we'd have an all-male crew."

"Nut Roll Queen! Nut Roll Queen!" The sound bounced around the basin and then rose up into the deep navy of the night sky, and I had the feeling right then that being a Piker was the greatest, most glorious job in the world.

Chapter Thirteen

WHEN WE REACHED THE FIRE LINE, WE stayed quiet for a moment, made a little reverent by the hike in, the dense green cloak of the forest around us, the bright ferns drooping lazily to dip into the singing streams. There the fire line was a twenty-four-inch slash through the underbrush, a fierce scrape down to mineral soil, brutal in its disruption of the forest floor. "This'll be your first burnout, huh, Julie?" Sam asked.

I nodded. "We were gonna do one the other day, but then the fire blew up."

"It's a crazy thing to stop a fire by lighting more fire," Sam said, "but it works like a charm."

I had learned by then that if a fire burned toward a crew, they could dig a fire line and then light off of it, setting the forest between their fire line and the main fire ablaze. If everything went as planned, the main fire would suck the newly lit fire right back into itself. Then the fire—having already burned out what was behind and what was ahead—would have no fuel and thus peter out.

Douglas began briefing the crew, "Today we'll be doing a burn off of the line the Mormon Lake shots dug last night. Since you carried the drip torch, Miss Nut Roll Queen, why don't you go ahead and do the honors?"

The drip torch looked like some sort of diabolical watering can, silver and full of a mix of saw gas and diesel. Sam showed me how to pour a little of the diesel mix over the wad of cloth situated just below the little spout. Then he lit the cloth so that it burned with a slow, steady fire. "Pick it up now," Sam said, "and pour a little gas out." I walked over to a bush, held the drip torch above it, and tilted the silver watering can. Gasoline spurted out and fell over the burning wick, turning into a little stream of fire that set the bush to crackling.

Here it was, the thing that, in the early days after my parents' death, had burned away the intensity of my pain and given me a respite from grief. The thing that I had given up the same day my creeping certainty that my grandmother had not wanted me at all was confirmed. And I had not had the dancing flames to assuage that fresh pain. I clung to my promise to my grandmother with a surprising stubbornness, never again wanting to be accused of putting her house and all she held dear at risk.

I walked between the towering pine trees, spilling fire from the drip torch, and the forest floor began to crackle and blaze. I breathed in the purifying scent of burning mountain sage. I couldn't have imagined on that grief-stricken day nine years before that I would be given this great gift.

"Let 'er rip," Hawg yelled, punching his fist into the air above his head. The Pikers around me lit fusees, which looked like long red sticks of dynamite. The fusees sprayed burning slag out of one end and let off a sulfurous smell. A shower of slag landed on Hawg's pants, making sickly yellow spots on the fire-resistant green cloth. The Pikers moved with me along the fire line, all of us going to work setting the forest ablaze. The fire started out small, just grass and little clumps of bushes. Pretty soon, though, the low limbs of the big trees caught some of the heat, and things started rocking and rolling. A bunch of ponderosas torched out, and Sam said, "Whoo-whee."

Just out ahead of us stood a cluster of old growth trees, and I had a sudden, irrational hope that the fire would pass them by, perhaps blackening their bark, but leaving them essentially unharmed. A mama fox took off running, her little baby foxes trailing behind, and I could see how they would inevitably be trapped between the main fire and our burnout. The fire we'd lit suddenly looked like some sort of Old Testament retribution, not something we could've loosed ourselves with nothing more than a silver drip torch and a few fusees.

We all stood looking up at the burning trees, listening to them blowing apart with the heat. Archie stood next to me, a radiant heat coming off of him only I could feel. If I'd looked at him, it would've made my eyes ache, like staring at the too bright flames. "You're good with that drip torch."

"Isn't it ferocious?" I asked. "I feel kind of terrible about it, but it's beautiful, too."

"Like a church you build with your own hands and then peek through the door and see God inside." I looked up at him, surprised, and he looked away. "Growing up I went to church with my family—my folks and my little sister, they were always into it. But I was more into football and partying. But then the winter of my senior year, this shit heel I went to school with, he was a junior, and my little sister went on a date with him. And he . . ." Archie shook his head. He couldn't go on, but he didn't have to. "She didn't tell my folks; it was my other little sister who told me, and I went to school that Monday with a pair of brass knuckles in my bag. I'd barely had a chance to fuck him up before the assistant principals pulled me off him, but the school has a zero-tolerance policy, and they kicked me out. And I wasn't about to tell them or anyone else why. That would've been the worst thing I could've done for my sister.

"I was all-state in football and had a clear shot at playing college ball, but of course I lost that chance. Everybody in town knew what I'd done, everybody at my church, my folks. That's when I really started praying, alone in my room, kneeling on my bed, crying. I prayed and prayed and then I started school at the community college up in Denver. I drove up there every day for a couple of years. Until I got hired on the Pike. And then I really started to have faith I was being taken care of." For a long time we stayed quiet, watching the fire burn in front of us, feeling its heat.

"Your sister?"

"It was all hard for her, too. She felt bad about what happened to me, but I told her it wasn't her fault. She was glad, in a way, too, I think. That I did what I could for her. She's fine now. It's been a few years.

"I've never told anyone all that before. Well, except for Rock Star."

"What about Bliss?" I asked.

"Talking to you, it's easier," Archie said.

The words hung in the air between us. "You and I, we do okay."

"I'll say. Half a season on the same squad, together twenty-four seven, sleeping out on the ground." We'd turned to face each other, the fire burning hot alongside us. We teetered there, on the verge of leaning into each other, but of course we never would.

"I'll tell Bliss someday," he said. But I wasn't sure exactly what he'd tell or what it was I'd want him to say to her.

"I bet you miss her." The words came out just to keep others from escaping. Before Archie could respond, the wind shifted, blowing embers high in the air over our fire line. Bright red points of light floated down into the unburned forest.

"Watch the green for spot fires," Sam called. We all turned to survey the green side of the fire line for smoke in the unburned trees and bushes. The low-hanging limbs with their fresh needles and leaves looked so delicate and lovely that, despite the drip torch in my hand, I wanted to do what I could to protect them. And in some crazy, complicated way, I was.

"I'm so glad Big Sweet Sam is our squad boss," I said, low enough so that only Archie could hear.

"I see a spot!" Archie pointed to a smoke rising from the bushes, and we hustled toward it. That first spot was about five feet around, but it was hot and putting off a good bit of smoke. Rock Star appeared with his chainsaw to cut the flaming bushes, and Archie swamped for him. I quickly scratched some line around the spot, but the smoke was blowing right up into my eyes. By the time I had it lined there were tears and ash and snot and spittle all over my face.

"Archie. Douglas," Douglas said, his voice coming out of Archie's handheld.

"Douglas. Archie." Archie pushed the black button on his radio down while he talked.

"Give me a yell."

"Oooooh," we yelled, so that Douglas would hear where we were.

Douglas told us to hustle over to another spot fire about fifty yards to the west of us, so the three of us set off at a run. My pack bounced and my chest burned from the smoke and the digging. Sam met Archie and Rock Star and me over at that spot fire, and we lined it together, but that was just the beginning. All twenty of us chased them for three hours, slipping and sliding on the steep slope covered in rocky shale. The other Pikers acted as if there was nothing to it, and I wondered if I was the only one near to keeling over. I hoped that the rest of the Pikers were just pretending, as I was, that the work wasn't all that hard. When it finally looked as if we'd caught all the spots, we headed back to our line to monitor the burn.

I was walking in front of Sam when the toe box of my White's caught on a stob sticking out of the ground. The fire had burned away the little tree or shrub, and all that was left was a little stump, sharp and hard as steel. It cut clean through the tough leather of my fire boots, leaving a two-inch gash in the toe box. Sam said, "Well hell, Julie, your White's are finally gettin' broke in."

Sam and I walked down our fire line, assessing the situation. Several giant, burning trees along the fire line began to teeter perilously, threatening to fall across the fire line into the unburned forest. Hawg and Rock Star walked up to us as we studied the snags.

I had already done the fantastical and breathtaking—I'd been paid to burn down an entire forest. The realization of such a dangerous and forbidden desire filled me with an unfamiliar confidence. "Let me drop one," I said.

"Now the Nut Roll Queen wants to run a saw?" Hawg said. "Contumelious."

Archie joined us as I pointed to a dead and flaming tree that wasn't leaning as far over the fire line as the others. "You know I can take that one. No problem." I spoke to Sam alone. He'd seen me drop plenty of more complicated snags during our late afternoon saw lessons. Sam hesitated. "What were you teaching me for then?" I asked.

Sam looked at Rock Star and nodded. Rock Star shrugged and handed his chainsaw to me with a look that said, "This'll be good." The chainsaw felt unexpectedly heavy in my hands. I rested the saw on my leg. Hawg and Rock Star smirked at each other. But on the first yank, the saw started up. I stepped up to the teetering, flaming tree and put in the first horizontal bottom cut on the side of the tree facing the fire. But when I tilted the saw to put in the second cut that would allow me to pull a pie-shaped wedge out of the tree trunk, I struggled to hold the saw at the necessary angle. I managed to make the cut, but it was lopsided and jagged.

I pulled the pie-shaped wedge out of the tree trunk and tossed it away from the tree. As I began to step back around to put in the final cut on the other side of the tree trunk, the tree began to really teeter.

Hawg's panicked voice cut through even over the roar of the saw. "Falling!"

I leapt back as the flaming tree crashed over in the wrong direction to land on the unburned side of the fire line, which was steep and covered in grass and gravely shale. Horror and a sick sense of self-reproach hit me.

Sam ran downhill to begin digging line around the burning tree so that the fire wouldn't spread on the wrong side of our fire line. But as he stepped along the uphill side of the tree, he lost his footing on the slippery shale. He fell onto his right side, his legs sliding under the tree trunk, his left thigh pinned against the flaming tree.

Sam howled in agony as his leg burned. Hawg, Rock Star, Archie, and I all barreled down the slope toward him. Hawg and Rock Star grabbed onto Sam's arms, pulling him out from under the tree. Sam buckled and sagged to the ground. For a moment we all just stood there, taking in the scorched, steaming mess of Sam's burned thigh.

Then Douglas was there saying, "There's a ridge about a quarter mile down the line where we can cut a helispot. I radioed for a medevac." Hawg and Rock Star lifted Sam's shoulders. Archie grabbed his feet. And I ran forward and took one of Sam's legs from Archie. I felt right then that I could carry Sam a long ways before I gave out on him, but I knew that failing my squad boss was something I'd already done.

Douglas led the way up the line, Tan hiked behind him, carrying a chainsaw to cut the helispot. Hawg, Rock Star, Archie, and I followed behind lugging Sam. Archie and I walked side by side, so close together that our shoulders jostled and pressed up against each other. I walked and walked, holding up Sam's burnt leg all the while, my hands cramping, my back and shoulders aching, but I knew I couldn't drop that leg no matter what. After a while, I couldn't hear the forest burning or the sound of our footfalls. If anyone spoke, it didn't register. All I heard were the noises Sam made, his clenched groans blending with the awful stench of his scorched flesh. I didn't see the woods around me, either, green trees to my right, blackened ones to my left. I even lost consciousness of the fact that Archie was so close to me that we moved together like two oxen in a yoke. The only thing I saw was that ghastly mess of Sam's charred thigh, the blackened edges of his pants framing a stretch of meat oozing white.

When we made it to the ridge, we set Sam gently down on the grass. Finally, I knelt down beside him, running the flat of my palm over his hair, murmuring, "I'm so sorry, Sam. I'm so sorry."

Tan yanked his saw to life to cut the helispot, and Archie and Hawg swamped for him. They'd barely cleared ground for the helicopter to land when we heard the chopper. I stayed crouched low by Sam to shield his leg from the rotor wash, my eyes searching his face, but it had turned blank, and he kept staring off toward the sun. Two paramedics jumped out of the open door and ran toward us, their bodies crouched low to protect their heads. They lifted Sam onto their stretcher, and he gave us all the thumbs-up sign.

"Take care, Sam," I cried, but there's no way he heard me, not over the steady beating noise of the rotors. The two paramedics and the stretcher carrying Sam disappeared into the chopper. It lifted into the air and then moved away from us, shrinking smaller and smaller into the pale blue sky until it could've been a hawk gliding along above the blackened, smoking forest.

"Good job, Pike," Douglas said. "IC will radio me with any information about how Sam's doing." He took a deep breath and let it out in a long sigh.

My feet carried me along numbly behind the others as we hiked back to the crew. I seemed to be floating along just above my own body. Back at our fire line, I stood alone, staring into the green forest. The smell of Sam's burned flesh had seared itself into my nostrils, making it impossible to elude the dark reality of the day.

As dusk finally began to fall, Douglas radioed for us to line it out and we did, walking silently through the Idaho landscape, the needle duff buoying our footsteps, the clear streams singing mournful dirges to us as we hiked. Usually as we made our way through the forest, banter skipped lightly up and down our line, but that evening we moved in complete, funereal silence.

I sat alone eating my meatloaf and potatoes au gratin, just as Sam had eaten dinner alone the day he fell out. I remembered Sam's gloves, how he'd written I FELL OUT across the knuckles, the hotshot equivalent of a scarlet letter. I looked up to see Lance coming toward me, unwilling to pass up an opportunity to comfort me. "I need to be by myself," I said, my tone unequivocal, even harsh and, blessedly, he turned and left me alone.

The other Pikers seemed too caught up in their own thoughts to be concerned with me. They ate in quiet clumps of two or three. None of them had said anything to me about my failure, but I didn't need them to do so in order to feel its sting. I looked down at my plate of food, and part of me wanted to refuse to touch it, the other part wanted to scarf down the whole plate and then seconds and thirds and then take the shameful creep into the darkness of the forest. But for whatever reason I ate most of the food on my plate and let it be.

I was worried I'd be unable to sleep, but I fell into blackness as soon as I slid into the bottom of my sleeping bag. I woke up at four in the morning sitting bolt upright, screams flying out of my mouth like bats smoked out of a chimney. The high-pitched shrieks echoed off the mountains before rising up into the clear black night. As my eyes adjusted to the darkness, I could make out firefighters all throughout fire camp sitting up, grunting and disoriented.

"Jesus Christ," someone muttered.

"What the fuck?" another cried. I tried to take deep

breaths to calm myself down. I didn't want to be one of the ones that fire destroys.

"Motherfucker," I heard someone say, "the Nut Roll Queen made me piss my bag."

"I'm sorry," I murmured, "I'm sorry, I'm sorry." And I wasn't sure if I was apologizing for waking the entire fire camp or for letting Sam down or even for presuming that I could hold my own on the Pike in the first place.

"Get your shit together." It was Tan's definitive military bark emerging from the darkness, and I was almost relieved to hear it. "Goddamn splittail, if you can't handle the fire line, you shouldn't be out here."

"I can handle it. I'll fucking handle it, Tan."

Chapter Fourteen

I HEARD FROM THE IC THIS MORNING," Douglas said, as we stood in an expectant circle around him. "Sam was transported to the burn unit in Boise. They said he's stabilized. As soon as he's in a little better shape, they're going to do a skin graft from his right thigh onto his left."

Tan whistled solemnly and the rest of us looked down at the ground. The torn leather of my toe box stared up at me like a reproach.

"We're gonna work today and then head out tonight to drive back down to the Fire Center for our two days of R and R," Douglas said. "It's been a hard tour, and I think all of us could use a couple of days."

I'd been asleep in the back of our crew rig for hours when I woke up to find myself slumped over onto Archie. I could feel his hand sunk wrist deep into my hair, his warm fingers against my scalp. I stayed perfectly motionless, pretending I was still unconscious, feeling his chest rise and fall with each breath. I finally stretched, and Archie slipped his hand back into his lap as I sat up. "Good morning, sunshine," Archie said. "We're almost home." Hawg was driving, Rock Star riding copilot.

"The rig feels empty without Sam," I said, and the others nodded. But the sun shone on my face, and despite my worries, it felt good to be riding down the blacktop with the mountains to the west of us, dark blue and capped with snow like a reflection of the wispy cirrus clouds above them. I saw a warmth to the familiar peaks of the Front Range after the stark, austere rise of the Idaho mountains. Hawg pulled off I-25 at the Monument exit.

"Can't wait to see Big Sweet Sam," Rock Star said.

"Sam's coming home?" I asked, suddenly hopeful.

"We're driving up to see him for our forty-eight hours of R and R," Rock Star said. "Nurse says not even family can visit yet. But I got a way with nurses."

"Who's going?" I asked.

"Me, Archie, Tan, and Hawg."

"Hawg, we got room in the car for one more?" Archie asked.

I saw the chilling look Hawg shot Archie in the rearview.

"Nah, man. You know with our bags, Hawg's rice burner is gonna be full up," Rock Star said.

Hawg pulled off down the long dirt road to the Fire Center. The pond blinked at us in the late afternoon sun, and the rows of trees flashed by as our rig kicked up a long cloud of dust. Up ahead lay Mount Herman and below it, the Fire Center, the cluster of old buildings looking like home. Archie glanced over to smile at me. I realized that without him at the Fire Center, R and R would feel like a wasteland of swirling ash.

I spotted the Llama helicopter rising into the sky.

"Looks like helitack is going to catch that fire over by Devil's Lookout," Hawg said.

"Seems I'm gonna miss out on seeing Rock Star's girl," Archie said. And everyone laughed but me.

When I woke up, darkness had settled in around the quiet bunkhouse and with it the full weight of my loneliness. Stepping out into the bunkhouse hallway, I could sense the emptiness of the place. Probably all the Pikers who were still around had headed over to O'Shea's Pub for a beer. I thought about driving there to join them, but realized that with Sam in the hospital and the rest of my friends out of town, it wouldn't be any fun. And I certainly didn't want to have to deal with seeing Lance.

In the kitchen I ate a sandwich, and when I was done drummed my fingers on the table, antsy and feeling a little desperate to get rid of it. I thought about being carried around the basin on the Pikers' shoulders, all of them chanting, "Nut Roll Queen." And I wanted that to have been the last time. Looking for a distraction, I pulled on jeans and a T-shirt; grabbed my sleeping bag, headlamp, and a bottle of water; and headed out up the road past the Saw Cache and the office, toward Mount Herman. Making my way up the hill, I veered off onto Anklebreaker Creek, a craggy trail that only ran with water during the spring thaw. The rough, uneven ground had injured more than one Piker jogging down it. My headlamp illuminated a circular patch of ground just in front of me so that I could make out the white pebbles and uneven footing as I took each step. Rocks crunched beneath my running shoes, and in the distance I heard the lonely sound of an animal howl.

When I crested Anklebreaker Creek, I stepped out onto the trail winding through Bitch Meadow, so named because the long, slow incline of the meadow that met the base of Mount Herman was a bitch to run. I'd last sprinted up it on my own just before the Pike left for the Idaho tour. That day the meadow had already exploded with waist-high red, yellow, and orange wildflowers, and as I ran along, startled butterflies burst into the air around me, their wings glowing in the sun. Now the light of the stars and the lopsided moon illuminated the meadow, turning the field of waist-high flowers a deep purple only a shade darker than the air above. I laid my sleeping bag down on the trail and slid inside, pulling off my shirt to use for a pillow. Looking up past the three-foot wildflowers to the wide-open night sky above, so full of stars, I felt my loneliness and inadequacy stretching up and out to the far corners of the heavens.

I lay like that for what seemed like hours before I could fall asleep, thinking of Sam and the smoldering mess of his thigh, wishing that Rock Star and Archie were on the ground in their sleeping bags on either side of me, missing more than anything the comforting sound of their breath. I would've given anything just to hear Hawg's terrible snores, to know that my friends hadn't left me behind, that I wasn't alone in the world.

Chapter Fifteen

WHEN I FINALLY WOKE UP AND PEEKED OUT of my bag, the sun shone high and bright above me. The first thing I saw when I sat up was Mount Herman in front of me, a vibrant green against the sky. I stood up and stretched, remembering that Rock Star and Archie told me that once, the year before, they'd woken up at four in the morning on a dare and had climbed all the way to the top of Mount Herman and then back down to the Fire Center in time for crew PT.

In the light of day, the flowers had turned back from a dark midnight purple to their cheerful yellows, oranges, and reds. With the sun hot on my face and blooms all around me, I felt a little ashamed of my night loneliness. A glance at my watch told me it was already eleven o'clock. Despite my nap the afternoon before, I'd slept late, exhausted by my nightmares, the long tour, and my worries about Sam.

After stuffing my sleeping bag and headlamp in my sack, I headed back up Bitch Meadow. But at the turnoff down Anklebreaker Creek, instead of heading toward the Fire Center, I stashed my gear behind a big rock and walked straight ahead up the trail toward Mount Herman.

I picked up my pace as the trail moved up out of Bitch Meadow, rising into the dense forest covering Mount

Herman. I moved light and strong without a forty-pound pack on my back. The trail passed through a small meadow bursting with primrose and fireweed, and then back into the timber. Every once in a while I'd stick my hand in my pocket to finger the arrowhead that Sam gave me after we visited Paloma Canyon.

Dry as it was and heating up with the sun, I took only small sips of water when I was very thirsty, hoping to make it back down to the Fire Center without running out. A stream cut across the mountain, but I didn't want to risk giardia by drinking from it. It was one thirty—I'd been walking for a couple of hours already, and I'd begun to think Rock Star and Archie's claim that they hiked all the way to the top of the mountain and back down before morning PT must've been brag talk.

When I finally stood at the top of the mountain, a little spacey from dehydration and heat, I raised my fist above my head in triumph. Looking down at the Fire Center surrounded by ponderosa pine, I realized that even though it was beautiful, a fairy-tale summer camp, what made it home for me wasn't the place so much as my friends. Without them there I was as lost and lonely as I'd be anywhere else.

Swaying a little with hunger, the memory of my debut overcame me suddenly, without warning or cause. My grandmother had threatened to quit paying my tuition if I didn't take a semester off from Colorado College to deb in Dallas. My rancor against her for feeling my presence in her house as a burden had long ago come to define me. The fact that she coerced me to be a debutante was just another stone to add to the teetering pile of my resentments.

After making my bow onstage in my big puffy white dress, after the forced humiliation of it, I'd quickly drunk enough at the open bar to be sloppy and had let myself be clumsily seduced by my escort. The ladies' room was fancy enough to have real wooden doors for each toilet, and we'd closed ours before he'd pulled up my dress from behind, but in our drunkenness we hadn't managed to lock it. It was white-haired Irene Mavis, one of my grandmother's closest friends, who opened the door. A couple more women who'd played bridge with my grandma for years stood at the sink washing their hands, and I saw the shocked horror of their reflections as they took in the image of my date mercilessly fucking me from behind in the bathroom stall. I felt it then, a swirling of terrible triumph and the old familiar guilt. For this transgression my grandmother would never forgive me, and perhaps I'd been out to commit the unforgiveable ever since that long ago day when I'd forgotten to lock another bathroom door and my grandmother had walked in to see my parents' names in fire.

I heard footsteps and stumbled backward, startled. Lance came around from the big rock in front of me wearing his fancy Oakley sunglasses, a Snow Monster T-shirt, baggy shorts that hung below his knees, and expensive trail shoes. A Camelback sat on his back, the plastic straw coming around over his shoulder. His dark hair hung down around his face, perfectly framing his fine features.

"Hey hotshot, you following me?" he asked. He looked pleased to see me, and I realized that I was glad to see him, too.

"Just headin' for the hills. Those the Lance Martin pants?"

"You know it," he said. "What do you think?"

"Nice," I said.

"Want to hike back down with me?" Lance asked. "I came up the trail that runs straight from the Fire Center."

"All right," I said. "You can be lead tool."

"Nah, you."

We walked along in a comfortable silence down the switchbacks, the trail sheltered by towering ponderosa pines, sunlight sifting through the branches, the air sweet with the smell of summer. And it felt good to hear the crunch of Lance's footsteps behind me. After we'd been hiking awhile, I unscrewed the cap of my water bottle and took a tiny sip. Despite my efforts at conservation, the bottle was almost empty and my throat felt parched.

"Want some water?" Lance asked.

"Are you sure?" I asked, almost too proud to accept the offer.

"Yeah, I'm sure."

I stopped and turned around as Lance grabbed the straw dangling over his shoulder and reached it out to me. I stepped close enough to him to drink from the straw, and as soon as the water hit my mouth I began sucking greedily. Lance and I stood face-to-face, no more than ten inches between us. When I glanced up at him, our eyes met. "Thanks," I said.

"Why don't you wear it?" Lance asked, sliding the Camelback off his shoulders and holding it out to me.

"No, no," I said.

"Come on now, even tough guys need to hydrate."

"Okay, but let me know if you need a drink," I said.

"Deal," he agreed. I slipped my arms through the straps of the Camelback, and the weight of the water sitting on my back felt good.

"I didn't bring enough water 'cause I wasn't planning on hiking."

"But you ended up on top of Mount Herman? You're hard-core."

"Nah, just doing my thing," I said. But I realized that if someone had told me a few months before that I'd head out into the wilderness alone just for fun I wouldn't have believed them. I looked down again at the Fire Center below us, the rows of trees beyond it, and beyond that the untamed forest. More beautiful than any place I'd ever imagined myself living.

"Where are you headed when fire season ends?"

It wasn't a question I'd asked myself. Truth was, I didn't want the season to ever end. I understood now why Sam just stayed holed up in his house during the winter, collecting unemployment, drinking beer, waiting for the spring sun to come out and thaw the snow and dry out the timber so that fire season could finally begin again. "I don't know, maybe I'll go into hibernation," I joked. "Sleep until next season rolls around."

"Maybe you could come down to Purgatory. I'll give you a snowboarding lesson."

"I don't think I'm into paying to fall on my ass all day in the freezing cold."

"If you're with me on the slopes, you won't be paying."

I rolled my eyes.

"I'm serious," he said. "I hope you'll think about it."

We popped out from the trail onto the dirt road running down to the Fire Center. I realized I didn't want any of the Pikers to see me walking with Lance.

"Hey, I'm going to run up Anklebreaker and grab my sleeping bag."

I handed him the Camelback and started to run off.

"Hey, hold on," Lance called. I turned back to him. "Let's go into town later for a beer."

"I'd love to, really, but I have some stuff I need to do," I said, a little pained. "Anyway, thanks for the water."

"Anytime," he said. He turned to walk back down to the Fire Center, and I headed back up Anklebreaker to fetch my sleeping bag. I'd only gone a few steps when I glanced over my shoulder at Lance's retreating figure. He looked back at me at the exact same moment, and we both laughed, maybe a little wistfully, and then we both turned and went our separate ways.

The bunkhouse was deserted again. Surely everyone had headed out to O'Shea's for steak and liquor. I tried to call Sam, but no one answered his cell or the phone in his hospital room. A long, hot shower left me faint with hunger, so I drove into town to eat Chinese alone, half-regretting having turned down Lance's offer. On my way back to the Fire Center I stopped in at the liquor store. When I arrived home, the place was still deserted, and I walked up to the classroom, put in a romantic comedy, and collapsed on the couch to watch it and drink the bottle of wine I'd bought. The couple in the film faced so many impediments of class, character, and circumstance that it seemed certain they'd never get together.

When the movie ended, I headed back down to the bunkhouse, wobbly from the wine, and crawled under my blanket. Though my bed still felt strange, I just wanted to go to sleep and wake up in the morning knowing my friends would be home that very day.

I heard the screams from deep inside the tunnel of my dream where Sam twisted and burned on a spit above a campfire. My bedroom door flew open, a dark figure standing there. I opened my mouth to scream again, and a voice said, "Julie. It's me."

"You scared me," I said, disoriented and still a little drunk.

Lance walked toward me. In the darkness I could see he wore pajama bottoms and no shirt. "May I?"

"Sure."

Lance sat on the edge of my bed. "Bad dream?"

I nodded. "Sam. He was burning."

"You were already worn out. We'd been working for hours."

"Worn out? Too weak is more like it. Tan can run a chainsaw for twelve hours. Rock Star and Archie, too."

"You had a bunch of hotshots staring at you, waiting for you to screw up." He paused. "Besides, that chainsaw weighs fifteen pounds more than the one you've been training on."

I looked at him, surprised. "How do you know that?"

"I was taking my laundry to the washer one time and I spotted you and Sam out the back classroom window.

Then I started to notice you would both disappear after work on the regular. Easy enough to figure out what you were up to. With a little more practice, you could run a saw on a fire just fine. And hell, at this point you can out-dig most of the crew. Just 'cause nobody mentions it doesn't mean we don't all see it."

I was so grateful for the kind words that I reached up and put my hand on the back of his neck, and then he leaned down and kissed me, gently, but with a confidence I hadn't expected. I pulled back the covers, and he slid underneath them, and we kept kissing as we peeled off each other's pajamas. I told myself I wasn't doing it out of anger at being left behind, but still there was spite in the act, a gloating self-satisfaction at indulging in the forbidden that felt all too familiar.

A couple hours later we could hear the other Pikers come clomping drunkenly into the bunkhouse from the bar, and we made sure to be perfectly silent as we clung to each other in the darkness.

When I looked at my watch again it was almost five in the morning. "You have to go back to your room now," I whispered. Our legs were tangled together with the sheets.

"Why?" Lance kissed my collarbone, my neck.

"Because I don't want anyone to see you coming out of my room in the morning, that's why."

"I want to fall asleep next to you."

Tempted as I was, I said, "I'm sorry, you have to go."

"Maybe when fire season is over we can sleep together," Lance said.

"Go on now."

"One more." He leaned over and gave me a kiss I felt in the arches of my feet and then he was pulling his silk pajama bottoms back on and then he was gone, leaving me to snuggle down into my blankets and fall asleep.

Chapter Sixteen

WHEN I WOKE UP TO THE SUN SHINING through my window, the memory of the night before hit me along with a wave of absolute panic. I didn't understand how it could've happened, how I possibly could've slept with Lance. The day before, tired, dehydrated, and hungry though I may have been, I'd had the good sense not to even go out for a beer with him, but only hours later I was scrogging him like a crazed weasel. It was the late hour, the wine, my desire for comfort from my nightmare, the fact that Lance came into my room in the shadowy land between sleep and waking. But even in my panic, I realized there was more to it.

I climbed out of bed, slipped into the bathroom, and took a long hot shower, washing off the night before. I quickly dressed and went to the kitchen, which at that early hour was still empty. With the receiver to my ear, I dialed the number for the Boise Burn Unit. The receptionist put the call through to Sam's room, and he answered on the second ring. "Sam?" I asked.

"Julie." His voice was thick with morphine, but still it sounded beautiful to me.

"Oh, God, I'm so glad to hear your voice. How are you doing?"

"Not so good."

"Are the guys still there?"

"They left."

"Is Cheryl there yet?"

"She was but—" Sam's voice wobbled, as if he couldn't bear to go on.

"Sam, what is it?"

"She took one look at me and told me I had to promise her I'd never go out on the fire line again. But, Julie, that's the one promise I could never make. Truth is, the only thing that's getting me through this is the thought of rehabbing my leg and getting back out there with the Pike."

"I totally understand, Sam."

"I mean, a woman who doesn't get what fighting fire means to me—"

"Doesn't get you at all, I know. So, what happened?"

"She kept saying she wanted me to go to work managing her dad's factory. Julie, I can't work in a factory! I'd, I'd—" Sam searched for the words. "I'd end up feeling the way I felt before I found the Pike, except worse, because back then I didn't know there was another way to live. Back when I worked wiring houses, I couldn't stand the day in and day out of it. I didn't even know how numbed out I was till the Pike thawed me out. I can't go back to that."

"I know," I said. "If there's anyone who knows what you're saying, it's me."

"Cheryl could see I wasn't going to budge at all, so she left me."

"She just left?"

"She was here maybe three hours total."

"I hate to think of you there all by yourself."

"The nurses, they're sweethearts. They check on me about every five minutes."

"I'm sure they can't help themselves," I said, trying to sound lighthearted. "Well, hey, want me to head up that way?"

"Don't be silly," Sam said. "The crew goes back on the boards tonight. And I'm gonna be fine." But he didn't sound fine, not at all.

I put my head down on my arms on the kitchen table and wished I didn't feel so alone. Suddenly I thought about my grandmother. I hadn't bothered to call her since we returned from our Idaho tour. But I could hear Archie's voice telling me I really ought to check in with her more because she'd raised me, after all. She was my blood relation, all the family I had, and I sure enough needed to talk to somebody. I picked up the phone and dialed her number, half hoping that her answering machine would pick up. The message I'd leave would be friendly and cheerful—I'd end it with a "Love you," spoken lightly, as if easy to say. But my grandmother answered on the first ring. "Frosty," I said.

"Julie, is that you?" she asked, and for a moment I thought I heard a quaver in her voice.

"It's me," I rushed in. "I'm so glad you're home. I was afraid you'd be out." Now that I'd heard her voice, the thought of leaving a message seemed intolerably lonely. I wanted to tell her all about fighting fire, to explain to her what it meant to me to be on the Pike.

"I'm right here. *I* haven't gone anywhere."

I ignored her implication, determined that the conversation would go well. "My crew went to Idaho for three weeks." I felt foolish; there was nothing I could say to explain Idaho to my grandmother: the prison crews, spiking out in that basin in the mountains, the singing streams, the way I'd failed to drop that snag where I wanted, the terrible smell of Sam's burned thigh.

"It's certainly been a while since you called." Her voice was calm and cool again, all hint of a quaver gone.

"Yeah, it's been really busy and there's no cell reception at the fire camp," I said.

"I don't need excuses. You could call if you wanted to." I heard Frosty take in a deep breath. "You know, you could've done anything in the world, anything at all, you had every opportunity. And then you threw it all away, your education—" she almost choked up, but didn't. "Anyway, I'm glad to hear that you're safe." My grandmother paused, and I could almost see her drawing herself up, using all her steely reserve to rein in her anger at the ways I had wronged both her and myself. "You're such a pretty girl. I ran into Nancy McGraw's grandmother at the Art League the other day. Nancy never was half so pretty as you, and she's marrying an investment banker in the fall, a smart girl marrying a smart man."

"Lots of guys on my crew are really smart. This one guy, Clark, he's getting a PhD in forest resource management and, Hawg, he can define any word in the dictionary."

"Hawg," Frosty sniffed delicately, as if she smelled something rancid. "He must be a delightful young man."

"Forget it," I said. "It was stupid for me to call." Stupid of me to think things would be different from how they've always been. "I'll talk to you later." I hung up the phone. "Love you," I said, into the still, thin air of the kitchen, and then I started to cry.

I went for a long mountain run. The pain as I pushed up the switchbacks made me feel a little better. The sun felt hot on my neck during the open stretches, but when I passed under the pine trees, the air turned cool. I ran through a giant stand of quaking aspen and thought about what Archie had told me, that the whole bunch of aspen were one organism, connected below ground by their roots. I ran the trail down the mountain, looped around Monument rock, a giant tan piece of sandstone jutting up from the ground, and then made my way up the last stretch of road to the Fire Center.

I spotted a group of Pikers grilling fish and milling about the picnic tables in front of the kitchen. Regret at having slept with Lance coursed through me, but I was pretty sure he would keep his mouth shut. I certainly wasn't going to tell any of the Pikers about my lapse. What had happened the night before had happened, but it was over and done with, and none of my friends would have to know about it. Archie and Rock Star threw the Frisbee back and forth with an effortless, animal grace. "Hey, Julie," they all called as I approached. Archie's face lit up when he saw me, and I felt my own skin flush.

"Hey, everybody, welcome home," I said.

Hawg gestured to the grill, covered with trout and bass. "We caught some fish on the way back. We were hoping you'd come home in time to eat 'cause we're grilling one for you."

"Thanks," I said, my spirits lifted—my friends were home.

I sat down next to Clark on one of the picnic tables. His face looked boyish and tan beneath his thick, blond hair.

"How's Sam?"

"They did the skin graft. Took a bunch of skin off his good thigh and pasted it over the burn. Pretty fuckin' brutal."

I shuddered and wrapped my arms around myself. "I talked to him this morning." I realized that even though Sam sounded terrible, speaking with him had helped me realize that, as hard a time as he was having, he was no longer howling in agony as the flesh burned from his thigh, the way he'd remained in my dreams.

"Yeah?"

"He sounded upset about Cheryl."

"It's a real bummer for Sam, though I hardly blame her. He's crazy not to realize hotshotting isn't a job he'll be able to do forever. It's a job for the young, really, and Big Sweet Sam ain't all that young." Clark paused. "He said we should've brought you with us." The words hung in the air.

"Guess what?" Rock Star said, to no one in particular. "I wrote a new song during R and R. Do you all want to hear it?"

"Sure," I said.

"Of course, we do, buddy," Archie agreed.

Rock Star trotted off to his room and came back a
moment later carrying his guitar. "Are you all ready?"
he asked. We nodded. Rock Star sat down on top of the
picnic table directly across from the one where Archie and
I sat. "The song's called 'Fishing with My Best Friend,'"
Rock Star said. "Archie, buddy, I wrote it for you." Out of
nowhere, my eyes teared up. Rock Star started strumming
his guitar hard. The song came out of him, fast and full,
and there was more happiness in it than I'd maybe felt in
my whole life.

Well I woke you up at seven, you said you didn't want to go.
But I got the dog and the truck's filled up and it's time to
hit the road.
I'll get you some coffee and you can put in a fresh ground
scrod.
'Cause it's our two days off and the sun is up and we both
got brand new rods.

We can fish all day to a six-pack of beer and some Keen
on the radio.
But the fish ain't bitin' and you and me's fightin' 'bout
what you got on my mo.
When the day is done after bakin' in the sun we can drive
to the Horse Creek Inn.
Turn on the grill and cook up some steaks.
I'm fishin' with my best friend.

All the Pikers within hearing distance broke into whoops
and applause and Archie and I stomped our feet on the seat

of the picnic table. "You like it, buddy?" Rock Star asked.

"Course I do," Archie said.

Rock Star glowed, as pleased as he would have been had Archie said he had the best buddy in the world.

Tan, Hawg, Clark, Archie, Rock Star, and I sat at a picnic table eating our fish. "Hawg, what is it with you and big engine girls?" Tan asked.

"They're grateful. They're easy. And it's always a challenge to figure out a configuration that works in the cab of an engine. I like a challenge." We all laughed as Hawg turned to Archie. "You ought to try a big engine girl sometime. Now that you've dumped the ball and chain."

I looked at Archie, surprised. He shrugged. Rock Star wrapped an arm around Archie's neck and rubbed Archie's head with his knuckles. "Didn't take my boy long to figure things out."

"Anybody need another beer?" I asked. A chorus of "I do" rose from the guys. I stood up to walk to the cooler, and Archie rose to go with me. I opened up the cooler. "What happened?" I asked, low enough so the others couldn't hear.

"She wasn't the girl for me."

I felt my eyes widen.

"We both knew it."

Hawg yelled from the picnic table. "Where's my beer?"

Archie turned to take a beer to Hawg, leaving me reeling with this new information. I grabbed a couple more beers and went to sit down, just as Lance and his weaselly roommate, Gary, came out of the bunkhouse, walking down the sidewalk toward us. I'd stayed away from the Fire Center all day and hadn't seen Lance since he'd slipped out of my bedroom at dawn. The remorse I felt was almost sickening. I focused on Archie's face across the table, his green eyes calm, and Lance and his roommate blurred blessedly out of focus.

"Good to see you, guys," Lance said as he came up alongside the picnic tables. "How was your trip?"

A muscle in Tan's jaw twitched. He didn't like Lance, his designer clothes, or his bragging. Lance looked at me, our eyes met for the briefest of seconds, and then I glanced away. "Great," my buddies grumbled.

"How about you?" Archie asked.

"It was good. Didn't do much, laid low," Lance said.

"Laid's about right," Gary said, snickering.

Lance nudged him and glared.

"What? I got up to piss at five this morning, saw you coming out of Julie's room."

Pikers paused with forks lifted halfway to their lips. Birds stopped chirping. I forgot to breathe. I passed over the look of shock that came over Lance's face and the disgusted expressions of the other Pikers to gaze straight at Archie. There was nothing in the world for me except his face, his reddish brown hair, strong cheekbones, and jaw that disappeared beneath a full goatee. He stared right at me, his face still and impenetrable as stone.

Clark cleared his throat and coughed a dry, pointed little cough and time started moving again.

"We're headed to town," Lance said, as if the situation wasn't happening at all. "Can I bring you guys anything?"

"We don't need nothing from you," Tan said. As Lance and Gary hurried away, I saw Lance give his roommate a hard shove on the shoulder.

Tan turned to me, his eyes hot. "Sounds like we weren't the only ones went fishing over R and R. Some of us caught trout, some of us caught bass, and some of us caught the elusive one-eyed burping worm." A nightmare blur of laughter rang in my ears.

"That's disgusting," I said.

"You got that right," Tan continued. "It is disgusting. Jesus, Julie, not only can you not drop a tree to save your life, you can't keep your pants zipped either."

My face went numb and tingly and then rage boiled up from my stomach. I rose to my feet. "Are you kidding me? Are you serious? Hawg here fucks every big engine girl he can get his hands on, in *fire camp* for Christ's sake, none of you guys say jack. Archie misses a dispatch 'cause he's out in his hazmat tent scrogging Bliss, nobody gives him a hard time. Me? I get laid once, and you think you can fucking talk to me like that? You guys weren't even here. You guys were gone. So don't act like it's any of your goddamn business what I do."

I stood up, chunked my beer bottle in the trash, and hurried toward the bunkhouse, leaving a stunned silence in my wake.

Chapter Seventeen

I N MY ROOM, I SHOVED A CHANGE OF CLOTHES in my backpack and grabbed my car keys. I peeked out the window to make sure the Pikers had wandered away from the picnic tables before making a break for my car.

I drove north on I-25 until I crossed the border into Wyoming. At Cheyenne I headed west on I-80, driving across the great, weeping plains as darkness fell. Already I missed the mountains. I wondered if it would always be this way for me, if I'd always create some great pile of rubble that I'd then run away from.

I drove all night, stopping only for gas and cheap coffee. I pulled into the hospital parking lot in Boise a couple of hours after dawn, bleary-eyed and a little bewildered. As I headed down the hallway of the Burn Unit I passed a man, terribly burned, walking down the hallway trailing an IV. I looked away so as not to seem to stare, and I had to work to keep myself from shuddering.

I knocked and entered Sam's room. And though I'd steeled myself for the sight, it was still a shock to see so many tubes running out of him. He looked pale and terrible, and I was glad that the hospital sheets covered his bandaged thighs. I forced myself to sound cheerful.

"Sam!"

He opened his eyes, drugged up and barely awake.

"Who's that?"

"It's so good to see you."

"Then act like it! Come over here and give an old man a hug!"

I leaned over to hug him, trying to make sure not to catch on any of his tubes. Then I pulled up a Naugahyde hospital chair and sat down. I could see Sam struggling to appear in good spirits.

"So, how are you, Sam?"

"Can't complain, and even if I could, wouldn't do no good."

"Oh, Sam. I'm so sorry. If I had—"

"Burned trees go where they want to go. I slipped and fell, pure and simple. Unless you think you're God, nature has a mind of its own."

"But—"

Sam put a finger up to his mouth to silence me. "I'm gonna get through this. Be fine soon enough. Here, push this button thing for me. Nurse's got my meds up too high." But before I could reach the call button, Sam had drifted off to sleep.

For the rest of the day I sat there beside him while he slept, and whenever he woke up I was ready with a quick smile. I only left the hospital a couple of times, to fetch Sam snacks or a milkshake.

I woke up the next morning, stiff from sleeping on the fold-out hospital chair.

"Morning, sunshine," Sam said. "You sleep okay?"

I smiled at him—he did look better. A nurse came in carrying fresh bandages.

"You Mr. Sam's daughter?" she asked.

"I only wish," I said.

"Be careful what you wish for," the nurse said. "I need a couple minutes alone with this old goat."

"She just wants to peek at my pecker," Sam said with a wink.

"Yeah, give me an hour to find it. Now, shoo," she said to me, so I scooted out of the room.

When I returned, I set a coffee and a croissant down for Sam on his tray and swung it around to be sure he could reach it. As I settled into my chair, Sam started with the line of questioning I'd been dreading since my arrival.

"So you gonna tell me why you're here? The crew's been back on the boards for two days."

"I just needed to see if you were okay."

"Yeah, and that's why you didn't come with the guys."

"Well—"

"Something's up. What is it?"

"Shit, Sam, I slept with Lance."

Sam lifted an eyebrow. "If there was a handbook for girl hotshots, that'd be rookie move number one."

"I know. I know. But I didn't do anything they don't do all the time."

"But with Lance?" Sam shot me a teasing look.

"After the accident . . . he was the only one who'd talk to me."

"And you felt sorry for yourself. Come on, Julie, you're tougher than that. And being here, you're just making it worse." He paused for a minute. "You promised me."

"I know I did," I whispered.

"You promised me you'd make me proud."

"I know I did."

"And do you think running away makes me proud?" I shook my head, suddenly feeling the crushing weight of all my failures. But then Sam took a deep breath, exhaling as he spoke. "Look, Tan called when you were getting coffee. The crew's about to be dispatched, but with me out, and you gone, the crew's down to eighteen. They need nineteen for a dispatch. You wanna go, you better hit the road."

It was night when I pulled up to the Fire Center. Pikers walked through the darkness around the rigs, packing tools and red bags. As I jogged past them toward the bunkhouse I heard Hawg say, "It's about time."

"We're rolling in thirty," Douglas called out to me. "Better hustle up."

I ran down the hallway and opened the door to my room, startled to see Bliss there, packing a duffel bag.

"Hi."

"Hey," she said. "I heard you went to see Sam. You doin' okay?"

I shook my head and started to cry.

"You must be exhausted," she said.

The story of sleeping with Lance spilled out of me.

"Good for you," Bliss said. "I don't know how you've made it this long without getting laid. I'd be going crazy."

"But Bliss, it's not good for me. I feel like I'm not cut out to be a hotshot."

"Needing to get laid has nothing to do with whether or not you're a good hotshot. It's fucking bullshit. It's like you told them, all the guys get laid and it's no big deal. Even I can get laid, and the guys don't like it, but they don't slap me any shit. But because you're a woman and a hotshot, you're supposed to be a nun, too? Give me a break. Hotshots' ideas about women and fire aren't going to change until women quit playing by their fucking rules, that's what I think. You did the right thing. And Lance? How was he?"

"Not bad. But he isn't the guy for me."

"Just keep your head up," Bliss said, "and keep doing a good job, and you're going to be just fine around here." She spoke so confidently that for that moment I couldn't help but believe her.

"I'm so glad you're back. I don't know what I'd do without you," I said, realizing I meant it.

"You're about to find out."

"What do you mean?"

"I have big news, too. Some guy on the Mormon Lake hotshots tore his ACL and is out for the season. I just found out this afternoon they offered me the job."

"Oh, my god, Bliss, that's great . . . I think. But why don't you just apply to go out as an alternate on the Pike? Sam's position is open."

"The Pike is Archie's turf. Now that we're done—" She shook her head.

"Bliss, I—"

She cut me off. "Look, don't worry about it. It was clear as day. I couldn't help but see it. It's nobody's fault." She paused before speaking. "You're going to be okay. You just need to stop being so hard on yourself. Have some confidence that you know what you're doing."

"When are you leaving?"

"Tomorrow," she said.

Part Three

Part Three

Chapter Eighteen

IT FELT STRANGE AND SOMEHOW WRONG TO BE headed out to a fire without Sam. Archie drove and Hawg rode shotgun, so that I was in the backseat with Rock Star, all of us quiet and pensive. By the next morning we were digging line in the Black Hills, through the stands of aspen, paper birch, and American elm, whose thick green tops created a dense shade above us. With Sam gone, Hawg worked lead tool, and I dug line beside him, the rest of the diggers trailing out behind us to do the easier work of clearing the ground we'd already broken.

When I wasn't bent over digging line, I kept to myself and even ate alone, still feeling angry and empty, still telling myself I didn't need friends who'd impose bullshit double standards on me. But on our fifth day at the fire, as I walked by with my dinner plate, Rock Star yelled, "Julie, get your skinny ass on over here and sit down." After that I sat with my friends again sometimes, but there was still an uneasiness among us.

Clark sat across from me at the table at breakfast. He took his third bite of breakfast burrito and then paused as he examined the burrito's contents. He quickly spat the unchewed bite out onto his plate. "What is it?" I asked.

Clark held the offending burrito out in my direction so that I could see inside it. He looked like a baby-faced kid grossed out by the contents of his lunchbox. "Eggs," he said.

"Well, you only ate a couple bites," I said. But by the time the rest of us were done with breakfast, Clark's eyes had puffed up so that he had to peer out of tiny slits, and the other Pikers were looking at him with shock from seeing one of their buddies turned freaky-looking in the span of a few moments.

"You're going to be okay," I said, as I walked next to Clark. I held the crook of his elbow with one arm and put my other arm across his shoulder so that I could simultaneously steer him and give him the sense he wasn't alone in his egg-induced blindness.

"Thanks," Clark said. "I think Tan was put out that you're taking me to the med tent. He's my best friend in the whole world, really—but to be honest, I'm glad you're with me."

"How come?"

"Much as Tan loves me, you're a lot more comforting than he could ever be."

"He hates me."

"True. Tan hates most people, though, so don't take it too hard." Clark laughed. "You know, you screwed up pretty bad when you screwed Lance."

"I know," I said. "But I don't think it was fair for me to be treated like crap."

"Probably not. But that's just how it goes. Nineteen guys and one woman out in the woods together, only way she's going to get along is if they forget she's a woman at all. Otherwise she reminds them of what they leave behind to fight fire. Tan hasn't seen his girlfriend in months, you know. Neither have I."

"That's not my fault," I said.

"Whoa there, I'm not saying it is. And I'm not saying the way hotshotting goes is perfectly just. Fire's got its own laws, that's all, and if you're going to make it as a shot, you're going to have to follow them. Sometimes you've got to let go of your principles and everything you're pissed off about and just roll with things."

We stepped through the medical tent. The scrawny, young medic leapt to his feet when he saw Clark's eyes, swollen shut and turning purple. "What happened?"

"I had a run-in with a breakfast burrito," Clark said.

"Burrito, one, Clark, zero," I said, and Clark laughed.

Once Clark was all settled in on a cot in the medical tent, I patted his forearm. "Well, I better get back so I can hike in with the crew."

"God, I'm jealous," Clark said. "You know this makes me feel so bad for Sam. He's pretty much fucked, you know?"

My eyes stung unexpectedly and I was glad Clark couldn't see me wiping them. "We'll come check on you tonight," I promised. I put my hand on Clark's brow.

"Thanks, Florence Nightingale," Clark said.

"Anytime," I said.

As I headed back out of the medical tent, I bumped

into Lance, who fell into step beside me. "Hey, I just wanted you to know, the way the other guys have given you such a hard time pisses me off to no end. You deserve to be treated better."

"Thanks."

"I'm sorry about Gary blabbing."

"It's okay."

"But that's not the real reason, is it."

"Reason for what?"

"That you don't want to be with me." I looked at Lance, a little surprised that after all his pushiness, he had finally figured things out without me having to tell him anything. "The real reason you don't want to be with me . . . I come off like a bit of a shrimper, I know. But it's just that the things I've got going for me, they don't get props on a shot crew."

"You do have a peach loofah."

"The thing is, I like my peach loofah. I'm not going to try to change so guys like Tan and Clark will want to hang with me."

"I can respect that," I said. "I completely respect that."

"I wish you had less respect for me and more of a desire to have your way with me."

"Oh, I had my way with you, all right."

"But that was it for us, wasn't it?" I nodded, and Lance smiled at me, a little sadly. "Even as it was happening, I knew. You're not the sort of thing I could fool myself about." He made a fist and slowly held it out. I bumped my own fist against it.

Lance and I reached the other Pikers as they gathered around Douglas. "What's the report?" Douglas asked, scratching a particularly inflamed ingrown hair.

"The medic said Clark needs to lay low for today and probably tomorrow," I said. "Pretty much what we expected."

"So that means Tan will need a swamper. Julie, why don't you give it a go?" Douglas looked at me, and I wasn't sure, but I thought I saw him give me, a quick, sly Sam wink.

A murmur of disbelief rippled through the Pikers. "Sir?" I said.

"You heard me. Tan needs a swamper."

"That's right," Tan barked. "I need a swamper, not a splittail. Give me Hawg."

Douglas spoke with the sternness of one not about to see his authority challenged. "If Clark was well, he'd be swamping for you. But since he's blind as a bat and laid out on a med cot, Julie will be working with you today. And that's an order." The Pikers chuckled gleefully.

We walked from fire camp over the flat stretch of dry prairie grass waving in the sun to the line of helicopters that would fly us in. When we landed at the helispot, we still had a considerable hike over rolling hills and through the conifer forest that made the landscape look black from a distance. The hike gave me a chance to work out some of my nervousness. By the time we arrived it was 9:30 and still cool enough that the relative humidity was high and the fire lying low. I walked over to stand next to Tan. He had his sunglasses on, but I could guess at his expression.

"Okay, Rookie, here's the drill. Anything I cut, you grab and throw way the fuck away from the fire line. You got that?"

"I got it."

"I'm expecting you to keep your man pleaser shut and bust your ass." All three sawyers started up their saws, and I headed out with the saw team, looking over my shoulder at the diggers leaning on their tools, watching me go. We were cutting hot line, moving along the edge of the burning forest, clearing out limbs and brush so that the diggers could work behind us. Even though I was terrified of the roaring saw bar, I jumped right in and grabbed whatever Tan cut, aware at every moment that with one false move Tan could accidentally cut off one of my hands or I could trip and be impaled on the saw. I threw the limbs and bushes as far away from the saw line as I could, so that they wouldn't create a berm right on the edge of our fire line. The work went hard and fast and within a couple of hours I was completely covered in dirt and bits of sawdust and bark. Dust had made its way down my collar and covered my chest, stomach, and back in a fine, gritty layer. Douglas radioed, and Tan turned off his saw to listen. "Rock Star, Douglas."

"Go, Douglas."

"Good work. The fire's cooled off a bit back here, and I'm seeing a bunch of gnarly snags really close to our line. Come on back this way and drop some." I saw Archie raise his fist at Rock Star and Rock Star grin his mischievous grin. The saw team lived to drop snags. The sawyers had told me plenty of times it was the most dangerous work of fighting fire, especially if the tree had been burned out and had widowmakers hung up in its branches. At that point, it was a science for the sawyer to decide where to put his cuts in so that the tree would fall where he wanted. And each swamper had to be the sawyer's eyes and ears while the sawyer was dropping a snag. It was the swamper's job to stay alert and yell as soon as the tree showed a sign it was going to fall so that the sawyer could get out of the way. More than because of his general dislike for me, Tan didn't want me swamping for him because he didn't trust me, and a sawyer has to trust his swamper—so much depends on it.

Tan dropped a few easy snags, and I stayed jittery and alert. He paused to size up a snag that was right on the line. Flames climbed up the trunk of the tree, and Tan yelled at me that he figured he could drop it against its lean, back into the black. I stood behind him with my head back, watching the top of the tree without daring to blink so I could see the first movement when it started to go. Tan stepped up and put in a pie cut right above the big burned-out catface. That couldn't have been that scary for him because the tree was leaning away from him, back over our line into the green. The flames were licking up and down the trunk, and I knew the saw bar must be heating up. The trunk of the tree was all black and ashy and flaming. Tan pulled the pie cut out and flames filled up the empty sliver. Suddenly, I had a respect for him that I'd never had before. Watching him pull his pie cut out of that burning trunk, I realized that he held himself to the high standards he imposed on everyone around him.

Even I could see the back cut was going to be the tricky part. The tree was leaning back and over Tan. He put the cut in, set his saw down, and then pushed an orange plastic wedge into his cut. A certain comfort existed in the sound of the saw idling on the ground. I pulled the FST—a long-handled sledgehammer—out of the loop where it hung from the top of Tan's pack and handed it to him, all the time keeping my head back and my eyes on the top of that snag. Tan pounded away at the wedge, but he had to put another one in and then another. I watched him swing the FST, driving those wedges deep into his back cut. I could almost feel how the blows must've rung all the way up his arms.

As I saw the top of the tree begin to quiver, I yelled, "Falling," as loud as I could. Tan ran to the side and turned to see the tree crashing down. It'd torched out, so there weren't needles or branches left on it to cushion the fall, and I felt the impact. Tan and I stepped up to read the stump. His cuts looked perfect, pretty much. The back cut was exactly parallel to the pie cut, and the flat pie cut went about a third of the way through the trunk. "Nice," I said, burning with the memory of the snag that I'd tried to drop falling back over our fire line onto the steep, shale-covered ground. Tan just picked up his saw and kept walking down the line looking for another snag to drop.

The next snag we sized up was small and looked easy. It stood straight up and down, so Tan decided to drop it away from the line. He put in the pie cut and stepped around and put in the back cut. He'd just set down his saw so he could push the tree over when I heard a crack and yelled, "Falling," at the top of my lungs. Tan heard me and dove to the side as the tree snapped back and crashed down right where he'd been standing. I took a deep breath and let it out as Tan rolled over and saw how close he'd come to being smashed by the tree. It was my yell that had kept him from being killed.

The stump was barber-chaired, and I walked up to look at it and see what the fuck had happened. Tan climbed to his feet and walked over, too. We could see from studying the top of the stump that his cuts were a little screwy, and the branches must've been weighted heavier on the backside than he'd figured. I could've stood there staring, sort of awestruck, at that stump all day. The realization that sometimes even Tan failed to drop a tree where he'd aimed it floored me. Sam was right; sometimes nature has a mind of its own.

The snag had fallen across our line and into the green, and Tan was already hustling to buck up the trunk into pieces. I carried them across to the black side of the line. A couple of diggers trotted over and scratched a line around where the tree had fallen, just in case there were stray sparks in the brush. Tan dipped his chin in my direction. I gave a solemn nod back at him and then he was walking down the line again, looking for more snags.

Chapter Nineteen

T HE SUN HAD STARTED DROPPING DOWN IN the sky when the fire blew up. I hiked at the front of the line with the rest of the saw team, and we made good time to our safety zone, a big flat rock about a quarter mile down our line with a good view of the smoke column rising into the sky. We lounged around there for a while, eating snacks and bullshitting. The fire started putting up a good-sized, mushrooming smoke column. "Looks like we're not going to get much more work done today," Archie said.

"Shit," Rock Star said, "with a smoke column like that, it'll be a wonder if they can fly us down off this fucking rock.

Tan, Rock Star, and Archie started talking about a spades game. I couldn't help hoping they'd ask me to be their fourth since Clark was out, but I knew that even though I'd held my own swamping for Tan, he wouldn't have me as his spades partner.

"Gather up," Douglas yelled, interrupting the momentum toward a card game. We all stood up and gathered around him.

"Okay everybody, here's the deal. I just talked to the IC, and there's no way we're flying off this mountain tonight."

"Coyote!" Hawg yelled.

Coyote camping meant we'd have to spend the night stuck out on the fire without our sleeping bags or a hot meal. When that happened, we ate MREs for dinner and slept on the ground with only the metallic space blankets we kept in our packs to cover us. The Pikers all loved coyoteing because if we didn't have our sleeping bags and a meal, the Forest Service couldn't take us off the clock, and we racked up overtime and hazard pay all night. The others could all sleep just fine without sleeping bags, their bodies like furnaces, but coyote camping meant I'd be awake all night shivering on the hard ground. I pretended to like it fine, but in truth I'd rather spend the night off the clock and in my sleeping bag with a hot meal in my belly.

Douglas scowled. "Actually, the IC's pretty determined to try to fly in our sleeping bags and some chow. They think they could pull off one sling load. The air's a little clearer about a half mile to the west, so I'm gonna send a saw team to cut a helispot out that way. If the helicopter manages a drop, we'll all hike over to grab our red bags."

"Send me and Archie," Rock Star cajoled.

Douglas ignored him. "Tan, Julie, you two up for cutting a helispot?" We both nodded. "Good. I want you two to hike about a half mile to the west. When you hit clearer air, cut the spot and then radio me."

"Will do," Tan said. He turned and started walking to the west, and I followed him, glancing back over my shoulder at the rest of the crew grinning after me. By the time I turned back around, I had to hustle to catch up. The hazy air and Tan's fast pace left me short of breath after only a few minutes.

"Fucking goat rope," Tan muttered as he hiked. "Uncle fucking Sammy risking some pilot's fucking life to fly in our fucking sleeping bags just so they can fuck us out of some overtime."

I for one wanted my sleeping bag and something to eat besides the preservative-laden omelette with cheese and dehydrated fruit cocktail in my MRE, but I didn't say so. I could almost hear Tan's thoughts trailing out behind him, a string of epithets about having to put up with the danger and indignity of working with me as his swamper.

"I bet Clark is bummed to be stuck down in fire camp," I finally said. "He'd hate to miss the overtime." Tan didn't respond. "I sure hope he's feeling better."

"You and me both," he retorted. "Sooner he can see again, the sooner I'll be rid of you." I decided then that I'd take an awkward silence over another attempt at conversation. Even though Tan hiked so quickly I suspected he was trying to drop me, it was a long half-mile through the forest, around rocks, scrambling over downed trees.

"It's funny," I said suddenly, as the air around us began to clear of smoke, "the radio sure has been quiet." We hadn't heard a bit of Piker radio chatter since we left the big flat rock where the crew hunkered.

"Hmmpf," Tan said. We hiked on until finally he stopped and said, "This looks like as good a place as any for a helispot." The area was flat with a few smallish trees and a couple of bushes. Tan held the button down on his radio. "Douglas, Tan." When there was no reply, he held the button down again, "Douglas, Tan." Nothing. "Damn batteries must be out." Tan shucked his pack, but before he opened it up he stopped. "Goddamn cocksucker."

"What is it?"

"Spare batteries are in Clark's pack. This is what happens when Douglas sends me out with a fucking splittail for a swamper."

"Look," I told him. "It's not my fault you don't have any spare batteries." Tan gave me an icy stare. "So should we hike back?"

"Long as we're here, let's clear the spot first."

Tan started up his chainsaw and cut through a couple little pecker poles. I pushed them over and dragged them away from the area we were clearing. He moved to cut through a bush with a thick, gnarled base. I grabbed onto the top, careful to keep my balance. He leaned in to slice through the bottom of the bush, but the saw bar struck a knot and kicked back hard. The saw made a zipping sound as it cut through his chaps. Looking down at his left leg, I saw that the chainsaw had sliced clean through the protective material. Tan turned his saw off and set it down. "I'm cut," Tan said, calmly.

"Oh my God," I said. "We need to radio Douglas."

"With no batteries?" Tan said.

"Oh my God," I said, as it slowly dawned on me that we were half a mile from the crew.

"I can't believe it," Tan said. "My saw's kicked back like that a million times. I've never even nicked my chaps." I knelt down behind him to undo the plastic clasps on his chaps. There was one behind each calf and each thigh and then one at his waist. When the last clasp was undone he threw the chaps on the ground. "Turn around," I said.

Scared as I was to look at his leg, I made myself do it. Blood seeped through his Nomex, but the cut through his pants was no more than four inches across. I let out a sigh of relief. "It's not as big as I thought," I said.

"It feels kind of deep," Tan said. "Fuck, fuck, fuck, fuck."

"Sit down," I said, and to my surprise, Tan lowered himself to the ground. I pulled a clean bandana out of my backpack along with a red wool long-sleeved shirt that I wore on cold nights. I pressed the bandana against the cut, rolled the shirt, and then tied it tight around Tan's leg to hold the bandana in place. "Look," Tan said, "you need to hike back to the crew quickly and tell Douglas to call for a medevac."

"Okay," I said. "I'll be right back." I took off through the woods at a near run, but I hadn't gone sixty yards when I was coughing from the haze. Looking up, I saw that the smoke column was growing and seemed closer than it'd been before. As I started ahead again, I pulled up in my tracks. After a long moment of indecision, the boiling smoke column prompted me to turn and head back toward Tan.

When he saw me appear through the trees he barked, "What the fuck?"

"The fire," I said, gesturing toward the smoke column. "It looks like it's really rolling this way. I'm not going to leave you here."

"You've got to fucking leave me," Tan said. "You've got to get me some fucking help. Now get the fuck back there."

"My sense of direction," I said. "It sucks. What if we

can't find you again?" I gestured toward the smoke column. "Douglas wasn't expecting that kind of fire behavior when he sent us out here." Tan could see as well as I could that the smoke column had quadrupled in size since we left the crew. "I'm not leaving you," I said.

He nodded. "All right," he said. "But we can't stay here."

"You're going to have to try to walk," I said. Tan nodded. "I'll help you." I pulled him to his feet.

"I don't need your help," Tan insisted. "You just carry the saw." I lifted up the saw and balanced it on my shoulder by the bar. With no saw pad on my backpack strap, its teeth cut into my shoulder. Tan took a painful, limping step, paused for a long moment, and then took another. Another pause and then another step. His face had turned deathly pale. "We're going to have to move faster than this," I said, and when Tan looked at me his eyes showed that he knew it was true. I set the saw on the ground. "We're going to have to leave it." Tan started to protest. "Come on, Tan," I said. "Don't be stupid. Now come on, put your arm around me." Tan gave me a look of utter distaste, but he slung his arm over my shoulder, and we moved along, him limping slowly, painfully beside me. He dragged me down, but I tried to bear as much of his body weight as I could. "Clark sure picked one hell of a day to eat eggs," I said, and Tan started laughing so hard that we had to stop walking.

We started up again, but with each step an agonized grunting sound escaped him. We made our way along like that for what seemed like hours, having to pause every second or third step for Tan to grit his teeth and become ready to go on. "Tan," I said, "if we don't hit that rock before the fire does, it's going to roll right over us. We're gonna have to pick up the pace." We both looked up at the smoke column, a force far greater than the two of us, and its menace brought us together in a way nothing else could've. "Look, I've got an idea."

"What is it?" Tan said.

"Empty everything out of your pack except your fire shelter."

"What the fuck?"

"Come on, Tan, just do it." I thought surely he would bow up, but he took off his pack, threw his FST on the ground, opened the pack up, and dumped everything out. His fire shelter remained folded up in its little box attached to the bottom of his pack. "Dump all your water. Come on, I've still got plenty." I helped him pull out his water bottles and then he put his pack back on. I took off my own pack, pulling out only the fire shelter, which I put into Tan's empty pack. "Okay now look at me." I stood facing him and we met each other's eyes. "I'm going to get us back to the crew, okay? But you've got to trust me on this. Don't fight me now, Tan." I bent over and walked forward so that my shoulder hit his abdomen. "Bend over me," I said. I half expected him to push me away, cursing, but instead I felt Tan's chest lying against my back and I yelled, "Huuughhh!" as I straightened up, picking up Tan as I did so. I wrapped my right arm around his legs, which dangled down in front of me. His stomach pressed against my shoulder and his torso hung down my back. I started lumbering tentatively forward, my heart pounding. I'd thought Tan would protest, but he must've realized the danger we were in as much as I because, aside from percussive grunts of pain, he stayed quiet. I wasn't making the best time, but still I was walking a lot faster than Tan could on his hurt leg.

I thought of a program I saw on television once about people who exhibited feats of superhuman strength in times of crisis: a man who lifted up a car to free a trapped baby, a young woman who picked a fallen tree off of her fiancé. Carrying Tan's 145 pounds over my shoulder would hardly constitute such a feat, but I did wonder if I would've been able to manage it if we weren't at imminent risk of being burned over.

"Good thing you're just a tiny, little banty rooster of a man," I said. Tan responded with a grunt.

As I trundled along, placing one foot in front of the other, I told myself, "Just one more step, just one more step," over and over again. I could feel blood dripping from Tan's leg down onto my yellow Nomex shirt. Every once in a while I'd glance up at the progress of the smoke column. Tan started grumbling, "Fucking Douglas should've checked the weather before he sent us off to cut a helispot."

"Don't worry, Tan," I said. "We're getting there." But I was worried. My back ached, and when I couldn't take another step I set Tan down. "I need a rest," I said.

"We don't have fucking time," Tan said. Up ahead, we couldn't see the Pikers' safety zone, but we could see trees exploding and torching out, the flames licking over a hundred feet into the sky, the air above a churning, boiling column of smoke. "Fire could've very well burned past the safety zone by now," he said.

"If it did, we're going to have to deploy," I said. I imagined Sam at the top of Paloma Canyon looking down at all of those firefighters who'd died in their shelters, the silver pup tents collapsed with the heat and melted into their flesh. Tan put his arm around my shoulder and we hobbled forward. When I'd caught my breath, I had him fold himself over my shoulder again, and I hoisted him up and staggered along as quickly as I could carry him. My whole right side felt crushed down by his weight. After ten minutes or so I tripped on a root and almost pitched us both to the ground. "I got it, I got it," I said as I wobbled back and forth, trying to regain my footing. I set him down again. "Let's walk a little more." Tan threw his arm around my shoulder. "Come on now," I said.

He grunted with each step, and when I looked down, I could see blood soaking a huge patch in his Nomex. "I'm surprised you haven't left me behind, way I've treated you," Tan said.

"You've been a dick," I acknowledged. "Here, bend over again." I hoisted Tan up on my shoulder. The haze was so thick and the sun was starting to set, turning the horizon a staggering pink. The glare and the smoke made it hard to see more than twenty feet in front of me. There was no telling if I would see the flames first or the flat rock of our safety zone. Suddenly, through the trees I saw the blur of two blue hard hats. "Hey," I yelled. "Hey, hey!"

The bobbing blue hard hats came trotting in our direction, Archie and Rock Star coming at us through the trees. "Julie! Tan!"

I set Tan on the ground.

Archie reached us. "Julie!" he cried. "What's wrong? Are you all right?" He sounded almost frantic with worry. Looking down, I saw blood spattered all across the front of my shirt.

"I'm okay," I said. "He's not."

"We need to hustle," Rock Star said. "Douglas, Rock Star."

"Go, Rock Star," Douglas's voice came from Rock Star's radio.

"We've found them."

"Pike, Douglas. Missing Pikers have been located. Come back to the safety zone ASAP. I repeat, return to the safety zone ASAP," Douglas said. Rock Star and Archie each grabbed Tan under one armpit and, without prompting, I picked up his feet and we started moving as quickly as we could.

We made it there as the other Pikers were straggling in from the forest where they'd been searching for us, and we set Tan down on the rock. Fire burned hot and high three-quarters of the way around us, and it was clear Tan and I wouldn't have made it back to the safety zone in time if Rock Star and Archie hadn't found us. The sun glowed burnt orange and luminescent pink through the smoky air as it dropped halfway below the edge of the horizon. The other Pikers clustered around until Douglas told everyone to back off. I stayed where I was, on my knees beside Tan. I told Archie to grab me the red wool shirt out of his pack, and then I put it beneath Tan's head so that he'd be more comfortable. "Lance, check him out," Douglas said. Lance rushed forward with his first aid kit, looking proud to be the crew EMT.

"I want Lance to keep his dick skinners off of me," Tan protested. "That's my dying wish."

"Tan, we're not going to be able to get a medevac out of here until tomorrow morning." Douglas's tone brooked no argument. Lance knelt down beside Tan and cut away his Nomex with a pair of medical scissors. The torn skin hung open in two ragged, bloody flaps, and below I could see the pink of exposed muscle. I gave Tan another clean bandana to bite down on while Lance poured hydrogen peroxide on the wound. Lance then packed it with gauze and bandaged it. "It doesn't look good," Lance said. "But you're not going to bleed to death before morning."

Lance slipped Tan a couple of prescription pain pills he kept in his pack for emergencies. I didn't think Tan would take them, but he gave Lance a grateful look and tossed the pills back without protest.

"Nice work, Lance," Rock Star said, and all the other Pikers nodded.

"You done good," Tan said.

Lance struggled not to look too pleased at the Pikers' approval. I looked away, but Archie caught my eye and gave me a little nod that said I was the one who should be proud.

Archie, Rock Star, and Hawg came and sat around

Tan and me, not saying much, just wanting to be near him. Tan's face was still pale and his forehead covered with beads of sweat. He was rigid with pain, but as the meds hit his bloodstream, he seemed to relax a little bit. "Those fucking chainsaws," Archie said.

"At least you didn't plunge cut yourself," Rock Star added.

"Some fucking consolation," Tan said ruefully, but he managed a small smile. "I tell you what, if it wasn't for this splittail here," he gestured toward me, "I would've been burned the fuck over."

"My name is Julie," I said. "And I want you to start calling me Julie, goddamnit."

They all smiled.

Chapter Twenty

ARCHIE AND I STAYED NEXT TO TAN ALL night, long after the other Pikers had eaten their MREs and wrapped themselves up like burritos in their crinkly space blankets and conked out. Finally even Tan fell asleep. The fire glowed orange in the night all around us, moving like lava down the hillsides. It was beautiful.

"I never thought I'd see the day Tan would let a girl haul him out of a tight spot," Archie said, laughing softly. I giggled in spite of myself. "From day one of the fire season, Tan thought you wouldn't be able to keep it together when the shit hit the fan on the fire line. But he figured you wrong."

We sat together in silence, the night close all around us.

"Hey, Julie."

"Yeah."

"We should've taken you with us to see Sam."

"I know." I paused. "You apologizing?"

"I am."

"Accepted." We sat together in silence for a long time, our longing for each other filling up the wide open night, burning like the orange glow on the hills around us. "What are we gonna do?" I asked.

"We're just gonna hang tight," Archie said. "We're not gonna do a thing."

Neither of us spoke again until the sun finally started its inevitable rise. A brilliant fireball, its rays came through the thick, smoky haze in purple and pink. Tan opened his eyes. "I never thought it would be light again," he said, through teeth clenched with the agony that must have been slowly returning as the pain pills wore off.

"Neither did I," I said. Douglas had kicked off his space blanket in his sleep. I could see him stirring and knew he'd be waking up at any moment, radioing the IC to go on and send us that medevac and send it quick.

Once Tan had been loaded on a stretcher and the helicopter had flown away, we went back to digging line through the understory vegetation that grew on those rolling hills of dark conifer. Chokecherry sagging with the weight of their black berries, wild rose, and skunk bush grew along the edges of the saw line. I wore Tan's pack since mine had been burned over. I was working with the diggers again, but this time Hawg actually let me be lead tool, so that I was the one to guide the line of diggers through the saw line. I was the one to break ground and decide exactly where the fire line was to go. It was harder work physically to be the first to swing into the undisturbed grass, roots, and caches of needle duff. I had to pay attention to the saw line and the fire and decide how to best use natural fuel breaks to our advantage, making sure we tied into rocks and gravelly patches because "dirt don't burn and rocks are our friends." I enjoyed the challenge of it. "How come you'd never let me work as lead tool before?" I asked Hawg as I went swinging along.

"'Cause you were a rookie and maybe a shrimper."

"It's still my rookie season."

"But you're not a rookie anymore, Julie. After yesterday, nobody could call you that."

"And I never was a shrimper."

"We weren't sure there for awhile."

"Clark," we yelled, as we walked toward the Pikers' tents in fire camp.

"Clarkie, m'boy," Rock Star bellowed in a fake English accent. Clark's head popped out of his tent, his eyes wide open. "It's a miracle," Rock Star cried, "the blind can see."

"How you been?" Hawg bellowed.

"Better now," Clark said. "Hey, I talked to a couple of fire gods over in the IC tent this morning, and they said that a little girl hotshot carried an ex-Navy SEAL half a mile on her back, saved them both from being burned over. Could it be true?"

"Good thing Tan only weighs about a buck and change," I said.

"Atta girl," Clark laughed. "Soon as I heard about it I found the IC. He said the doc at the hospital reported Tan had emergency surgery, but that he's gonna be fine."

"That's what Douglas told us," I said.

"So it hurt his pride worse than anything, huh?" Clark giggled. "Don't get me wrong, I love the guy. I'm worried about him. But I've been laughing my ass off."

Chapter Twenty-one

WHEN WE PULLED UP AT THE FIRE CENTER at the end of our Black Hills tour, Tan stepped down from where he sat on the picnic tables and came walking toward us with barely a limp. We spilled out of the rigs and crowded around him, all of us asking at once how he was doing. "Doctor says how fast I healed after he sewed me up was a goddamn miracle," Tan said. "But I know better." I knew Tan meant that he'd willed himself to heal.

"It's that strong SEAL blood," Clark said.

"Hooyah!" Tan gave a war cry and we all laughed.

Sam was a different story. He came back from the Burn Unit in Idaho, and as soon as we were off the clock we headed over to his house. We were surprised to find Cookie there with the baby, frying him some shrimp. She kissed Sam on the top of the head as she set the plate of shrimp and a baked potato heaped with sour cream and cheese down in front of him. He looked happy to be pampered, but whenever he stood up to hobble anywhere on his crutches, he was obviously still in pain. I scanned his refrigerator and the shelves over his breakfast nook for photographs of Cookie or their baby Caitlyn, but all I saw were flames and slurry bombers and Pikers looking tough in hard hats and sunglasses.

Caitlyn toddled over to the kitchen, opened the cabinet, and pulled out an empty bottle of Hot Damn. Clark laughed. "She's her daddy's girl, all right. She likes the sweet stuff." Cookie lifted the bottle from Caitlyn's hands, and the baby began to cry. I scooped her up and carried her over to the kitchen table on my hip.

"You look good with that baby," Archie said, a secret something in his smile.

Sam pushed back from the table and came awkwardly to his feet. Hawg stood up to help him, but Sam brushed off his outstretched arm. "I don't need your help," he said gruffly and hobbled toward the fridge on his crutches for another beer.

Some nights Tan, Clark, Archie, Rock Star, Hawg, and I would all sleep over at Sam's, a couple of us on the living room floor, one of us on the couch, another in the recliner, and one or two out in sleeping bags in the yard. More than Sam, even, it made us feel better to be there with him. We weren't as restless as we usually would've been stuck at the Fire Center doing project work, waiting to be called out to a fire. Sam kept talking as if it was almost a certainty that he'd be back on the fire line in no time. He swore the doctor would be impressed by improvement none of the rest of us could see. The Pikers always partied so much that I don't know if the others noticed how many pain pills he was taking, or how much he was drinking, but I saw it. But the ultracompetent, nurturing Cookie was over almost every night with at least a couple of her kids, and with Cookie looking after him, I figured Sam had no choice but to be all right.

Those nights we slept over at Sam's, Archie and I would stay up talking long after the others had drunk themselves into a stupor and passed out. And always there was a great desire between us. We never spoke of it, but I knew without him saying it that he didn't want to mess things up for me on the Pike.

"Tell me some more about your mother," he asked one night.

"I don't remember too much."

"When I was a kid, my mom always made lasagna. What did your mom cook?"

"Why does the mom always have to be the cook? For all you know, my dad was the one who cooked."

"Oh, come on. Don't be stubborn."

"Actually, neither one of them cooked, but my mom baked all the time. She'd make these little flaky cheese balls, and then sometimes we'd drive around town and give them out to homeless guys." For a second I was there in the car beside her as she rolled down the window and held out a brown bag full of baked goods to a shaggy man with dirty hands holding a cardboard sign.

"Wild," Archie said.

"Yeah, only I just figured it was something everyone else did, too. After my parents died, my grandma Frosty, she didn't want me talking about them at all, so I just quit. So now it's hard to do."

"It must've just wrecked your grandma," Archie said, "to lose her daughter like that."

I looked at him. It was honestly something I had never thought about much. I'd always been so focused on the fact that I'd lost both of my parents, I never really considered much that Frosty had lost her daughter and son-in-law, too. Her grief had been invisible to me, and what I saw was her icy reserve, her desire to control me.

"I was the kid," I said.

Archie took a long swig of beer. "That you were," he said, but I could tell he wasn't entirely agreeing with me. "And what are you now?" We sat there for a moment in obstinate silence. "You ever thought maybe she did the very best with you that she could?"

What I'd always thought was that what she'd done hadn't been good enough. Archie always seemed to side with Frosty, and I needed him to understand. "She told me, right after my parents died, that she'd had to take me in. She said it was my dad who got them killed. She told me it was his fault. And that I was just like him."

"She said that?"

"Yes, she said it."

"How did she say it exactly?"

"She said," I gulped in air, preparing to speak the words aloud that I'd held high up near my heart, a burning resentment with me for these ten long years. "'You. Are. Just. Like. Your. Father. He took her from me.'"

"That could mean anything," Archie said. "Anything at all. But it doesn't sound to me like she meant it was all his fault they died." In my head it had always been so clear. "Ask her," he said. "Just ask her about it."

I stepped outside the bunkhouse, breathing in the thin mountain air for courage. The ponderosa branches whispered to me in the breeze. The mountains rose up above me, looking their darkest against the brave blue of the sky. I dialed her number on my cell. Frosty answered and we talked for a few minutes, our usual pained, stilted conversation. And then I forced myself to say the words. "Frosty, that day you caught me . . . setting the tile on fire in the bathroom—" We had never spoken of it. Not once.

"My Lord, you scared me half to death." Frosty sounded almost relieved to talk about it.

"You said . . . you said you had to take me in. Because I was your only daughter's only child."

For a moment a silence buzzed between us.

"Julie, I would have taken you in no matter what. You were the only joy I had left in the world."

The words vibrated in my head. The only joy. "Why didn't you ever say that? Why didn't you ever tell me?"

"I've never been good . . . at that kind of talk. I thought you knew."

"I was twelve. How could I have known? All I heard was that you didn't want me." My voice sounded like the voice of a lost child.

"No one on earth could have pried you from me," Frosty said, a sudden fierceness in her words. I leaned my back against the side of the bunkhouse and slid down it until I came to rest on the grass. "You have always been the most precious thing to me. It kills me to think you haven't known that."

Tectonic plates shifted in my mind, smashing into each other, buckling up, causing mountains to rise. I wanted to cling to the way things had always been, to stay on those barren plains of loneliness. I wanted to hang on to the truth I had always known, no matter how bitter.

"You said it was his fault. For killing her."

"Julie, what ever do you mean?"

"You said he took her from you. You said he took her."

Again, a long stunned silence, and then my grandmother said, "I thought you knew. Your mother. She was driving the car." I saw black spots in my vision. I pulled my knees into my chest, put my head down, and pressed my eye sockets against my knees. "Didn't I ever tell you that?" Frosty asked.

"No. You. Never. Told. Me. Anything," I said.

"I was sick," Frosty said. "I was sick with grief. Talking about it. That's one thing I couldn't stand."

"Then what did it mean? 'He took her from me—' What did you mean by that?"

"Your mother and I. We were always so close. And then she met your father. They were very much in love. She stopped. She stopped listening to me. And then you were born. And it was the three of you together. And ever after I was . . . I was always on the outside. That's what I meant. That's all. I never should have said that to you. It was selfish. I was just a sad, broken-down woman. You are my precious. You are my precious grandchild. My very own."

"I wish you had told me," I said, starting to sob.

"I'm so very sorry," Frosty said. "But I'm telling you now. You are everything to me. I'm so proud of you. I'm so very proud."

One night just after Tan's doctor had cleared him to go out with the crew on fires again, we all sat around the kitchen at Big Sweet Sam's, drinking and laughing and telling fire stories. Cookie was at her own house with the kids that night. With the end of fire season in sight, we were all appreciating each other a little more than usual. We all knew that at the end of September, fire season would end, and we'd be laid off and turned out into the world on our own for six whole months. "Doctor's sure to give me the green light at my next appointment," Sam kept saying. Although we'd nod in polite agreement, he didn't have anyone other than himself convinced.

"I could still make it out for a late California tour. I went to California at the end of one season," Sam said. "The Pike had already disbanded, but they patched together some extended season crews from all the guys who didn't have nothing else going on. They were lucky there were some of us around, too." He pointed to a picture on his fridge of an intersection draped across with a huge banner that read, WELCOME TO HOLLYWOOD. Behind the sign were the hills, and on them houses like no Piker would ever own. And behind the houses flames, and above the flames that funny orange glow that only comes to the sky when there's a fire raging.

"You guys have never seen a fire camp like that one in SoCal," Sam said. "We could see the mansions on the hills from where we pitched our tents. And they didn't serve normal fire food. They served California cuisine. And there was an ice cream stand set up right there in the middle of the fire camp. After a big day fighting fire we all had ourselves a double dip ice cream cone. Rocky road. After a day on the line, imagine it." I nodded and laughed with the rest and drank my beer as Sam talked about that fire camp as if it was Disneyland.

Sam had a true gift with that camera. His photos of us showed the fire more fiery than it ever really was. They showed us stronger and braver and in more danger than we had known at the time. They showed me that for Sam, fighting fire was the only real thing.

Sam grabbed on to his crutches and tried to stand up from the kitchen table.

"Don't get up, Sam," Clark said. "What do you need?"

"I need a smoke," Sam said.

I followed him out onto his back deck. He leaned against the deck rail, the crutches alongside him, and I sat on the rail, my legs dangling. His thumb came down on the lighter, one, two, three times, and then it caught, the tiny flame illuminating the crannies of his face, his cheeks hollowing as he sucked on the end of his cigarette. Its tip flared up like an ember floating through the darkness.

"You know, Julie," Sam said. "I was young once. Ox strong. Invincible. Fighting fire was my big adventure. Then I fell in love with it, head over heels, and I knew I never wanted to do anything else. Being on the Pike, that was it for me. I been on the crew fifteen years now. I'm forty-five years old.

"It's different now 'cause of this," Sam gestured down toward his burned leg. "This has got me worried. I used to be Archie, I used to be Rock Star, and now—. Maybe

I could get a job as an engine slug, or even work as an Assistant Fire Management Officer. But it wouldn't be the same. To be forty-five and know the good stuff is already behind me. To lose my place on the Pike." Sam stopped for a minute. When he spoke again there was a certain uncharacteristic hardness to his voice. "And look at you. For you, fighting fire, it's not gonna be your whole life." I opened my mouth to protest, but Sam wouldn't let me. "No, no it won't," he insisted. "For you, it'll only be that adventure it was to me at first, something to mention to people you want to impress, people who otherwise might think you're just another pretty little gal. 'I used to be a forest firefighter,' you'll say to people who wouldn't know what a hotshot is. Braggin' rights it'll be for you, maybe a long-gone something that you cherished. I'm jealous of you for that. For me . . . well, I don't want it to be a goddamn tragedy."

"Sam, there's nothing tragic about you. You're the opposite of a tragedy. Your ex-wife cleans your house, for Christ's sake." We both chortled. "Far as we're all concerned, you're the man." We giggled again and then settled back into quiet, and I could tell Sam's mood hadn't truly lightened.

"But Julie, there's more to it. What I'm getting at, what I want you to tell me is . . . aww shit. I mean, what's it all been for? What's it all been about, really?" Smoke from Sam's cigarette drifted in front of me.

"When the smoke's really bad," I said, "out on a fire and we've all got our faces pressed down in the dirt, you're the one who can stay standing and watch for a clean patch of air blowing through. You're the one to tell us when it's safe to breathe." It was true, the gift of being a heavy smoker, Sam's lungs could tolerate what the rest of ours could not.

"You're wrong about me," I said. "For me, this isn't a fling. It's not some summer camp. My parents . . . I don't know if it was the actual impact of the wreck that killed them, or if it was the car exploding. But it burned them down to teeth and bone. And after they died—I was only twelve—I turned into a total pyro. Any time I was alone in the house I was setting things on fire. I was careful about it, sure. I wasn't stupid. But it was the only thing that made me feel the slightest bit better."

"Fire," Sam said. "I've found it can burn away most any grief. At least for a moment."

"Yes," I said. So he understood. "My grandma. She caught me. She was so outraged that it scared me. Made me feel ashamed, I guess. Made me feel like I was repaying her for taking me in by just about burning down her house. I quit after that. But it was still with me. Always has been. This crazy urge. This obsession." I quieted before speaking again. "Back then I didn't even know that hotshotting existed. Never even heard of a forest firefighter."

"Life's funny like that," Sam said. "It finds a way to get you where it wants you to go."

Sam sat in his easy chair telling burly, farting Hawg stories about finding the different arrowheads that filled up the glass cases along one wall. Hawg pointed out his favorite bottles from the collection that ringed the room on shelves high up by the ceiling while I lounged on the floor and petted Sam's wild cats, touched the split place on the steer's skull where the arrowhead stuck out of the white bone, and looked at the feathers hanging off of Sam's dream catchers. And I wondered why Pikers always wanted to talk about their adventures. I mean, there was a whole wide world out there, and all my buddies ever wanted to talk about was *fire*.

Rock Star and Archie played their guitars, and I sat around and watched and sang along. I was a good audience because I knew exactly what they could play—I never requested anything they couldn't. Our phones went off just after midnight, and we tried not to act excited when we read the text, "Return to Fire Center. Dispatch. Southern California. Five a.m. flight from DIA," because a dispatch meant we'd be leaving Sam behind. Rock Star was too drunk to be tactful, and he hollered that Big Sweet Sam sure had the fire mojo working, telling his SoCal fire stories and all. He said the gods of fire, they must've been listening.

We stood around the table in Sam's breakfast nook and slammed water, glancing at our watches every minute or two to make sure we wouldn't be late getting back to the Fire Center. "Sam, I wish you were coming with us," I said, and the others nodded solemnly. The first raindrops sounded on the tin roof, and by the time we said good-bye to Sam and ran outside, it was coming down hard.

We loaded up into an old school bus at the LA airport and drove into the hills and then the mountains, which were green and steep and cooler than the city, arriving at fire camp after dark. We set up camp, and then I lay in my sleeping bag and listened to Clark, Tan, Rock Star, and Archie playing spades. Hawg was sitting nearby, too, listening in. I felt happy to have Tan back among us.

On our hike to the fire the next day, we went up the steep slopes of the San Gabriel Mountains, the Coulter pine and California walnut a deep green that made the mountains in the distance the color of emeralds. When we finally made it to our division of the fire, we started putting in line through manzanita, which grew up over five feet tall in a close, twisting thicket, its wood reddish, shiny, and beautiful, its root system tangled and endless and deep, a veritable hell for diggers.

By late afternoon my hands were cramping up around my tool, and I was looking forward to heading back to fire camp for dinner. The time after dinner was what I liked best, when dark came up on the fire camp and all the Pikers unrolled their sleeping bags.

But word came over the radio that we were going to work all night. All of the boys were excited about the overtime, and I tried to look happy, too. Dusk came and we hiked down into Division G to burn off of a line another hotshot crew put in that day. The burnout was to ensure the line would hold. Lance spun a weather—winds were favorable. Tan had suggested he take up the job until Sam returned. Lance took pride in it, though he was still slow at it and a little clumsy.

We spread out down the line, and Hawg walked in front of us with the drip torch. The diesel mix shot out of the spout and over the burning wick. The fire splashed and danced down into little clumps of bushes, and Hawg passed over a ridgetop ahead of us and out of sight. Dark came down around us. The moon rose up, just a sliver of white, and the flames flared up, red and yellow and orange. The temperature dropped, and the heat coming off the flames felt good, so I stayed close to the fire.

Archie stood down the line, and I kept wanting to look over at him. We held the line like that for a long time. The fire swelled and spread back away from us and into the unburned forest, where a deer bounded away from the flames, illuminated by their light. I was sorry to know something it didn't, that it was headed straight toward the main fire. If Sam had been there, he would've taken silhouettes of Archie and me walking in front of the flames, and the pictures would've come back perfect, both of us outlined blacker than black in front of the fire.

The wind shifted suddenly, sending what looked like the embers of Sam's cigarettes flying through the air above us. And then the smoke blew across the line like fog. I stood for as long as I could, but when I started dry heaving, I dropped down to my hands and knees because there's always more oxygen low to the ground.

Lying flat on my belly and dry heaving smoke, I dug at the ground with my hands and pressed my face into the hollow. Sam wasn't there to stand through the worst smoke, to let us know when patches of clear air blew through. When the smoke let up, I lifted my head. "Hey Archie," I called, "where's our safety zone?"

"It's in the pond," he yelled.

"Pond?" In the darkness, I saw Archie jerk his head toward the chain-link fence running about thirty yards from the green side of our line. I hadn't seen it before through the dark and the smoke.

"The pond's on the other side of that fence."

"Oh, that's helpful."

Archie shrugged again. "That little fence wouldn't stop me."

Right then I heard someone yell, "Spot fire!" And then we were up and running. I could barely make out figures moving like ghosts between the trees. I could see them flitting between the bushes to catch the patches of light springing up where the sparks landed. I worked hard chasing spots, and I only stopped digging when my lungs belched the smoke back out, or when I just had to wipe my eyes.

The smoke cleared, and I saw Archie, walking toward me with his chainsaw slung over his shoulder. I could see behind his safety goggles that his eyes were completely bloodshot, but he was grinning around his mouth and all through his red eyes.

Hawg came out of the smoke behind Archie and then all three of us were chasing more spots together. The more we lined, the more sprang up around us. Then I saw that the spots were growing together on our green side of the line. Douglas was yelling, "Pike, we've lost our line! We've lost our line!" The spots had grown up and into each other, and there wasn't fire on the black side of our line and spots in the green. There was just one big fire and our line hadn't held.

"Get to our safety zone," Douglas was yelling, and I ran toward it, but spot fires had popped up between me and the fence, all of them melting together, and I was leaping back and forth to dodge them. Rock Star made it to the fence before the others. He set down his saw and started climbing the fence, vaulting over the top.

I picked up his saw and yanked the cord to life as the other Pikers came barreling up behind me. They all began leaping and dancing because the flames were under us then. I stepped up to the fence and sliced through it with the chainsaw, creating a hole big enough for us to pass through. Archie grabbed the fence and pulled it wide open.

Archie slapped my shoulder and raised his chin to say go, and I scrambled through. A whole army squeezed through behind me, and then we were splashing together out into the foul pond water. We stood there, waist-deep, as the fire burned all around us, an impenetrable sea encircling our little island of water.

When dawn finally came, the sunrise was orange and pink and lovely through the smoke. We hiked out to a road and sat alongside it. By looking at my friends I could see that I was soaked and dirty and my eyes were red as hydrants. On the fire line there weren't any mirrors, and so I had to look to my buddies to see my own reflection. We sat down and joked about how the dirt would stick to our wet butts and make us look like we'd grumped in our Nomex. We stretched our legs and leaned back on our packs. Rock Star said he'd better watch out or I'd take over his position on the saw team. Hawg passed out damp cigars, and all the Pikers puffed away at them, the cigar smoke blending right in with all the smoke around us.

Rock Star fell asleep with his head tilted back against

his saw pack and the lit cigar hanging from between his lips. I took his picture because Sam would've, and we were all sure to be quiet about laughing so we wouldn't wake Rock Star up. And I was truly part of it.

Chapter Twenty-two

FIRE CAMP LAY IN AN ENORMOUS MEADOW with tents clustered together in bunches of twenty and huge catering tents and lines to eat or use the Port-a-John. There wasn't any ice cream stand, but the hills were pretty, and from where we'd set up we could see the waterslides to the east and the concert stage to the west. Sam had been right about Southern California fires after all. We didn't have to be back on the line until five the next morning; seventeen hours off the clock was an unheard-of luxury. After a nap, the bus driver took us to Walmart, so we could spend some of the overtime and hazard pay money we were racking up. I bought a bikini and a shimmery, purple sundress. I knew I was in trouble, too, because I wanted Archie to notice when I wore it.

They let firefighters into the waterpark for free. We laughed at each other, because our faces were so tan and the rest of us so pale we could've glowed in the dark. When I was floating on my back in the water, it was like I'd dreamed all the smoke I sucked in the night before. It was hard to remember how awful it had been not to have enough oxygen. The boys played football in the water, and I floated and watched. Later we went down the waterslides over and over. "What do you think Sam is doing right now?" I asked, as Hawg and Archie and I raced up the wet stairs toward the top of the slide.

"Letting Cookie sit on his face, I hope," Hawg said.

"Oh, God," I groaned. "That's awful." I could hear Archie laughing behind me.

"It's true. That's pretty much the best thing that could be happening to him right now," Hawg insisted.

"I hope more than anything that he's gonna be okay,"

"You fight fire long enough and it'll wreck you, doesn't matter who you are," Archie spoke quietly. "Sooner or later he's gonna have to give it up."

Rock Star spent the afternoon hanging on to the base of the lifeguard stand and talking up at the blonde on duty. He came over saying he had big news, but he wouldn't tell us right off what it was. He made us guess who was playing that very night at the big concert stadium we could see out on the other side of the fire camp. We all asked, "Who? Who? Who?" And finally he told us. "Lynyrd Skynyrd."

"No way," Archie said.

"Way," Rock Star insisted.

"That can't be," Clark said. "The singer for Lynyrd Skynyrd's been dead for decades. He died in a plane crash."

"That sucks," Archie said, "but it'd be better than burning to death. At least a plane crash would kill you quick, like spitting Copenhagen on an ant."

"Lynyrd Skynyrd's got a new singer," Rock Star said. "Big Sweet Sam told me so just a couple months ago. The new singer is the dead guy's brother."

Clark was the only Piker who wouldn't go. He didn't like that the singer had been replaced by his brother after the plane crash. He said it was cheesy and spooky. Clark said he'd rather stay in his tent and read a new book about the effects of prescribed burns on the American elm.

A whole stream of firefighters made our way across the open field between the fire camp and the stadium. As we walked out of the fire camp, I felt like we were really going somewhere. Some of the other firefighters wore their crew shirts, but Pikers knew better than to identify themselves when they're out drinking. I wore my dress, and it slid easy against me as we walked. I felt half naked, I was so used to wearing a hard hat and Nomex and my White's. I'd showered and washed my face, but left the smudges of ash around my eyes like makeup. When Archie first saw me, his eyes got big, and he said, "Where'd you get that?"

"Wallyworld," I said.

"Well, all right."

The concert organizers let the firefighters in for free, but only into the cheap section. There weren't any seats, just a long stretch of mowed grass, which suited us fine. Once we were inside the stadium, Archie and I bought a huge paper cup full of beer to share, and we sat on the cool grass and picked out Rock Star in the front row. The lifeguard sat next to him, her bleached hair looking like a halo. We cheered when we saw his arm sneak around her shoulders, even though there was no way he could've heard us down there so far below that he and the lifeguard looked like dolls. And I felt a little jealous of the lifeguard, that she was able to be a woman on a date, plain and simple.

Archie and I sat and shared beers through all the opening bands. The beer tasted good and cold, and Archie and I showed each other foam mustaches and laughed.

When Lynyrd Skynyrd finally came out, the crowd went nuts. Archie and I made fun of the audience, scanning the crowd for the worst tattoos and the biggest hair.

The band rocked out, and then halfway through a song the singer suddenly spun around and raised his arms up above his head. On the back of his shirt there was a huge drawing of his dead brother's face. He stood with his back to the audience for a long time, still singing into the microphone, as if it was Ronnie up there. The crowd loved it. All the tanned, big-haired women shook their asses, and the fat biker men raised their fists, and it was like they were trying to punch through some imaginary ceiling to the hereafter where their dead rock star had gone.

I looked over at Archie to see if he was feeling what I was feeling—glad that we weren't dead ourselves. We weren't dead, but just barely. I wondered if he was feeling how alive that made us. I felt plugged into some invisible socket, like my veins were running blue with energy. I was liquored up enough to wonder if the blue lines running through me would've showed up in a picture. I thought that they would if Sam could've taken it—a picture of Archie and me sitting on the grass drinking beer, listening to Lynyrd Skynyrd, all pink from a day at the waterpark. My veins full of beer and lightning, because all of us Pikers were alive still.

A bunch of diggers behind us laughed raucously. They'd made a pile of paper cups and twigs and leaves and they were holding a lighter to them. Pretty soon a good flame kicked up, and I watched them dance circles around it. They were howling and laughing and I could tell then that the great current I felt was running through them, too. They howled, "Freebird," even though the band had already played it. I could still make out Rock Star in the lights coming off the stage. He looked small so far below. He and the lifeguard were mugging down, and his hands were sunk in her bleached-out hair, and I knew that he felt it, too. That it was in all of us, that we were one Pike, because we'd each crawled through the hole I cut in the fence, because we splashed out into that nasty pond water together. More alive because we'd almost lost the living, and the thought of it scared me and turned my skin electric.

I pushed myself up and headed to the ladies' room, dingy with crummy lighting and crumpled streamers of toilet paper floating around on the floor. The busty, tanned women waiting in the long line obviously thought there was no other option, but I couldn't stand there with them like I would've before the Pike. I walked back outside and waded out into a clump of bushes, lifted up my dress, and squatted there. But suddenly, midstream, I had a drunken flash of insight. Right then I knew I'd been out in the woods with men for too long and that I wasn't the way I'd been before. I missed it then, the waiting with other women. I missed complaining with them about how there never is a line for the men's room.

Chapter Twenty-three

WHEN I PULLED UP AT THE FIRE CENTER after a run to the grocery store in Monument, my backseat full of beer, baked potatoes, and steaks to grill, Sam was in front of the kitchen. I hadn't seen him since we'd arrived home a couple of hours before, and at the sight of him my heart lurched. As we hugged, I spoke quietly so that none of the others would hear. "I ran into Cookie at the grocery store. You okay?"

For a half a second Sam's eyes shone with tears and then he blinked and they were gone. "I'm gonna be fine. Don'tcha see me walking?" Sam took a couple of steps to emphasize how well he was doing. "You know what she told me, Julie?" he said in a low voice. "She said I'll always have a string of women, and I'll always, essentially, be alone."

"Oh, Sam."

"But don't worry about me. I'll be fine. Let's us just have a good time now."

Clark was in charge of grilling steaks, and I made guacamole. Hawg acted as my royal taster, instructing me to add more lime or cumin until I had it right. Tan recited a few dirty limericks he learned in boot camp. Rock Star and Archie played guitar and sang. I knew Rock Star would be throwing up or wrestling with someone within the hour.

When the two finished singing "Mr. Tom Hughes's Town" they put down their guitars to rest for a minute and drink their beers.

I spotted Oscar the fox skirting the area looking for handouts, and if I'd been by myself I would've gone over to pet him. Clark said, "That damn fox needs to learn he's a danger to himself." He disappeared into the bunkhouse, reappearing with a string of Black Cat firecrackers in his hand. I wanted to say something, to stop him, but I just looked on. He lured the fox out into the center of the dirt parking lot with a bit of raw meat, then he lit the firecrackers, tossed them, and jogged back to the picnic tables. The firecrackers went off like machine gun fire, not four feet from where Oscar gnawed away on his bloody prize, and the little fox skittered away into the woods to Piker laughter and applause. I felt suddenly shaky and sick. "A good scare like that is what that fox needed," Clark said. "It'll probably save his life."

Everyone was still laughing and talking about the firecrackers when Clark went up to Sam, put a hand on his shoulder, and said, "We hate going to fires without you."

"I feel like I'm ready to be back on the fire line," Sam said. "I'm barely walking with a limp. My doc's appointment's in the morning. I'm sure he'll give me the go ahead. I'm sure he'll sign me off."

"I hope so." Clark kept his voice sympathetic, but he knew as well as the rest of us that Sam had been having trouble keeping up on the fire line even before he was burned.

"Where's Cookie and her little ear screwin' monkey?" Rock Star wanted to know. I held my breath.

Sam cleared his throat; the pause before he spoke was painful. "She got me through the hard patch. I guess I can't expect more than that."

"You mean—" Rock Star began.

"She loves her horses and her kids more than she loves me, and I love fire more than anything, so maybe it was inevitable. I liked the idea of it, though—being with Caitlyn's mom."

"When did you all break up?" Archie wanted to know.

"When I proposed."

"Ouch," I muttered.

"Yeah, but she said something that really hit home for me. She said she thought I didn't really want a wife, just a backup plan for when I can't fight fire anymore. And what woman wants to be some old hotshot's backup plan?"

Archie and I sat at the far picnic table in the darkness, talking low to each other about inconsequential, silly things—Hawg's drunkenness, which of Rock Star's songs we liked best. But what we felt for each other stuck in the air between us, the inevitability of it had taken on a weight and a momentum stronger than our own resolve.

The sounds of Hawg heaving behind a nearby bush reached us, and we joined in the general cheers. Then Rock Star came up with a beer in each hand, wanting to know what in the hell Archie and I were whispering about.

We all went on like that, talking and drinking, singing and eating steaks, partying into the night. It was just the usual thing, but suddenly I could see how beautiful it was. Somehow everything had the tinge of premature nostalgia, like I was remembering back to a lost, enchanted time, only it was happening right then and there. I told myself it was only because it was already September and the season was coming to a close. Still I kept waiting for Archie to search out my hand in the darkness, to give me some sort of sign, but he didn't. I think he didn't want to make any sort of decision for me.

At about midnight Rock Star yawned, and Sam said he was going to head home. He looked so liquored up I couldn't help but ask, "You okay to drive?" But he said he was fine, just fine, and I left it at that. Too drunk to hide his limp, he made his way slowly to his car. The sight of his lopsided gait made my heart ache.

The evening was obviously winding down, and suddenly I couldn't stand the idea of going off to my room alone. I considered whispering something to Archie when the others were out of earshot, but realized that I didn't want either of us creeping down the hallway in the darkness as if we had something to hide. "Hey, Archie," I said, in front of the others. "I think I'm going to sleep in the attic above the Saw Cache. Want to come?"

The silence hung thick in the air, and then Tan spoke. "Damn, Julie, you've got the biggest fucking balls of any woman I've ever met. Propositioning another hotshot in front of half your goddamned crew. Goddamn." The others burst out in friendly laughter and I shrugged.

"Look at him," I said. "I just can't help myself."

"So, Archie, you got a response for the lady?" Rock Star asked, with good-natured curiosity.

"Oh, so Julie's a lady now?" Archie asked, and we all laughed again. When we quieted down, he said, "Sure,

Julie. I'd be up for that." And the other Pikers didn't cheer or say anything derisive. They just nodded slowly, as if what was happening between Archie and me was respectable and right, something they could approve of.

Archie flipped on the downstairs light as I followed him into the Saw Cache. The room looked dusty, eerie, and timeless with the hand tools hanging suspended in rows along one wall and the potbellied stove hunkered in the corner. The times I'd come in to talk to the sawyers as they worked, Clark and Hawg would spit tobacco juice on top of the hot stove, and their spit would curl into balls and sizzle and dance. I'd felt like an intruder on the Pike's last bastion of pure masculinity. "It feels a little sacrilegious to be in here like this," I said.

"Sure does," Archie said. He gestured at the ladder leading up to the attic. "You first." I climbed the rungs carefully. I'd only been up in the attic at the very beginning of the season when Big Sweet Sam and Douglas issued us our gear. Peeking my head over the top of the ladder, I found the spacious, dusty room still empty except for a few fold-out chairs and the front seat of an old Chevy that had been ripped out and somehow manhandled up the ladder. Light from the moon and the stars drifted down through the three overhead skylights. The wooden floor creaked as I stepped out onto it, Archie following behind. He grabbed two sleeping bags and a headlamp from the walk-in storage closet. With the headlamp on, he zipped the two sleeping bags together. I shivered in the darkness, nervous and almost unbelieving.

"How does all this feel to you?" I asked.

Archie looked up, but not quite at me. He knew as well as I did that when you're wearing a headlamp, you can't look directly at the person you're talking to, or else the light will blind them. His profile became a silhouette etched against the lighter darkness, his nose straight, his jaw strong. "Not quite real. I never thought I'd be crawling into a sleeping bag with you, that's for sure."

"But it's okay with you, right?" I asked, feeling suddenly uncertain.

"Oh, Julie," Archie said, slipping his arm around my waist, pulling me to him, and burying his face in my hair. "It's more than okay." And then we stripped off each others' clothes, our goose-bumped skin exposed to the cool night air. When we slipped into the downy warmth of the sleeping bags, every place that our skin touched glowed like a fire burning ruby red through the distant forest. I felt like a tree torching out, exploding from the earth into the night sky with the heat of what I felt for Archie, with the pure joy of finally being with him.

Chapter Twenty-four

AT 6:30, MY WATCH ALARM BEGAN BEEPING with an annoying insistence. "Time to get up," I sang, giving Archie's shoulder a shake. He rolled over in his sleeping bag. "Come on, Archie, we've got to meet the guys up in the classroom to lift weights in five minutes." Archie groaned, but climbed out of the bag and onto his feet. "I'm not going to shrimp out on a morning workout just because we hooked up."

When it was my turn at the pull-up bar, I cranked out nine. I struggled for a tenth, and it was Tan who stepped up and put his looped hands under my ankles. "One for the Chief," he barked and, with his help, I hauled my chin up to the bar.

"One for the SEALs," I said, and he helped me with my last pull-up, both of us laughing and all of our friends around us laughing, too.

After we finished lifting, we headed down the hill to the picnic tables. Most of the crew had already gathered up for morning PT. Sam was there, wearing sweatpants. "Sam!" we all cried, glad to see him down from the office where he'd been doing time sheets and paperwork for Douglas.

"You gonna PT with us today?" Rock Star asked, trying to hide a note of skepticism.

"I can't run just yet," Sam said, as if he might be out doing wind sprints any day, "but I'm going to go for a little hike. I have my big doctor's appointment today. Since he's for sure going to clear me to go back out with the crew, I need to hurry and get in fire line shape again." I studied Sam's face, taking in the puffiness around his jaw I'd never noticed before, the purplish circles under his eyes; he hadn't shaved for days.

The rest of us glanced at each other. "Well, we can't wait to have you back out with us," Archie said, sincerely. "We're certainly not the same crew without you."

"Isn't that the truth," Tan said, putting a hand on Sam's shoulder. I didn't ever remember seeing Tan voluntarily touch another Piker before, not even Clark.

The whole crew stood around, all twenty of us taking our final sips of coffee, still waking up, waiting for Douglas to come on down from the office and head us out for our crew PT. When he finally came walking down the hill, he was grinning from ear to ear. "Good news," he cried. "I just heard that the Pike National Forest is ripping over by Gunnison. I'd bet my job we'll be called out within the day." We all cheered, but not as loudly as we would have if Sam had for sure been up for going.

"My doctor's appointment is at one," Sam said, hopefully. "So I bet I'll get to go with you guys."

"We're here for you, Sam," Archie said. "I'm praying for you." The rest of us nodded. Even those of us who didn't have Archie's faith could see that Sam needed our prayers.

"Here he comes," Clark said, taking a bite from his sandwich. Rock Star stood up from the picnic table where he sat with the rest of us eating lunch and pumped his fist into the air as Sam came down from the office, almost able to mask his limp.

"Jesus Christ," Tan said under his breath and looked away. The rest of us stood up from the tables and flocked around Sam, a little awkwardly, our hope and worry fluttering in the air around us.

"Soon as I get the all clear from the doc, I'm gonna race back here and throw my red bag in the rig," Sam said. "If you guys get the call to Gunnison in the next little bit, stall for me. I ought to be back here in an hour and a half." His words hung for a moment. Hawg shuffled and coughed, and then we were all clapping Sam on the back and wishing him luck.

Sam's monster truck kicked up a cloud of dust as it drove down the road.

"Look at that," Hawg said. "It's dry as fuck." Then, "Fuck!" He kicked at the dusty ground with his heel.

"I know," Clark said. "I want to be rooting for Sam, but I gotta hope the doc has the good sense not to send him limping out onto the line to get himself and who knows how many of the rest of us killed."

After that none of us really had the heart for project work, so we all wandered in and out of the Saw Cache, getting in each other's way, sharpening our stash of tools and straightening up. Rock Star showed me how to take apart and clean out a chainsaw, teasing me about how I'd be taking over the saw team soon enough. All of us kept glancing at our watches, but nobody mentioned Sam.

"It's him," Hawg called, and we all ran out of the Saw Cache to see the monster truck rolling slowly, so slowly up the road, trailing its parade of dust. We followed after the truck to where Sam parked it in front of the kitchen. The cab door creaked open as we stood in an expectant horseshoe gaping up at Sam. He unfolded his long limbs slowly and climbed down with the care of an old man. We all half-waited for the joke to be over, for him to crack a smile and say, "Gotcha, I'm in the clear," but he just looked at us and shook his head.

"He said," Sam started, but choked up. "The doc said—" He shook his head and turned to go back up to the office.

"Sam!" Archie called, but Sam ignored him.

That day up on Paloma Canyon all the Pikers had left Sam alone to hike up to where his friends had died and sit with his grief, but that had been the grief of losing his two **buddies**. This was different. This was the grief of losing life on the Pike. Tan gave me a push from behind. "Go on," he said. "You're the one who can talk. Go on and talk to him."

I came up beside Sam and took his arm, and we mounted the stone steps curving up to the office. Almost to the top, we sat down without speaking. Below us, we could see the cluster of Pikers breaking up in the shadow thrown down by Mount Herman: Rock Star and Archie headed back to the Saw Cache, Hawg scratched his butt and looked lost, Tan popped the hood of one of the Suburbans while Clark stood by with a clipboard so that they could go through a weekly vehicle inspection. Sam sat silently and

I stayed there with him for a long time. Finally he spoke. "It's over then," he said. "It's all over for me. I'll never fight fire again. I'll never run again. Doc says no way will I ever be able to hike with a forty-pound pack. This time next season, I'll be working in the district office, wearing a pickle suit. I'll spend most of the year inside, maybe get out now and again for the smell of smoke. Oh God, Julie, I'm forty-five years old and it's over for me."

"You've fought fire longer than most," I said. "Most guys make it a couple seasons on a shot crew. The diehards make it nine or ten. You've been on the Pike for fifteen years, Sam, a hell of a run. It's just that it's work for the young and none of us stays young forever." I sounded convincing, but didn't believe it somehow. Archie would always be young, and Rock Star. It was just Sam who'd slipped through the cracks of aging.

The rest of us, Clark and Tan and Hawg and I, we'd always be on the Pike, always be together. Even sitting there next to Sam, I needed it to be so. "I'm like you. You guys are it. You guys are what I've got. So I get it, I think. I know it must feel like dying."

"Working under fluorescent lights in a goddamn pickle suit," Sam said. "That ain't dying. That's being buried alive." I leaned my head against his bony shoulder, tucking my hand into his elbow's crook.

Chapter Twenty-five

JUST AS WE WERE ABOUT TO GO OFF THE clock for the evening, Douglas received word from dispatch that a fire had started outside of Gunnison. When he came down to the Saw Cache to let us know, we all stood there looking at him, none of us with the heart to whoop or holler or dance. All the Pikers shook Sam's hand or clapped him on the back, and I gave him a good-bye hug. Then we all loaded up in the rigs, and Sam stood in the middle of the dirt parking lot between the Saw Cache and the kitchen to watch us go. I turned around in my seat and waved and waved until he was just a tiny ant I could barely see down the dirt road.

We climbed out of the rigs when Douglas came out of the Gunnison District Office, a squat little Forest Service building in the small city's downtown. "Since we're the first crew to arrive here, I've been named Incident Commander. IC picks the fire's name. So I was wondering what you all want to call it." We all stood there thinking. I must've not been the only one remembering Sam waving good-bye to us, because Hawg said, "How about the Big Sweet?" We all nodded approvingly, and Douglas said, "The Big Sweet Fire it is."

The plan was to sleep on the ground outside the district office that night and drive as close to the fire as we could in the morning, then hike in. I pulled my sleeping bag out of its stuff sack and laid it down between Rock Star and Archie. I was more than half expecting a crack from Rock Star or one of the others. Something along the lines of "Don't you want to go ahead and snuggle up with your man, Julie?" But none came, and as I lay there in my sleeping bag, it finally settled in that I'd slept with Archie the night before and that the whole crew knew about it and that somehow, after all we'd been through together, it was okay.

We lay on the ground for a long time looking up at the sky, the stars a bit faded by the lights of Gunnison. "I wish Sam was here to point out the constellations," Rock Star finally said, and only after that could any of us sleep.

"Gather up," Douglas barked, once we'd parked the rigs in a crease between two mountains and geared up. The pine trees and firs reached up thick and dry, their needle duff carpeting the brooding peaks looming above us. Douglas took off his pack. "I want you all to know that from now on, Julie will be wearing a radio." He pulled a chest harness and radio out of his pack and handed them to me. I strapped on the harness, the Pikers all looking on.

"What the fuck?" Tan said. "I was on the Pike two seasons before I got to carry a radio." But he was joking, pretending to be his old self.

"Hush," Clark said, and that made me smile. I'd never

heard anyone tell Tan to hush before.

"Tan, if I'd been carrying a radio earlier this season, I wouldn't have had to pack your ass back to the safety zone," I said.

"Tell it, sister," Hawg said.

"Thanks, Douglas," I said. "Radio today, saw team tomorrow."

"The girl doesn't know her place," Tan said.

"You got that right."

"Back to business. We're gonna need a lookout," Douglas said. "Dry as it is it's gonna be a crucial job. Lance, you up for it?"

Lance nodded solemnly, obviously proud of the assignment.

"No napping now," Douglas said.

"Just catnaps," Lance said. He and Hawg knocked fists, and then he climbed into one of the crew rigs and drove farther up the road so he could walk up the mountain across from the one we'd be digging on and watch for fire below us.

The morning air was cool, and it was quiet and peaceful hiking along through the pines. I had to scramble to climb over fallen tree trunks most of the other Pikers were tall enough to step over, and the thick cover of duff and leaves made the ground springy beneath my White's. The fallen trees, the dead and down, were rotting back into the soil, many of the trees certainly home to birds and mice, squirrels and other forest creatures. But the forest floor was choked too thick, it had long begged for a small fire to come through, licking out the undergrowth, clearing an open space, leaving the giant trees to continue their slow and majestic growth. Its wish had not been answered, and now the dead and down was dense enough to cause a conflagration so hot it would surely set the larger trees ablaze.

We spent all morning digging fire line up a steep mountain. I'd glance up from digging now and then, tilting my head back on my neck to gaze up the steep slope. If I turned around and faced downhill, toward the south, I could look directly across at the mountain where Lance was surely sitting lookout for us. So far he didn't have much to do, but once we started our burnout, he would be crucial in watching to make sure there was no fire spotting below us.

Looking out to the east, we could see the main fire smoldering on the other side of the next mountain. At lunch we sat and ate together as a crew, and then we dug until mid-afternoon, cutting a seam up the side of the slope. We crested the ridge of the mountain and tied our line into a big rockslide on the other side of the ridge at about 14:00. After that we hiked back down to the bottom of the mountain to start burning off our line.

Rock Star ran the drip torch, and we spread out, following him slowly up the hill, walking our fire line. He could've laid down a big strip of fire as fast as he could walk, but the forest was dry and the dead and down thick, so he knew better than to waste fuel. He knew better, I think, than to let the genie out of the lamp too quickly. I thought of fire as a genie because it's what hotshots want more than anything, but also because nobody knows how to put a genie back in a lamp. Diesel mix splashed out of the drip torch and over the burning wick as Rock Star walked back off the line and into the forest to the east, through the tinderbox ponderosa and spruce. When we were about halfway up the ridge, we spaced out and held the line.

The fire burned hot, and by the time Rock Star came walking back out of the trees, the flames behind him kicked up two hundred feet at least. The sun beat down, a fire in the sky, and the burn Rock Star lit rose up and moved toward our line. By then I knew well that fire rips uphill— the convective heat rises and dries out the fuel above, so that when the fire takes off it explodes more than anything. I'd seen it myself plenty of times. The fire wasn't exploding then, but it was moving uphill at a good clip and burning slowly downhill. I looked across at the rock pile I figured Lance was sitting on, and I saw the flash of a mirror.

The fire that Rock Star lit on the east side of our line worked its way toward us. First it moved through the grass and bushes, then it climbed up the fallen trees and blazing bushes into the branches of the standing trees, and then the trees began going up in flames. Then the fire bumped up against our fire line, and the line held it. The conflagration moved no farther, and, as always, it seemed to me a miracle that our little scratch in the soil could contain the raging force of nature that was a forest fire. My skin was dry, and I only knew I'd been sweating because I was all crusted with salt. When I moved to walk back into the green to the west, a little ways from our line where it wasn't as hot, my Nomex burned the backside of my legs where it touched me. The other Pikers stepped back too. We were spread out with about a hundred feet between each of us, all up and down the side of the mountain.

Rock Star was still moving up the line lighting, and just above me I could see Tan holding our line. Hawg was below me, and below him was Clark, and below him, Archie. We all stood on the fire line we'd dug and watched the green for spots, our backs to the flames. From that distance the warmth felt good, like the comfort of the fire in the potbellied stove in the Saw Cache. There wasn't a bunch of chatter coming over the radio, either. I turned to watch the flames and the trees exploding, and looking back through the forest was like seeing into the heart of a ruby. I remembered the feel of Archie's skin against mine, the friction like a forest burning deep inside us.

I watched these big lovely ponderosa standing there as the flames climbed up into their branches. They'd torch out for about fifteen seconds. Some of their tops would explode and throw sparks up into the air, and then all of a sudden it would be over and there'd just be these big, deadly looking, burned-out snags standing where the trees had been. We'd look up to watch the sparks float across our line overhead, and we'd watch the green closely to see if any of them landed and caught.

None of us wanted to lose that line, but everything was dry, the air in my lungs even. It was coming up on mid-afternoon, and that whole forest was ready to rip. There was nothing but our twenty-four inches scrapped down to mineral soil holding it back. Looking up the mountain I could see Rock Star, high up near the top, still disappearing in and out of the green with the drip torch.

I heard Clark yelling, "Hey! Hey! Hey!" so I turned and looked downhill to see what he was yelling about. I saw it then, streaking across our fire line, moving from the burning side into the green to the west. Long and thin and low to the ground with a big bushy tail that looked like a pinecone on fire. Its whole body was burning and the poor fox must've been trying to outrun its own fur, but of course the wind from the running just made it flare up hotter. It was probably a hundred yards down the mountain from where I stood, but it seemed like I watched it run for a long time. The fox passed through dry grass and over deep squirrel caches of duff. It disappeared into stands of bushes and then reappeared farther away from us. Tan yelled, "What the fuck?" And below me Clark and Archie gaped, because the grass that brushed the fox as it passed caught fire, slowly at first, and the clumps of bushes began burning and the squirrel caches started smoldering. Then the silence over the radio broke, but nothing any of us said could change the fact of that burning fox trailing fire through the unburned forest below us, making a mockery of the fire line we had spent all morning digging up the mountain.

Clark was first saying, "Douglas. Clark."

"Go, Clark," Douglas said.

"We've got a problem down here," Clark said. "Burning animal crossed over the line."

"Is there any spotting?"

"That's affirmative. It's too early to tell the extent of it, but there's definitely fire below us."

"Get your men on it," Douglas said. But by that time, those of us at the bottom of the mountain were already running toward the spot fires.

Archie cut flaming bushes with his saw, and Hawg swamped for him. I lined a small spot fire and then threw dirt on the flames. As I pounded line around to the uphill side of the spot, my tired muscles burned, my hands cramped around my ching, and the smoke blew up into my face. Coughing and gagging, I remembered to take shallow breaths, and then I was okay, not comfortable, but okay. Tan was cutting farther into the green with Clark swamping for him.

Douglas radioed Lance, who was still sitting lookout on the mountain across from us. "Lance, Douglas."

"Go, Douglas."

"I need you to spin a weather."

"I just spun one twenty minutes ago," Lance said, and for a moment I hated his arrogance.

"Lance, spin a weather."

"Copy."

"Can you see spots below us?"

"I can see a couple of little smokes, yeah," Lance said.

Most of the Pikers were still up near the top of the mountain, spaced out to hold our fire line, watching the green for spots. The burn Rock Star lit still raged right against the line up where they were. Gary radioed to ask Douglas if he should hike the rest of the crew down the mountain to line spots with those of us already farther below. It was a long time before Douglas responded. "No," he finally said, "I figure the Pikers near the top of the mountain better stay put. If any spots cross over up where you are, we need somebody to catch them." I knew then what he was saying. If spots crossed over into the green closer to the top of the mountain and there was nobody there to put them out, they would spread and block our escape route up the mountain. There'd be fire below and fire above, and we'd be completely trapped.

Then the radios were quiet, and Archie, Tan, Clark, Hawg, and I kept scrambling to catch those little spot fires started by the fox. Hawg had left off swamping and was lining spots with me. We'd been working since 6:00, and I was starting to feel beat, but I knew wearing out wasn't an option. And the spots we lined were small, most of them no more than two feet in diameter. We'd been through so much together already that season that I didn't see those little spot fires as anything like a real threat.

After what seemed like a long time, Lance radioed Douglas again from across the way. "Douglas, Lance."

"Go, Lance."

"Yeah," Lance said, and there was a quaver in his voice, "I'm looking at this thing from over here, and that animal's trailed fire all the way around the bottom of the mountain. RH has dropped three percent in the last twenty minutes, and the wind's kicking up to the north. I recommend that you pull our folks out of there. Hike them over the ridge to the rock slide."

Douglas's voice was tense. "Lance, you're aware that in doing so, we'll lose our entire division of the fire? And that there aren't any natural fire breaks from here to Gunnison?"

"I'm aware of that," Lance said, all business.

"Copy," Douglas said.

Up until that point I can't say that I knew what was at stake. Even though I'd been right there when Sam fell, even though I'd had to carry Tan after he cut his leg, somehow, up until right that minute, I'd never believed anything truly bad would happen to us. But from the time I heard Lance saying we needed to go over the ridge, I knew we were in real danger.

"Pike, Douglas."

"Go, Doug," Clark said, as I fumbled for the button on my radio.

"Go, Douglas," Rock Star echoed.

"We're pulling out. Let's hike it over the ridge. Make sure you've got all your people and go."

It was at least a third of a mile to the top of the ridge. Jackstrawed logs and thick bushes covered the steep mountain. The spot fires around us were spreading together, throwing off sparks about my height and sending up smoke, through which I could see the shapes of Pikers coming together. Clark counted heads to make sure that we had all five Pikers who'd come down the hill. He counted me and Archie, Tan and Clark and Hawg, then we all lined out and began hiking up our fire line, up the mountain.

By then it was so smoky that I couldn't see very well, and the fire below us was moving into piles of downed trees and patches of brush all on the green side of the fire line. My eyes watered and I coughed as we hiked. Clark was at the front of the five of us, with Tan and Hawg right behind him. Archie was the only Piker behind me. We moved uphill, staying together pretty well, all of us pushing as hard as we could. My calves and lungs burned and I tasted copper at the back of my throat. Even though Hawg had always been too tall to pace off of, I kept my eyes glued to the back of his heels, matching my steps to his. I could hear Archie breathing right behind me. "Hurry, hurry, hurry. Hustle, hustle, hustle," Tan yelled every few moments, and the sound made us all move more quickly. Blood roared in my ears, the veins in my temples fit to burst with each heartbeat. Suddenly I realized just exactly what the Pikers' macho posturing was all about, why they pushed each other so hard all the time. Because they sensed that when it really came down to it, when our asses were really on the line, pushing each other was our best chance of survival.

A glance behind me revealed that way below Archie, the spots were growing together, the flames seeking each other. I heard a couple of trees torching out. Our burn was on our right side, to the east, and it was still hot, the charred stalks of trees still glowing red, stumps and piles of dead and down still flaming, the ashy ground too scorching to stand on without getting a bad case of the hot boot. To our left was the green, the forest thick and dried out, looking like it'd be a lot healthier if it burned. And below us it was already burning, the wind kicking up to the north, ready to blow the conflagration uphill.

The line of us finally started rubber banding out a little bit, until there was twenty feet or so between each of us. Staring down ahead of me, I no longer saw Hawg's boot heels, just the lonely ground. I pushed harder, my lungs and the muscles in my legs screaming. Then I heard

Tan yelling again in his Navy SEAL voice. I couldn't tell what he was saying, but there was an edge of outrage in the sound, and perhaps of fear. Then I could make out a figure tearing down the mountain, toward us, toward the fire. Through the smoke I couldn't make out that it was Rock Star until he'd passed Hawg and was almost to me, yelling, "Where's Archie? Is Archie okay?" Rock Star's every instinct for self-preservation should've been propelling him toward the ridge, but here he was coming downhill toward the flames looking for his best friend, the person with whom he wanted to grow old.

Archie said, "I'm right here, buddy," and then I heard a sharp crack and saw a little torched out snag on the black side of our line snap and fall. The trunk just missed Rock Star as it fell, but a branch clipped him on the back of the head and knocked him down onto his face. Archie and I dropped onto our knees, shaking him. Rock Star came to, but he was groggy. Tan, Clark, and Hawg hadn't seen the tree fall, hadn't heard it over the great crackle of the fire below us, and they powered up the mountain away from us. We didn't have time for what was happening. Archie was yelling, "Get up! Get up! Get up!" and Rock Star staggered to his feet.

I propped him up on one side and Archie propped him up on the other, and we started back up the mountain. Holding up almost half of Rock Star's 210 pounds made every step an agony of endurance. Sweat streamed down, hot and salty, into my eyes. At first we weren't making any sort of time, but then Rock Star started coming around a little bit and walking pretty much on his own. Archie looked back down the mountain at the fire kicking up, and I could see he was trying to decide whether or not we should deploy. The last thing I'd ever wanted to do was climb alone into the hot, terrifying little space of my fire shelter and wait for the roaring flames to pass over me.

"Let's drop our packs," I said, shucking mine before Archie could speak. "We'll move a lot faster without them. Come on, guys, get your fire shelters." Archie helped Rock Star take off his pack, and then we all pulled our fire shelters from the bottom of our backpacks. "Let's go! Let's go!" I yelled, and when we started up the ridge again I was relieved to see Rock Star keeping up with us. We were careening up the mountain then, moving faster than I'd ever thought we could up a slope that steep. Suddenly I didn't feel it anymore—my screaming legs, my stinging eyes, the hot, bright pain in my lungs. Fear made us light and we flew over the uneven ground. We blew by a chainsaw laying eerily on the ground.

Without our packs and flush with adrenaline, Archie and Rock Star and I were able to start catching up to Tan, Clark, and Hawg. It must've only taken a couple of minutes, but it seemed like whole seasons since we started moving up that hill. I saw Tan first, and I pushed hard to reach him. "Come on, guys!" I yelled.

Archie, Rock Star, and I closed the distance as Clark started yelling, "Deploy! Deploy! Deploy! We're not gonna make it over the mountain. Deploy your shelters." Terror seized me. The smoke blew up from behind me, and through it I could see the rest of the crew, the guys who'd stayed near the top of the mountain, scrambling to make it up and over the ridge. God, how I wished that I was with them instead of standing there with the desperate plastic box that contained my silver fire shelter in my hands, a sick joke that such a thing should stand between me and the all-consuming flames blowing toward us.

Tan and Clark disappeared, and in their place were two silver fire shelters ballooned out with oxygen. Above me and to the east, Hawg stepped on the back of his shelter with his heels and dropped down onto his stomach. The shelter covered him completely, looking suddenly innocuous, like a little boy's pup tent.

Voices floated eerily out of those three fire shelters. Hawg was closer to the burning side of the line, and Clark and Tan were to the left of me in the green, where it was cooler, but where all the fuel was still unburned. A couple of jackstrawed piles of tree trunks lay near them. Their voices moved past me with the smoke like ghost voices coming out of the silver tents.

Clark calling, "Tan?"

And Tan saying, "I'm here."

"It's me, Hawg. Who's there?"

"Hold tight to the front of your shelters," Tan yelled.

Next to me Rock Star suddenly seemed addled again, as if that falling snag had knocked the sense out of him, so I pulled out his shelter and helped him step onto the back of it with his heels. His right heel missed once, twice, but I grabbed his ankle and placed his heel squarely under the edge of the shelter. I did the same with his other foot, and the back of the shelter was pinned securely to the ground. "I'll take it from here," Archie yelled, in a voice that brooked no argument. "You go on and deploy."

Archie helped Rock Star raise the shelter over his head as Rock Star dropped down onto his stomach. I fumbled to pull my own shelter from its box and started shaking it out. It was stiff and new and folded up tight. The wind from the fire below us blew uphill harder than anything I could've imagined, probably forty miles an hour, and I clung tightly to my shelter to keep it from blowing away. I turned around to see the tremendous fireball rolling up the hill toward us, incinerating everything in its path. I stepped onto the back of my shelter as Archie, who was just on the other side of Rock Star, shook out his. The radiant heat of the fire reached us then—the fire itself was almost to us—and I took a deep breath and started to fall forward, pulling the shelter up over my head. But as I fell, I could see a crumpled, tumbling, silver ghost flying up the mountain on the ferocious wind. I hit the ground on my stomach, the breath knocked out of me, my mouth full of tall grass, my hard hat falling off onto the ground. The shelter was all around me, but I lifted the side and peered out.

"Archie!" I screamed and there he was, standing empty-handed, his shelter snatched and whisked away by the hot, brutal wind. "Come inside my shelter with me," I screamed. He looked over at me. He couldn't have possibly heard my words over the deafening roar of the fire, but he understood. He took three steps toward me, Rock Star's shelter still between us, and then the heat hit the back end of my shelter. I ducked my head back down, pulling the shelter over me, sealing me off from the flames that blew over me like a moving furnace that waits for no one.

The flames crackled and devoured and burned all around me. In the dark shelter I was breathing hard and sweating. My gloved hands held onto the front edge, and my feet held down the back edge, and the deafening roar of the fire was my heart flying apart. The wind ripped at the shelter all around me, and I was cooking inside it. I knew my lungs would collapse and the shelter would melt into me, melt into my burning flesh. Everything in me wanted to explode out of that shelter and make a wild break for the ridge, but I stayed inside. It was too hot to breathe, and then the flames came burning under the edge of the shelter. They burned through the patch of grass I'd landed on, and the grass underneath me caught fire. My braid caught fire off the grass and then my braid was torching out.

I tried to put out my braid with my gloved hands, and I could feel the back of my neck and my right ear burning, a pain like I had never felt. I could smell my own scorching, melting skin. I still held the shelter down with my feet and one elbow, beating at the back of my neck and the burning grass and taking the shallowest possible breaths because I wanted as little of that scorching smoke and air in my lungs as possible. The sound of the fire blocked out every other sound, so that I didn't even know what noises I made, and the grass below me finally burned out to ash. When I realized my hair wasn't burning anymore either, I grabbed onto the front of my shelter again with both hands and tried to breathe through the incredible agony that the back of my neck and right ear had become. After a long time the sound of the fire moved up and away from us, and I felt the air in the shelter cooling, degree by degree. I was trapped inside with my pain and with the smell of my burned hair and flesh.

For a long while I didn't move. I didn't want to come out and find out what exactly had just happened to me. I couldn't bear to come out and see the larger hell outside the private one of my shelter, so I lay there, praying to a God I had never believed in to have been burned to death so that I wouldn't have to leave that shelter, knowing that my first prayer was already too late to be fulfilled. When I finally lifted the front end of the shelter off me, the outside air rushed in. It was smoky and there was an awful charred smell outside, too. But the air felt cool to breathe.

Still lying on my stomach on the ground, I looked toward Rock Star's shelter, still puffed up with oxygen. I couldn't see to the other side where I'd last seen Archie—had it only been moments before or years?—stepping toward me, toward the safety of my shelter. And no matter what, I didn't want to see. Instead, I looked up toward the three shelters above me. The shelter just above Rock Star looked all right, but the two shelters to my left, over on the green side of our line near the big smoldering piles of dead and down, didn't look like little silver pup tents anymore. They were charred black and collapsed around the bodies they covered. They'd been burned into the Pikers inside. The fresh air caught in my lungs then, and I just lay there.

The shelter up above me that was okay rustled and then flew back. Hawg popped up and out of it, staggering around, looking like he was all big belly and fire boots and red, red cheeks. I could've cried to see him, and for a second I felt a strange, piercing joy that he was still alive. But I watched him take in the two charred shelters, and I saw him smell them for the first time. I saw him look down to Rock Star's shelter and then take in the sight of what was on the other side of Rock Star. When Hawg turned back to me, his eyes were round with horror—he looked at me the way the living must turn to the dead in dreams—and said, "Julie, my God," and then he fell to his hands and knees, retching into the ash.

And then Rock Star's shelter stirred, and when he stepped out of it and stood up, the silver tent tumbling down the hill, I could finally see the blackened, burned, smoking mess on the other side of him, the smoldering stink that could not possibly have been Archie, my big buddy, my love. And the sound I heard then was a voice like angels and demons lamenting together. It was bellowing and curdled and high and low at once, and then Rock Star and I were both on our knees in the smoldering ash next to Archie's smoking corpse. I still don't know which one of us was wailing more.

Chapter Twenty-six

FOR A LONG TIME THERE WAS NOTHING BUT a drug-induced blur and the pain, dulled by morphine, but still excruciating, always the pain, my true companion, cutting through the fog. My mom and dad stayed in the hospital room looking down on me with unblinking eyes full of love, my mom in her overalls, my dad wearing his favorite thrift store shirt with pearl snaps. Clark would come and sit beside me and read big books on forest ecology. Tan would stop by for visits sometimes. He'd stand in the corner and scowl disapprovingly, as if my condition was the result of some inherent weakness in my character, but still his presence was oddly soothing.

Archie's visits were my favorite. He always laughed a lot and played his guitar for me, singing songs that reminded me how much there is to love about life. "Mr. Tom Hughes's Town," he'd play, and "Fire on the Mountain," and even some of Rock Star's originals, like "Piss up a Rope" and "Fishing with My Best Friend," and I always had the energy somehow to sing along. Sometimes he would set the guitar down and look at me fondly, and I would want him to tell me he was consumed by what he felt for me, but he was always silent then.

"Do you love me?" I asked him once.

"We were lovers for one night," he said. "And before that we were friends." Then he shrugged. "If it weren't for the Big Sweet Fire . . . but then who knows?"

"But do you love me?" I insisted, emboldened by death.

"You're my big buddy, of course I love you." And it wasn't the declaration of undying passion I wanted to hear, but it was enough.

And then, after what seemed like ages, whenever I opened my eyes, it was the living who had come to see me. Sometimes Big Sweet Sam sat making carvings of Kokopelli on bits of sandstone, often Hawg was there playing a handheld video game. Rock Star was there most, though I hardly recognized him—it was as if his careless, silly self had risen out of him like smoke, leaving behind the ashes of the young man he had been. I wanted to tell him not to worry, that Archie was still young and handsome and carefree, still playing his guitar, but I couldn't form my mouth around the words.

And then finally I opened my eyes to see my grandma Frosty perched on the chair next to my bed, stroking my forearm, holding my hand. Sam sat next to her, holding her needlepoint for her, as if they'd become old and dear friends. Somehow I knew the two of them would stay there for as long as I needed them.

The hospital released me in early November, and I felt like a Flame 'n Go finally leaving prison as I walked toward the exit with Rock Star on one side of me, Sam on the other, and Hawg just behind. With fire season over, Hawg had stayed in Monument working as a timber beast, and Rock Star had gotten a job framing houses just ten minutes from the Burn Unit. They didn't say so, but I knew they'd done it so they could visit me every day. Sam could drive up anytime with no trouble since he was just hanging out around his house drinking beer and collecting unemployment.

Rock Star had brought me jeans and a sweater from the Fire Center, and it felt good to have on real clothes instead of the flapping indignity of the hospital gown. The surgeons had grafted skin from my thigh onto the back of my neck, but I still hadn't had the plastic surgery I would need to reconstruct my right ear. What had been left of my charred hair had been shaved off for the operation. I kept a hand in my pocket so I could finger the arrowhead Sam had given me the day we hiked Paloma Canyon. I wore a too big Piker hat set gingerly atop my head. It covered some of my bandages, making me feel safer, a little more protected, a little less exposed to those who would inevitably gawk at the damage done by the Big Sweet Fire. And if I thought too much about the future, I would wish that I had died there on that mountain outside of Gunnison along with Archie and Tan and Clark. I'd wish I had died there instead of Archie—I would've traded places with him in an instant—but when I thought about just the day in front of me, I felt a certain excitement, my happiness at having the Pikers by my side sloshed together with the sharp sting of grief, like a shot of cheap tequila chased with the sweet taste of soda.

The automatic doors slid open. My White's hit the asphalt as the sunlight hit my face, bright and warm, and with my boys walking with me, I felt the grace I'd always been looking for. With the Pikers by my side, I knew I wasn't being turned out into the world alone.

Acknowledgments

This book would not exist without the unflagging support of Joy Williams and Stephen Harrigan. I am so grateful to you both.

Many thanks to my fantastic literary agent, Felicia Eth, miracle worker, destroyer of obstacles. Thanks to my amazing editors at Skyhorse, Jennifer McCartney and Julie Matysik, for patient editorial guidance, enthusiasm, and for making my dreams come true. Thanks to Lauren Burnstein at Skyhorse and Marian Brown for their hard work ushering the book into the world.

Thanks to my father for always believing in me and in this book—I needed it; to my mother for creative inspiration; to my sister, Margaret Lowry, for constant cheerleading; to my amazing bonus parents: Mary M. Lowry and Eric Becker. Eric, how I wish this had happened in time for you to see it.

For ongoing and much needed encouragement, thanks (in no particular order) to: Aaron Reynolds, Dawn Erin, Jennifer Jack, Domenica Ruta, Sam Baker, David Moorman, Jenny Hassibi, Alisha Medlock, Ann Williams, Melissa Mazmanian, Della Landes Pope, Carolyn Landes, David Mainhart, Melissa Bryan, Bo Day, Hilary Clausing, David Becker, Elizabeth Becker, Allison Chapman, Margie Becker,

Glenn Smith, and James Moore.

Thanks to Denis Johnson and Cindy Johnson for Chaos and for showing me the way.

Thanks to Bryan Jack for use of the lyrics to his song, "Fishing with My Best Friend," which he wrote for Brent Smyth.

I am indebted to Suzanne Warren, Bill Mechanic, Lynn Nesbit, Peter Straus, Murry Taylor, Jim Magnuson, and the Graduate Program of the Department of English at the University of Texas.

Thanks to H.P. for everything.

And finally, thanks and big love to George Dickinson. You bring all the good luck.